ACKNOWLEDGMENTS

My grateful thanks go to editors Shelly Shapiro (Del Rey) and Sue Rostoni (Lucasfilm); my agent Russ Galen; Jim Gilmer, for unstinting logistics support; Karen Miller, for being a good mate; and the 501st Legion, for revealing what really happened on Teth.

THE CLONE WARS

HUMANS MADE THE RULES IN THE GALAXY, SO JABBA THE HUTT felt morally obliged to ignore them all.

He would raise his son, Rotta, to do the same.

"I *could* tell you," he said, taking in the glittering throne room with a short sweep of his arm, "that one day all this will be yours. No. I want you to have more. *Much* more." He picked up a price-less string of faceted emerald beads, alive with light and a delicate tracery of internal veining, dangling them in front of his child's eyes. The assembled court—Jabba liked to admire his collection of talented, costly, and obedient beings—watched in silence while a solo musician plucked a soothing tune on gelen strings. "There. Isn't that lovely? Isn't that *valuable*?"

Rotta gurgled, foaming little bubbles of pearly drool, and grasped the necklace for close inspection as if assessing the carat weight. Then his face split into a grin. He shook the emeralds enthusiastically like a rattle.

"The more you own, the stronger you are." Jabba waited until Rotta tired of his impromptu toy and let it go. The Nikto guard stepped in to take the jewels from Jabba's hand. "Our bodies are slow, *pedunkee*, so our minds must be fast. You'll need to learn all these lessons before you inherit my empire."

Rotta stared into his face, bemused. He didn't understand his legacy yet. It didn't matter; Jabba would repeat the lesson anyway, each day, until Rotta was old enough to understand that the only way to hold your own in a galaxy dominated by those fast-moving, pushy, cocky bipeds was to use your brains, to play them at their own game, grab wealth before they did—before *anyone* did—and hire faster, deadlier beings to help you hang on to it. Hutts weren't built for mobility. They were built for Varl, their long-abandoned homeworld, where their size and shape hadn't been a handicap—until they began competing with humanoids.

But we learned to win. We filled a niche, as scientists say—the environment of crime. And now the bipeds come begging to us.

What's a crime, anyway? Who is the Republic to dare tell me what's right and wrong?

"It's nearly time for Rotta's daily excursion, Lord," said the Nikto. "Shall I summon the sail barge?"

Jabba blinked slowly and glanced at the antique Chammian ivory wall chrono he'd accepted to settle a gambling debt. Or had it come from that smuggler who couldn't deliver his contract on time, and bought just a thorough beating instead of a blaster bolt to the head? It didn't matter. It was still time for Rotta's *walk,* as his nurse called it, even though Hutts *slithered.*

Jabba leaned over slowly and tickled Rotta's chins before picking him up. The infant was already heavy, a sign of robust health.

"I have business to attend to, *meekie lorda*. Go with Nurse, and be good. I'll ride with you tomorrow."

Jabba often saw revulsion in humanoids' eyes. The skinny, untidy, short-lived things judged everything by their own narrow standards. They thought Hutts were repulsive; they said so. But Jabba cradled his son—his own flesh and blood, and *only* his, because Hutts needed no partner to produce a child—and was mesmerized by how *perfect* he was. This was the unbroken bloodline from his own father, Zorba, stretching back millennia across generations of Hutts. This was the heir to his carefully built empire; this was the Hutt who would eclipse all that Jabba had achieved. *Nothing* mattered more.

The opinions of bipeds definitely didn't.

The nurse today was a droid. Sometimes a Twi'lek or some other servant filled the role in a randomly changing roster; Jabba didn't want Rotta to become more attached to the hired help than to his own father. He also mistrusted everyone—*everyone*—and the less predictable the routine, the lower the risk. A security team of well-armed Gamorreans waited to accompany the nurse. Tatooine might have been Jabba's turf, but there was no sense in being complacent.

Jabba stroked Rotta's head before surrendering him to his escort. "Guard him with your lives."

They knew he meant it. The nursery guard trooped out, and Jabba steered his repulsorlift toward the ornate dais on which he'd recline while he received his next visitor—the viceroy of Bheriz. It was a grandiose title for a miner. But he'd be ready to trade processed teniline granules for access to Hutt-controlled hyperspace routes, and any substance that was critical to hyperdrive production would be at a premium in any war.

If the price wasn't right, Jabba would seize the mineral anyway. There were ways to do that. But it was still cheaper and easier to negotiate.

He glanced around the chamber, satisfied that his entertainers, bodyguards, assorted staff, and slaves were arranged in a suitably impressive way around his throne, to focus the Bherizian's mind on exactly how powerful a Hutt lord he was dealing with.

"Bring the viceroy in," Jabba said. He settled into a go-ahead-and-impress-me pose. "I don't have all day."

Actually, he *did*.

He might live to be a thousand years old. No Hutt was in a hurry with a life span like that. Jabba had acquired *lifetimes* of experience, contacts, and knowledge; he had these transient species beaten from the start.

The viceroy walked in, head lowered reverently—sensible start, *good* start—and bowed.

"Lord Jabba . . ." he said, in passable Huttese. "It's very good of you to see me."

"Yes, it is. How much can you deliver?" Jabba took a long rattling draw from his bubble-pipe. "I don't deal in small change."

How can they possibly understand the long game?

The viceroy of Bheriz was a sharp operator, but Jabba had been doing business for generations. "Lord," he said, eyes darting as if he was trying to avoid staring at the Twi'lek dancers draped around the throne. "I can offer you a quarter of our total annual teniline output in exchange for—"

"Half." Jabba checked the ivory chrono again. "I would ask for all of it, but parenthood has made me sentimental." His market analysts told him that teniline prices would collapse within five years now that hexophilenine-based drive components were being developed. There was no point being left with too much stock on your hands. "Do you have sons?"

"No . . . daughters," said the viceroy quietly. "Three."

The distinction between male and female was a temporary detail for a Hutt. But these frantic little bi-gendered species based their entire civilizations on it. Jabba wasn't sure if the viceroy was apologetic for not having reproduced male offspring, or just stating a fact. "Splendid," Jabba said. "Bloodline continuity is a fine thing. Now seal the deal, and you can have free passage on Hutt routes."

It wasn't free, of course. It was merely cheaper than it might have been if Bheriz had tried to dig its heels in.

"Agreed, Lord Jabba," said the viceroy.

Jabba waved him away and puffed at the pipe again. Sometimes it was too easy. Sometimes . . . every day felt the same as the last, decade after decade after *century*. He cast around for some novelty to pass the time, not exactly excitement—he had seen far too much in his life to think there was any thrill left to be sought—but simply something *absorbing*. The musicians provided that for a while. Jabba lost himself in the chords.

"Lord Jabba! *Lord Jabba!*"

One of the Nikto guards came running into the chamber. He fell on his knees, quite literally, skidding the last half meter on the polished tiles. Niktos didn't usually panic; he obviously had very bad news that he knew wouldn't be well received.

"This had better be important, *shag*," said Jabba.

The Nikto paused for a breath before he spoke. "It's your son, my lord," he said. "We were ambushed. Rotta has been kidnapped."

It wasn't the kind of excitement Jabba had been looking for. Every fiber in his body tensed with dread; then his fear reaction took over and he drew himself up to his full height, scattering dancers and musicians.

"Find him!" Jabba bellowed. "*Find my son!* If he's harmed—you'll all pay with your *lives*."

Yes, he meant it.

ONE

———◯———

We have to get access to those hyperspace routes that the
Separatist droids haven't seized yet. Without that, we'll
never be able to take the Outer Rim worlds. Unfortunately,
that means we need the cooperation of the Hutts.

CHANCELLOR PALPATINE, on the logistics problems
facing the Grand Army of the Republic

ZIRO THE HUTT'S PALACE, USCRU DISTRICT, CORUSCANT

"COULD YOU KILL A CHILD?"

Count Dooku thought it was an odd question, coming as it did
from Ziro. The Hutt had been perfectly happy to go along with the
idea of kidnapping his nephew's baby son. But if he'd thought
through the reality of grabbing Jabba's gangland power, then wiping out all rivals, even baby heirs, had to be high on his list of pri-
orities.

Maybe it wasn't. And that would be a fatal mistake.

"Could *you?*" Dooku responded casually. "Isn't he almost
your flesh and blood too?"

Ziro blinked, passing the nictitating membranes across his eyes
with slow deliberation. It was the Hutt equivalent of raising a sar-

castic eyebrow. The private chamber was deserted, with not even a serving droid to overhear them.

"You don't understand us, even if you speak our language far better than most realize," Ziro said at last. "He's Jabba's bloodline. Not mine. So I do whatever it takes, and my priority is my *own* offspring."

Ziro might have been playing the hard case, or he might have been serious. If he *was* serious, then Dooku hoped for his sake that he was ready to kill Jabba, too, because his nephew would send every assassin in Hutt space after him if he found out his uncle was responsible.

"Try not to be too hasty," Dooku said. *Don't blow this before I get what I need.* The ploy was buying time. "Extract maximum leverage from this."

"You don't have to explain long-term strategy to a Hutt," Ziro rasped.

Dooku tried to stop himself from falling into a chain of reasoning with Ziro. It would bring the delicate edifice of his own operation crashing down if he said anything that made Ziro wonder if this kidnapping was going to achieve anything for him. Dooku wasn't convinced that taking Rotta would dislodge or even weaken Jabba's grip on power, but Ziro thought it would reduce his nephew to mere clay in his hands—which was all Dooku needed.

Dooku was certain of one thing, though: harming the Huttlet would unleash a tidal wave of incredible vengeance, and Jabba was going to be around a long, long time to make sure he found everyone involved in the kidnapping and punished them in his uniquely inventive way.

Dooku was counting on it. He wanted the Hutt in the Separatist camp, and the way to do that was to frame the Jedi for Rotta's disappearance.

But if Ziro's cover is blown—then he has to be silenced. We can't have Jabba realizing he's been maneuvered by us . . .

It would be too bad if anything happened to Ziro. After Jabba was signed up, Ziro's fate was inevitable; he would have to be silenced before he implicated Dooku.

Either Hutt would do, though, in a pinch. It didn't matter if it was Jabba or Ziro who denied hyperspace passage to Republic forces. Dooku wasn't selling ideology, and he was sure neither Hutt was buying.

"Of course not," he said, smiling at a being he would kill without hesitation if he threatened his plans. He had no doubt that Ziro would do the same to him. "But you do have to consider what you'll do with Rotta in the longer term."

Ziro eased his bulk across the marble floor onto a platform strewn with shimmersilk cushions that he swept out of the way. Hutts needed smooth surfaces to move properly; carpeting and upholstery didn't go well with a lubricating layer of slime. But Ziro surrounded himself with the finest examples of furnishing anyway. It was as if he wanted to show the rest of the galaxy how powerful he was in terms that other species could understand. Dooku didn't despise that. He felt the faintest pang of pity. It explained the Hutts' need to flaunt Twi'lek dancers and other glamorous humanoids, so radically, physically *different* that no Hutt could possibly have found them attractive. They collected them because *humanoids* coveted them, and so it sent the message clearly: *I possess everything you lust after, so I have power over you.*

It all came from fear. Hutts felt threatened at a subliminal level. Once Dooku worked that out, it had been far easier to deal with them by pressing gently on their paranoia.

"Rotta should be on Teth soon," Dooku said, taking a slow turn to look at the doors. He could hear raised voices in the chamber beyond. He sensed anxiety; no unusual thing in a Hutt's palace with a capricious boss. Maybe the servants couldn't find whatever overpriced delicacy he'd sent them to procure. "Plenty of time to consider your position at your leisure."

"I'm expecting confirmation any moment. Tell me, why *do* you hate your Jedi family so much?"

"They're not my family, and haven't been for a very long time," Dooku said. "Does it matter?"

"Motivation is everything in business."

"Lord Ziro, I suspect you really have no need to ask. Would *you* put your future in their hands?"

"I wouldn't trust the Republic to do anything for Hutts except try to stop us from making a living."

Ziro saw Jedi and Republic as one entity. Dooku had reached a similar conclusion years before. "And anyone who doesn't want to be part of their happy Republic family must be a tyrant or an anarchist. If a world wants to leave, it's accused of being undemocratic, because the will of its inhabitants doesn't suit Coruscant. Such a beautifully embroidered veil of irony."

"You don't have to sell me on Separatism, Dooku. I don't care about your politics, but I know in which sauce my gorog is marinated." Ziro seemed the braggart in Jabba's extended clan, but sometimes Dooku saw hints of a subtler intelligence underneath. He kept a cautious eye on that. "You help me get what I want, I help you get what *you* want."

"Welcome to politics," said Dooku. "Don't delude yourself that it has to have party labels."

Dooku steeled himself to relax. The doors suddenly snapped apart; two droids strode in at a brisk pace, and Dooku slid quietly into a shadowed alcove to watch unnoticed from the sidelines.

"Exalted Lord," one said in a flat monotone. "We have bad news. Your nephew's son has been kidnapped by criminals."

Ziro reared up in feigned shock, then settled down again with a noise like slapping a wet stone. "It's an *outrage*! Have they demanded a ransom? This is an insult to all Hutts! Organize a search team. We'll find the scum who did this to poor Jabba."

Ziro wasn't a bad actor, all things considered. But even if he'd rehearsed it, his choice of words was revealing. Dooku noted that it was more about loss of face than concern for the child's safety. But Hutts didn't think like humans, and the social rules of organized crime were not those of middle-class Coruscant. He tried not to judge when his own species had so little to boast about at times.

Dooku listened, waiting for the droid to leave. *Now to the next stage. Now to making sure that we lure the Jedi to Teth . . .*

"There has been no ransom demand yet, Lord," the droid said. "Most unusual."

"I'll see the scum fed to a rancor." Ziro held out an imperious hand to the second droid. Dooku couldn't quite see the other droid around the edge of the alcove. "Get me the comlink. Let me console my nephew. I expect all Hutts to rally around and help him."

He's really getting into the role . . .

"Lord Jabba is said to be inconsolable. He has asked the Republic to help—to send Jedi to find the child."

Dooku was a hard man to surprise, but the thought of Jabba—*Jabba*—throwing himself on the sympathy of the Jedi hit him like a punch.

Why would the head of one of the most powerful criminal organizations in the galaxy, who could buy any number of bounty hunters and an intelligence network that many governments might envy, beg the Jedi for help?

It was an inexplicable move for a species—a gang lord—so concerned about loss of face, about looking weak, about being seen to be an easy target.

Not Jabba. And it will *be explicable, if I think about it . . .*

The Hutt was up to something appropriately slippery. Dooku wasn't sure what that might be, so he was instantly on his guard. But it was the most *perfect* stroke of luck—unnaturally perfect—for Jabba to ask the Jedi to walk into his setup and implicate themselves in the kidnapping.

Some would say it was meant to be.

And while Dooku didn't believe in luck half as much as he believed in the less random patterns of conspiracy, plot, and counterplot, he wasn't about to pass up an opportunity.

He hoped the Jedi Council would do the decent, upstanding, *moral* thing, and say yes.

He was certain that they would.

TWO

$-\!\!\!-\!\!\Diamond\!\!-\!\!\!-$

Communications with General Kenobi, disrupted they are.
So a messenger we are sending, with important orders for him.

MASTER YODA to Admiral Yularen, ordered to deliver
Padawan Ahsoka Tano to General Kenobi

CHANCELLOR PALPATINE'S OFFICE, CORUSCANT

"I NEVER THOUGHT I'D HEAR LORD JABBA SAY *THAT*," PALPATINE
murmured as the holomessage repeated in a shimmering blue loop.
TC-70, Jabba's droid, delivered the appeal for help to find Rotta
while his master looked on, blinking and swaying slightly, clearly
agitated. "He must be in enormous distress to ask for outside
help."

The Chancellor looked around at the Jedi assembled in his office
to gauge their reaction. He could *feel* it, but it was always interest-
ing to watch their little physical tells—the frowns, the twitches, the
slight lifts of the shoulders—that hinted at the anxieties within.

Mace Windu stroked his chin, grim and unmoved. The man
never looked so much as even slightly satisfied with his life. The
others—Plo Koon, Luminara Unduli, Bolla Ropal—seemed to be

leaving it to him to say what was on all their minds. Nobody was rushing to Jabba's aid.

Palpatine nudged gently for a reaction. "A suitable job for Jedi. Nothing can be hidden from you for long, after all." *Except me, of course.* Even now, after all these years of delicately careful planning, he had moments when the ease with which he moved undetected among them as a Sith Lord made him pause and marvel. *You don't deserve to be the guardians of the galaxy, do you?* "Come along, Master Windu, what's the problem?"

Windu leaned back in his seat. "It'll be a sorry day for the Republic when we divert resources to helping criminal scum."

"Harsh words, my friend. But I'm sure he speaks highly of you, too . . ."

"Chancellor, Jabba probably knows who's done this—no doubt some other gangster he's crossed." Windu's tone wasn't exactly serene. "He's never shied from kidnapping as a tactic himself. Why would he ask *us*? And why should we divert Jedi to a basic police task when there's a war to fight?"

"Because it's *right*, Master Windu." Palpatine had no real need to leap to the moral high ground, but it amused him to do it and labor the point. *Such blind spots, Jedi. This is how I shall remember you when you're long gone—unable to see what was right before your eyes, from me to your own duty.* "A child is *missing*. If it were a human child, would we be having this conversation? Does the parent's *lifestyle* have any bearing on the child's plight? Or do Hutt parents not feel the same grief that we do?"

"Would we be having this conversation," Windu said, not rising to the bait, "if the human child's father was the head of Black Sun?"

"We would, if he could deliver *this*." Palpatine sat down and activated a holochart. It hovered above his desk, a complex web of lines and clusters of light representing the major points of the known galaxy. He tapped the control to remove layers of detail, and entire star systems and planets winked out of existence—so easily done, so very *easy*—to leave a few snaking threads of colored light that ended in the Outer Rim. "A hologram, as they say, is worth a thousand words."

The threads were hyperspace routes. And they were all controlled by the Hutts.

Windu looked like a granite monument to disapproval. Eventually, he tilted his head slightly to one side. "I still feel uneasy. There'll be more to this than a simple ransom demand or a settling of scores. I sense it."

Palpatine allowed himself a sad smile, with just the right blend of I-share-your-concern and you-know-I'm-right. "You might not like doing deals with the Hutt, Master Windu, but these are trying times, and we can't be too exacting in our qualification requirements for allies. As long as they help more than they hinder, that has to be good enough for us. This Hutt has control of the hyperspace access we need to move troops and matériel to the Outer Rim, and we have the expertise to find the unfindable. Mutual advantage."

"I still say there's more going on here than a simple kidnapping. It's a sting of some kind, knowing Jabba."

"I didn't realize you were that well acquainted."

"Based on his track record . . ."

"Then you need to put as many Jedi on this case as you can . . . based on his track record."

"Chancellor, that's impossible. We're at overstretch. I have no Jedi to spare."

"And our *troops* will be spread even more thinly if we can't reach the Outer Rim and keep a resupply chain functioning."

"I'm inclined to agree with the Chancellor," said Unduli. She'd been totally silent until then. "Regardless of the reasons for this kidnapping, we *have* to negotiate with Jabba, and this would give us an excellent bargaining position."

"A win-win, as you might call it," Palpatine said quietly, in almost a whisper. "Save a child, and save our army."

Windu was silent again for a few moments, then spread his hands in reluctant concession. "Kenobi and Skywalker have just taken Christophsis. The planet's largely secured, so if anyone can be redeployed, it's them."

"Very well, send them," said Palpatine. "I'll contact Lord Jabba and reassure him."

The Jedi stood and bowed their heads politely, almost synchronized. Palpatine returned the nod and watched them file out of his office. In a few moments, he'd open a comlink to Jabba and set the wheels in motion.

Lord Jabba, you have our sympathies. You must be beside yourself with worry.

Windu had a point, even if he didn't know it. Why *would* Jabba expose his weakness like that so conveniently? Dooku would have to exercise appropriate caution.

We'll put our best people on it, Lord Jabba . . .

Jabba's plea saved time in the plan to take one more potential ally away from the Jedi, once they were suitably incriminated, of course. In the longer run, it was also one of the finely balanced thrusts and counterthrusts that would keep the war in an uneasy balance until everything was in position, until the Jedi were in just the right state of vulnerability, and Palpatine could choose to end the war—and with it the Jedi Order itself.

Fascinating, how they didn't jump into action when they heard the child is missing. He really is: Dooku's made sure of it. Jabba might be corrupt, but the child . . . he's still an innocent. Fascinating . . . *how the social acceptability of the parent affects the willingness to aid the child.*

They were very selective, these Jedi, about where they focused their legendary compassion.

Palpatine hoped nothing went wrong and that the Huttlet was returned unharmed when he'd served his purpose. Rotta was, after all, another *very* long-term potential ally in his plan.

But if anything happened to the poor thing—ah, here he was,

falling into the platitude trap of being a politician, lies repeated so often that they eventually persuaded even the speaker that he meant what he said, and had done no wrong.

There were always innocent casualties of war, but war still had to be fought. And Jabba would be even more firmly in the anti-Republic camp if anything happened to his son.

Fascinating and . . . yes, still strange *occasionally to play both sides of this game as if I want each to win.*

Palpatine opened the comlink on his desk. "I want to speak to Lord Jabba," he said. "This is the Chancellor of the Republic."

FORWARD AID STATION, CRYSTAL CITY, CHRISTOPHSIS

"Steady with the polish, sir," said the squad sergeant, checking the fluid level on a hemostatic hypospray. "If you shine it up any more, we'll have to put a camo net over you."

Clone Captain Rex paused in midsweep, razor held between thumb and forefinger as he shaved his mirror-smooth scalp, and ran his other palm over his head to test for missed stubble. Hair was just *annoying* under a helmet. And regrowth *itched*. Shaving was now both a necessity and a diversion in quieter moments, a comforting ritual.

Rex went on dragging the razor across his head in precise, slightly overlapping strips, one boot resting on his helmet as it lay on the ground. "Use me for signaling. Should be able to see me from orbit."

"You missed a patch, sir. Going for the tufted look?"

"Maybe a topknot." Rex allowed himself a smile, then pocketed the razor. "Or a fancy braid like those Weequay pirates."

It was the first chance he'd had to sit back and take a breather for days, and his head buzzed with fatigue. The armies of Separatist droids here had been reduced to scrap and a few pockets of resistance; Christophsis had finally fallen to the Republic. In the shelter of a colonnaded doorway that was doubling as a first-aid station, he took out his datapad to check the casualty reports coming in, conscious of an injured trooper sitting on an upturned crate while the sergeant—Coric—tended to the man's shrapnel injury. Plastoid armor was said to be the best credits could buy; Rex staked his life on it. But it had to have joints, gaps, and seals—and they were always vulnerable. The trooper had taken a spray of jagged fragments as razor-sharp and as lethal as fléchettes. Some had penetrated the gap between back plate and shoulder.

"How you doing, Ged?" Rex asked.

"Grateful it's just my shoulder, sir," said the trooper, not looking around. "At least I can still sit down."

Yes, it wasn't bad kit. Could have been better, like the fancy ARC trooper rig he'd seen, but it did the job. The relatively short list of names and ID numbers on his 'pad was testament to that.

Light casualties for a battle. Doesn't feel like that, though.

"Running low on bacta, sir," Coric said. There was a metallic tinkle as he dropped bloodstained fragments into a plastoid container. "Okay on analgesics for the time being."

Rex did a quick mental calculation of how long it would take the cruiser *Hunter* to reach the supply base, load up, and return. "They've sent the ship for replenishment. It'll be back in—"

Rex heard his helmet sensors blipping before he felt the blast. He snatched it up and lowered it into place just as something crashed into the street behind them.

Whoomp—whoomp. A massive explosion shook the ground, then another.

"Incoming!" a voice yelled over the clatter of raining debris.

Yeah, we noticed. Thanks.

Rex grabbed his rifle and sprinted for the street. He didn't look back at Coric or the injured trooper. The two Jedi generals—Kenobi and Skywalker—were already in the open, dodging blasterfire. When Rex got level with them, he could see a wall of droids, rank upon rank, marching toward them in that weird synchrony. It wasn't the same as a well-drilled army of human beings. The precision was cold, unthinking, inexorable, as if the tinnies would keep marching right on over you and crush everything in their path. It was the SBDs, the super battle droids, that really got to him.

He sighted up and aimed.

It was the way they ran with their firing arms extended. And they had *no visible heads*. Any tinny could kill you, but at least the regular droids looked vaguely *human*.

Do they think? Do they feel? Do I care?

No.

Us or them.

Rex squeezed off a few rounds, smashing into the front rank. It wouldn't do more than slow them down. It never did. The game was all about numbers, and the droids had them. Clone troopers, roused from brief sleep or caught while gulping down dry rations, took up defensive positions.

Clone Commander Cody sprinted to Kenobi's side. "Where the stang did *they* come from?"

General Kenobi didn't seem too pleased with his young general. "I told you they caved in too fast," he said, swinging his lightsaber in an arc to deflect a volley of blaster bolts. It was hard to hear him over the blasterfire. "Some victory, Anakin . . ."

"I wasn't the one who decided to send the ship for supplies . . ." Skywalker stood his ground, lightsaber grasped two-handed. *"Master."*

"Neither of us is perfect, then, and let that be our lesson— second wave incoming, men. Stand to."

Anakin swung around. "Platoon, *on me*!" he barked, tapping the top of his head in the signal to form up. Skywalker even *sounded* like a soldier. He was an easy general to follow. "Rex, see that building? The energy sphere? Best position, I think."

Rex flicked the macrobinocular setting on his helmet to get a close-up view. "You want to go around behind."

"It's risky, but we can make it."

"Okay, let's go for it, sir."

Chunk-chunk-chunk. The battle droids marched like a single machine. Rex hated that noise. It just *would not stop.*

Droids relied on numbers and keeping coming, and coming, and *coming.* Rapid reaction wasn't their strong suit. They also preferred a nice level battlefield and wide open spaces. Rex signaled to the platoon, indicating that they should melt back into the deserted streets and alleyways of Crystal City, then transmitted the coordinates of the objective via his helmet comlink. A chart of the streets leading to the energy sphere appeared in the head-up display in every trooper's helmet. Rex didn't really need to use hand signals with that level of communications tech, but it was an instinctive thing to do—and if the HUD systems went down, they all had to fall back on good old-fashioned, nondigital soldiering.

Coric grabbed his medical field kit. The FAS moved with the front line.

General Skywalker darted for the entrance to a deserted office block, Rex at his heels, to pick through the rubble and passages of the city and make their way back behind the droid lines. The route ran parallel to the main street. Kenobi, Cody, and a company of troopers returned the heavy fire raining down on them from the advancing droids; Rex couldn't see it, but he could hear it, and feel the shocks under his boots. Plumes of gray smoke bloomed into the air.

Keep 'em occupied, Cody . . .

Rex scrambled over a shattered fountain that was still gushing water from a broken conduit. This must have been a nice place to live, once; Rex tried to cast his mind back to just a few days earlier, when Crystal City had been a landscape that seemed carved out of glittering gems. The civilian population had already fled by the time ground troops had landed.

It felt like a lifetime ago, and he'd still not seen a live Christophsian. *Plenty of dead ones, though. Plenty of them.* His night-vision filter kicked in as he ran down a sloping passage into darkness and shapes resolved in the green-lit image, a chaos of shattered transparisteel, permacrete, and cables.

A light winked on a console torn from the wall; he hadn't realized there was still a functioning power supply in this complex. *Not a booby trap. No HUD sensor warning. Just a light.* Rex ran on. Skywalker's robes flapped, blotting out the faint lights beyond like a black cloud.

Rex glanced at the HUD icons set to one side of the main display to check for stragglers, counting the transponder blips and ID numbers of the platoon. Sergeant Coric was right behind him— and the injured trooper. He must have been tanked up on painkillers. The trooper's bodysuit had lost some integrity, too. Rex hoped he didn't get into a situation where he needed it to be airtight.

"You could sit this one out, Ged," Rex said.

"I get lonely, sir."

"We'll keep you company, then . . ."

It took maybe ten minutes to skirt around the droid lines, staying close to the canyon-like walls and covering as much ground as possible under cover to avoid aerial detection.

Skywalker leaped ahead—it would have been very handy to bound clear over obstacles like that, Rex thought—and was already on the roof of the energy sphere building by the time Rex pushed through the doors.

They edged to the parapet around the sphere. Troopers positioned themselves and sighted up, snapping anti-armor attachments onto their rifles. On the ground floor, the rest of the platoon hid in the lobby, ready to give the droids a street-level surprise from the rear.

Skywalker seemed to be sizing up for a jump. Two stories beneath them, three octuptarra droids marched forward in that three-legged staccato gait, each one a sphere supported by thin arching legs, spitting a stream of cannon fire.

"What's the plan, then, sir?" Ged asked, as if he didn't know. There was one surefire way to take a droid like that. But their narrow profile and relatively small spherical bodies made them a hard target to hit.

The general seemed to be focused on one of the droids. "Follow me."

"Right you are, sir . . ."

Rex secured his rappel line on the edge of the roof and signaled to the men behind. Skywalker didn't need anything fancy like that.

He just *jumped*.

STREET LEVEL, CRYSTAL CITY

Anakin landed on the back of the octuptarra droid just hard enough to balance on the flat section on top of its spherical body without tipping both of them over.

And the droid couldn't do a thing about it.

It spun and flailed as he rammed his lightsaber deep into its top panel. One of its comrades swiveled its cannon and fired. Anakin batted the bolts away with his lightsaber as Rex and the rest of the clone troopers opened fire and took down the two remaining octuptarras, running over the wreckage to engage the rear rank of battle droids, which had now realized they were facing a rearguard action as well.

Anakin knew he wasn't actually *thinking* at this point. An odd moment of mental separation left him able to run on some buried instinct at the same time as part of him took a step back and observed it all, both fascinated and appalled. His body had bypassed his higher brain functions, moving him around the battlefield without his consent. He was aware of the position of every droid, every clone trooper, but not *consciously*; he could see Kenobi's blue lightsaber blade, flashing intermittently through a smoky forest of battle droids. The noise was deafening—screaming, ripping metal, explosions so loud that they felt like a punch high in the chest—but he wasn't sure he was hearing or even listening. It was . . . a kind of blindness where he could still somehow *see*.

Images flared and vanished in front of him like flash-frames. He was swinging his lightsaber into a group of Tusken Raiders. *You killed my mother. Now it's your turn.* It was a memory; he'd done *exactly* that. For a split second, he wasn't sure if he was look-ing at droids or Sand People. He simply spun around the droid lines, swinging and slashing, buoyed up on a wave of reflexes. Metal fragments flashed past his face. Some veered away at angles, deflected not by his lightsaber but an instinctive and unthinking Force push. One moment he was rising explosively from a squat into the looming shadow of an SBD, thrusting his lightsaber through its chest, the next he was leaping onto the back of a battle droid and ripping off its head with a Force-assisted stranglehold.

And he could still glimpse Tuskens he didn't want to see, solid ghosts, running for cover in the forest of falling droids as white ar-mored troopers charged, fired, and even vibrobladed them. He sprinted after one: but Rex now stood right in front of him, smash-ing the butt of his DC-15 rifle hard down on a battle droid's frag-ile neck as it lay struggling to get up. Rex was almost *casual*. The clone hammered the droid right-handed as he reached into his belt pouch with his left hand to grab a reload. He barely paused as he snapped the new energy pack into its housing and started firing again. Another droid turned on him—perhaps to aid its fallen comrade, perhaps not—and got a faceful of blasterfire.

Anakin struggled to shut out the memory of the Tusken Raiders. They vanished. But in the melee he saw a tall gold figure with long black claws; a Blood Carver called Ke Daiv. He'd killed him, too, years ago.

It's not darkness.

I'm not dark.

This isn't anger—

It was okay; they'd always told him so. He was fighting to save his men, and if he did terrible things out of compassion, out of love, then he wasn't turning to the dark side. That was the Jedi way.

For my mother. For my men. For Padmé.

His body carried on anyway. He swung his blade through metal bodies as easily as if he were cutting grass. Rex and the clone troopers fought as hard as he did, as pumped with adrenaline as he was, too desperate to feel their own natural fear—and yet at that moment they felt unlike him in the Force, devoid only of that singular crazed frenzy, that throat-closing . . . *rage*.

I'm not turning dark.

This has to be done.

Don't stop to think: it'll get you killed.

Anakin shook off the doubt, but it scared him more than death. He charged past Rex into the next rank of droids, almost choking on smoke and flying dust. The thing within swept him along the way it had when he wiped out the Tusken village for his mother's murder, a strangely cold *frenzy*, equally consuming, equally animal in its intensity.

He went on killing. Somehow it didn't matter that those who fell before his lightsaber this time were droids. It was all the same to him. He leaped from octuptarra to octuptarra, driving his blade deep into each droid's sphere as he went. He felt that he could keep going for eternity, never running out of this—

Not rage. Not rage.

Whatever it was, he had to let it out.

The droids were crushed against one another, unable to maneuver. Clones pressed in on them, firing point-blank into their weak points. Shrapnel flew, peppering noisily against clone armor.

"Anakin!" Obi-Wan yelled. He whirled his lightsaber around his head and took out two battle droids in one sweep, cut in half at the waist joint. "*Come on!*"

Anakin suddenly ran out of droids. The cacophony of battle noise stopped. He was now face-to-face with Kenobi, and they were standing on a carpet of dismembered and shattered droids. A sudden silence descended on the battlefield, the kind that left Anakin's ears ringing.

"Are you okay, Anakin?" Kenobi was staring into his face as if he'd seen something.

Anakin took a deep, steadying breath. For a moment, Tuskens, Blood Carvers, and enemy droids were all gone. "Yes, Master." He turned to check how many of his men were wounded. "Rex? Let's evac as many as we can while we—"

But it was just a lull in the storm. The sound carried from farther up the road, that *chunk-chunk-chunk* again.

Another wave of droids.

"We're going to need reinforcements, *fast*," Anakin said.

Kenobi looked up as if he expected a ship to appear on demand. "I still can't get a comlink signal through to the admiral. Must be atmospheric conditions."

"Let's get these guys out, anyway," Rex said wearily. A trooper was calling for a medic; two men picked their way through the droid debris to a fallen man Anakin could see only as a tangle of limbs. There were at least a dozen troopers down. "Come on—I said, *let's get these guys clear!* Move it!"

The clones had been heavily outnumbered, but they were human—agile, motivated, and smart. The droids were just machines. They fell victim to their sheer numbers and inflexibility in every sense. Stick them in a tight spot, and they couldn't avoid one another's arc of fire, or even move. They had no room to fight the way they were programmed to. They couldn't use a rifle as a club like Rex would, or drop a grenade into a hatch and jump clear like Sergeant Coric, or care enough about their brothers' lives to fight like crazy men, or even *think*. They were machines. *Just dumb machines.*

I just destroyed machines. I didn't kill.

Anakin felt as if he were sobering up after a drinking spree, but he'd never been drunk. The moment left him disoriented and embarrassed in a way he didn't understand. He shook himself out of it. More droids were coming, and there were wounded men to evacuate. He rushed to check the casualties with Kenobi and Rex, helping those he could, moving those he couldn't.

Chunk-chunk-chunk.

"Patience, clankers," Rex muttered, hauling a trooper by his shoulders into the shelter of a doorway. Anakin took the man's legs. "I'll get back to you soon."

And then the metallic marching stopped. Anakin strained to listen; the close explosions must have affected his hearing. But he wasn't imagining it. He could see them now, a line of metal statues seeming to wait for orders.

The droid advance had ground to a halt.

"Let's hope that doesn't mean they're moving long-range artillery into position," Kenobi said. He wiped the back of his glove across his mouth, smearing dust and droid oil across his beard. The wretched things scattered debris and fluids for meters when hit. "We can't take much more of this."

Anakin heard it even before he felt it. It was a very distinctive sound, pure music. He looked up at the same moment Rex did, and what he saw was possibly even more wonderful than it sounded. It was so arresting that he almost missed the droids up ahead doing a sudden, crisp about-turn and marching away again.

An armed Republic shuttle banked above the street and veered off toward the plaza.

"That's more like it," Rex said. His shoulders sagged slightly, a blend of relief and fatigue. "They don't like the odds now."

Anakin turned to Kenobi, trying to look unmoved. He wanted to cheer. But it wasn't a very Jedi thing to do. "They're pulling back, Master. Looks like the reinforcements have made them see sense. Come on, Rex, let's give them a proper welcome."

"Where's the cruiser?" Rex asked, tapping his finger against the side of his helmet as if having comm problems. "I'm not picking up anything within landing range."

"It'll be here," Kenobi said, exuding energy. As always, he seemed—*felt*—invigorated by a fight. Anakin wondered if he had those frenzied killing moments too. Kenobi hooked his lightsaber to his belt and jogged toward the plaza, where they'd set up a landing area. "Time for reinforcements, supplies, and perhaps my new Padawan."

Anakin's stomach sank a little. *Dead weight.* It distracted him from his brush with darkness—not darkness, no—and he seized it. A change of problem really was as good as a rest. "This isn't the time or the place to train a Padawan, Master. They're a liability."

"Oh, I don't know." Kenobi picked up speed. He broke into a steady run and pulled ahead. "*You* weren't. Most of the time, anyway . . ."

"Most?"

"The best way to learn is on the job, after all. You should ask Master Yoda for your own Padawan, Anakin. You have a lot to teach. I really think you should."

"No, thanks." Anakin glanced at Rex and raised an eyebrow to Kenobi's back. The captain shrugged. "I'll teach when I think I've got experience worth passing on. And a learner would slow me down. We don't have the luxury of time at the moment."

Anakin could have sworn Rex was amused. He couldn't see his face behind that T-shaped visor, but he noticed a slight dip of the chin and felt his mood in the Force. Then the man gave him a discreet thumbs-up.

Anakin winked. *Thanks, Rex.*

The gunship touched down between two cannon emplacements, and the ramp went down. But no fresh clone troopers disembarked, or even supply droids steering fully-laden repulsors and ammunition crates.

A little female Togruta stepped onto the plaza instead. A tiny girl. A *child.*

Kenobi stood transfixed. "What's that youngling doing here? Where's the ship? Where's *Hunter*?"

The little Togruta drew herself up to her full height—which wasn't saying much—and craned her neck to look up at Kenobi. "Master Yoda was worried that you hadn't reported in, and he couldn't reach you, so he sent me with a message."

"*Sent* you?" Kenobi said. "So where's the cruiser? Where are our reinforcements? Our support?"

"The ship dropped me off. Master Yoda wants you to return to the Temple right away. There's an emergency."

"Funny, we've got one of those too, in case you hadn't noticed." Anakin gestured over his shoulder at the palls of smoke still rising into the air. He didn't dare look at Rex in case the dismay rising in his throat was contagious. After the blissful relief of the droid retreat, the realization that they were still under siege slapped him back hard. There was no end in sight, no resupply, no comm to Padmé to let her know he was fine. "Are you telling me they never got our signals asking for help?"

"I don't think they did. Perhaps we can relay a message via the cruiser that brought me."

"And who *are* you?"

"I'm Padawan Ahsoka Tano," she said.

"Ah, my new apprentice." Kenobi gave her a polite bow, as if grateful to salvage at least something from the situation. "Nothing like being thrown in at the deep end."

Ahsoka looked a little uncomfortable for a moment, then smiled as if she'd nailed it on with grim determination just to keep *their* spirits up.

"No, Master, I'm not *your* assigned Padawan." She turned to Anakin and bowed. "I'm *yours*, Master Skywalker."

THREE

Stand by to break orbit—Separatist vessels incoming.
Sorry, General Kenobi, but we're under fire—you're on your own.

ADMIRAL YULAREN, withdrawing
Jedi cruiser *Resolute* from Christophsis orbit

THRONE ROOM OF JABBA'S PALACE, TATOOINE

IT WAS NEVER A GOOD IDEA TO SHOW WEAKNESS IN FRONT OF THE
hired help.

Once they realized that you could suffer just like them, they
got ideas above their station, and the last thing Jabba needed right
now was to lose his iron grip on his empire. He was permanence,
stability, the unspoken law on Tatooine. Fretting was out of the
question.

Jabba kept his despair and fears for Rotta hidden behind a barrier of contemptuous anger. He worked hard at the act of lounging
on his dais, snacking on gorogs from a jar of brine even though
he'd lost his appetite.

"The slicers, Lord Jabba." A tech droid and his human associate—hackers for hire—were ushered in by a Gamorrean guard to stand in front of the throne. "Master Gaib and Tee-Kay-Oh."

Jabba waited the requisite number of beats before paying them visible attention. He swallowed a gorog headfirst with slow care, slurping the legs as they slipped over his lips, something that always seemed to repel other species. It appeared to work on the one called Gaib. His eyes widened for a telling fraction of a second. At least he didn't look away.

"Report," Jabba said casually. He clutched at every shred of information. He couldn't pass a minute without trying to imagine where Rotta was at that moment, whether he was afraid, or hungry—or even still alive. Did humans understand this? Did they realize that when you lived for a thousand years, when your child was *you*, the product of your genes alone and not something you could carelessly re-create over and over like their fast-breeding species, that your child was the entire future? He doubted it. They were such *temporary* things, humans. They only understood *today*. "You've found something."

It wasn't a question. It was a command. Gaib nudged the droid. "Tee-Kay, show Lord Jabba . . ."

"Air-traffic-control records," TK-0 said. He had a polished dome like an R2 unit. A small cylinder extended from the rim to project a holochart onto the inlaid tiles, where a star system magnified, resolving into a sun and a circling planet; one highlighted itself with a pulsing red glow. "Comlink-relay records. Medical-data-bank accesses. Correlating all that—which took some processing, I might add—leads us to the planet Teth."

Jabba had expected some lengthier explanation. He'd paid for it. "You deduce that from *what*, exactly?"

"Ships leaving Tatooine at the estimated time," Gaib cut in. "We . . . acquired the outgoing comlink records on all the main HoloNet nodes within a day's flight time. What pinned it down was checking access requests to the Galactic All-Species Self-Help Database." He paused, looking as if he were measuring his next sentence to see if it was long enough to hang him. "We hacked the access logs on that, too. It's a Republic-health resource. Tee-Kay examined all the requests for information on Hutt health and ill-nesses."

"We *rarely* sicken," Jabba said slowly.

"Well, we never said the Hutt file was an *extensive* one . . ."

Their line of inquiry was troubling Jabba. "Why would you even look there? Why a database for the sick?"

"How many beings know how to take care of a Hutt baby?" Gaib said. "Except a Hutt, and no Hutt would cross you, right? So the first thing you do if you kidnap a baby is worry about keeping it alive and well. You need to check what's normal if they start—well, doing whatever Hutt babies do. Crying. Being sick."

Jabba could only think the worst. Hutts weren't prone to every passing bug and infection. Most poisons didn't work on them. Something was badly wrong; he didn't have to work hard on his anger act now. "You have reason to think my son is *ill*?"

TK-0 carried on, unperturbed. "Someone on a ship outbound from Tatooine accessed the GASSH Database to download infor-mation on Hutt childhood illnesses, and that ship landed on Teth."

Jabba summoned TC-70, his interpreter droid. "Dispatch the bounty hunters to Teth immediately. And pay these two." He leaned forward slowly and fixed Gaib first, then TK-0, with slow-blinking eyes. "I'll *keep* you. Make yourselves available whenever I call, and you get a handsome retainer."

"What if we're busy?" TK-0 asked.

"Then you get a decent funeral . . . or scrapyard of your choice."

"You'd be amazed how fast our customer-response times can be," said Gaib, physically turning TK-0 toward the doors with both hands. "Pleasure doing business with you, Lord Jabba."

Jabba didn't even see them go. He'd closed his eyes for a mo-ment, every dread passing through his imagination. The scum that had taken Rotta might have botched the kidnap. They'd harmed him, accident or not, and when he caught them, he would harm *them*, in ways they couldn't even begin to imagine. He opened his eyes again. The silent, anxious faces of the entertainers, servants, and guards stared back at him. The palace had had the air of an interrupted funeral for the last two days. He fought an urge to travel to Teth himself, but that was what he paid others to do, and he needed to be here to oversee operations.

There was no telling what might happen if he turned his back and left Tatooine. Coups weren't unknown. But there had been no ransom demand; whatever the kidnappers wanted, it wasn't the usual pile of untraceable cash-creds or aurodium ingots, so there was every possibility that the leverage they were seeking was territorial, or it might have been simple revenge. A rival crime syndicate, or even a rival Hutt kajidic . . . Jabba had amassed a respectable list of would-be-if-they-got-the-chance enemies over the centuries, not that any of them had shown the courage or daring to take him on—yet. But wars created turmoil, and some fool might see this as a good time to take advantage of the chaos growing all around.

Black Sun? No . . .

They wouldn't dare. Nobody wanted a gangland war now that there were rich pickings to be had from the real one.

Or the Republic.

It wasn't the Republic's piously high-minded style, but he didn't trust Palpatine, and so he'd see what his request for Jedi help would shake down. If Palpatine put serious effort into it, the Jedi would pick up Rotta's trail; if they didn't, then Jabba would know that the Republic either wanted nothing from him, or had some involvement.

Win-win. Of a kind.

Jabba suspected everybody at the moment. He would rule them out one by one. Then he would punish whoever was left.

"Captain," he said. The Nikto waiting by his dais—the head of his security detail—snapped to attention. "Has the crew of the sail barge remembered anything else about the kidnapping? Any more useful detail at *all*?"

"No, Lord Jabba."

"Have they tried *very* hard, do you think?"

"Yes, Lord."

"Execute them, then."

Nobody in the throne room breathed. A thin wisp of smoke drifted toward the ceiling from a rare halamo oil lamp. There wasn't a twitch or a sigh, but Jabba was satisfied that the point had been made to his entourage. He wasn't lashing out in anguish, not at all. He wasn't mired in helpless rage. He was making it clear that failure on that scale could not be tolerated, and had to be punished.

No, he wasn't out of control, or weakened, he was certain. He was just managing his empire. Business as usual.

He took another gorog from the jar and swallowed it head-first.

DOOKU'S PRIVATE SHUTTLE, LAID UP SOMEWHERE ON KEM STOR AI

"Most inspired," said Dooku. There was a storm coming; he could hear the fierce wind starting to shriek around the unsealed hatches of the ship. "I really *am* impressed."

A shimmering blue hologram of Ziro the Hutt sat on the table like an ornament in dubious taste, the kind that had been given by someone important and so could not be relegated to a cupboard. "Jabba would suspect he was being set up if it was more obvious. A trail of crumbs works better at luring him than a flashing sign. So I had someone throw in a few electronic transactions that only a *good* security operative would spot."

And was this your idea? You are *more intelligent than you let on, aren't you?* It was always hard to find the balance between dangerously smart and *usefully* smart in a collaborator. "An he'd missed it, Lord Ziro, we would have given him a few extra clues."

"He *didn't* miss it."

I know. I wouldn't leave this entirely to you, would I?

"His bounty hunters are on their way to Teth, then. I'll take over from here."

Ziro wobbled a little. "Take over . . ."

"In that I need to ensure the information about Jabba's bounty hunters reaches the right ears inside the Grand Army, and that the Huttlet isn't actually rescued. A task best done by me. That's all."

"And then?"

"As I said before, simply leave the rest to me. I have a reliable associate who'll take on the next phase of the operation." Dooku bowed his head. "I'll keep you informed."

The hologram vanished as the comlink closed. Dooku rolled his head a little to ease the tension in his neck, then settled down at his desk—even on a shuttle, he needed some illusion of permanence—to study the ground plan and schematics of the monastery on Teth again. There was never a guarantee that any plan would unfold even remotely as intended, not even the small stages, the step-by-step increments of putting the dejarik pieces in place. But this was going well.

Dooku opened his datapad. There were so many layers to planning, so many flow charts to build in his head that would direct events this way and that, or implement the appropriate contingency plan when one coin flipped the wrong way. Planning was a science; he hated to see it reduced to less.

The kidnapping could have gone wrong, and the kidnappers seized. But there was nothing to connect them to Dooku, and he had contingency plans to try again without Ziro's assistance. There would be other wedges to drive between Jabba and the Republic. The clues about the flight to Teth might not have been spotted, but he would have nudged a few more Jabba's way. Jabba might not have called for Jedi assistance, but in the end Dooku had a cascade plan of operations to eventually place some Jedi with Rotta in an incriminating spot.

I've spent years preparing to break the Republic's stranglehold. Years. A long way to go, still, but it'll come. The galaxy is ready for it. Worlds want to run their own affairs. Make it happen soon, Darth Sidious. The Republic's the worst kind of dictatorship—a pseudo-democracy cloaked in smiles and tolerance, as long as you do as it says.

And I will not do as anyone says. I'll think for myself.

Dooku stared into the mesh of light that showed the plan of a castle-like structure full of passages, chambers, and high walls.

Don't think, Padawan Dooku.

"You were wrong then, Jedi," he said aloud. "And you're wrong now."

Destiny was not about *feeling*; destiny was about *thinking*, about rationality. Dooku didn't see reacting blindly to feelings as some mystic virtue, but as a weakness.

In a child, he would have punished it as giving in to impulses, a lack of maturity and self-control.

As a child, he had been trained not to think. As a child, he had been trained to be a Jedi.

Don't question so much, Padawan Dooku. Feel. Don't doubt. Believe.

Well, he questioned things now. And he didn't believe. The Republic was corrupt to its core, and the Jedi were its lackeys—sanctimonious mercenaries. Their comfortable little cartel was coming to an end. Darth Sidious would finish it off, and Dooku knew it was his moral duty to help bring about that day.

Then he saw snow again, not the polished apocia wood desk; a battlefield in winter, finally silent. The schematic's hair-fine lines of red light became spatters and trails of blood that Dooku feared he would never be able to wash from his hands.

He was standing ankle-deep in the muffled, ice-cold whiteness of Galidraan in winter. Jedi and Mandalorian dead lay everywhere. And he could still hear his own appalled voice, his own shame.

What have we done?

It was a massacre; and the Jedi had carried it out, pawns of the corrupt Galidraan governor, who had set up the Mandalorian army for his own agenda. Looking back on it, Dooku saw it was the tipping point that had changed his life. It was the moment he had started to *think.*

I believed my Masters. I didn't think for myself. They didn't question, either; they took the governor at his word. They just be-lieved. And we killed people. We killed them on the say-so of a criminal.

If you were going to take lives, go to war, then there was no benefit of the doubt to be given, no other's word to take. Dooku trusted only proof now.

What have I done?

You came to your senses.

But I'm setting up the Jedi now. That makes me as degenerate as they are.

Think of it as using their own complacency against them. Turning their own weapon on them. Poetic justice. Whatever it takes. They won't say sorry and step down simply because you point out the error of the Republic's ways, will they?

He had these arguments with himself more than ever lately.

The snow had melted; the dead were buried. But he couldn't erase Jango Fett's face, the face of a man back from the living death of a slavery that Dooku had delivered him into, etched with all the bitter lines of surviving only to have his moment of justice. It was always the last image to leave Dooku. It wasn't just that the millions of troops cloned from Fett made forgetting it impossible. It was that Fett hadn't lived to see the downfall of the Jedi. Fett's motive for sharing—aiding—Dooku's ambition hadn't been greed, he realized, but the same understanding that the Jedi Order was a destructive, destabilizing cabal.

The Jedi had killed Fett in the end. But most of him seemed to have died at Galidraan anyway, and only his insatiable hunger for justice had kept that formidable body moving.

We'll have our day, Fett.

Dooku opened the comlink again, this time to the monastery on Teth. It was time for the next stage of the operation.

"Ventress," he said. "Ventress, is the Huttlet all right? Bring me up to speed."

FOUR

You have to know the provenance of information to evaluate it.
In other words, who wants you to know this? Who doesn't? And why?
If you come by sensitive information too easily, it might be planted.
So if you check out Teth, go carefully.

INTELLIGENCE OFFICER LIEUTENENT KOM'RK, N-6, Special
Operations Brigade, Grand Army of the Republic

OBSERVATION POST, CRYSTAL CITY, CHRISTOPHSIS

ANAKIN KNEW HE HAD TO GRIT HIS TEETH AND TAKE A CERTAIN
amount of Jedi Council bureaucracy, but there was a war on. And
there was every chance that they'd die here.

He didn't have time for a Padawan.

He also didn't want to kick up a stink in front of Rex. There
was nothing more demoralizing for troops than a commanding officer who didn't look solidly in control. If his clone troopers could
take any onslaught without murmur, then he had to do even better.
It was what officers did. It was expected of him.

The abandoned skyscraper was a useful observation point.
When visibility was good, they could see for thirty klicks in every
direction. Smoke hanging in the air had cut that down dramatically, but it was still an excellent vantage point, and went some

way to making up for the lack of air cover and forward air control. He could direct long-range artillery from here.

We need reinforcements. Ground troops, a fighter squadron, an armored battalion, too.

Ahsoka stood on a rail to look out from the top of the abandoned skyscraper as if she were sightseeing. She wasn't tall enough to peer over unaided. Anakin grabbed her by the belt and pulled her back down.

"This isn't a training exercise, youngling," he snapped. "The Seps use live rounds. They're awkward that way."

"I know what I'm doing." Ahsoka readjusted her belt. "Why don't you send a couple of squads to infiltrate the—"

"Skyline yourself like that again and you'll get your head shot off, Jedi or not."

Rex had his head turned toward the droid positions. He might have been watching, or he might not; there was no way to tell. Anakin envied him his helmet at times like this. Rex didn't have to grit his teeth. He could just switch off his links and retreat into a private world. He could vent his spleen as much he wished, and nobody would be any the wiser.

The clones did that. He *knew.*

"I thought you said you'd never have a Padawan, sir . . . ," Rex said at last.

"Someone must have fouled up the flimsi." As soon as the battalion was relieved, Anakin would pack Ahsoka off to the Temple again. "I don't have a Padawan. I *can't* have a Padawan. There's normally at least some discussion about this kind of thing first."

Ahsoka stepped in front of him. "I'm still here, Skyguy. Stop talking about me as if I'm not."

"*Skyguy.*" Rex took off his helmet and laughed. "Skyguy . . ."

Anakin wasn't in the mood. He fixed Ahsoka with a don't-mess-with-me look. "What did you call me? Look, don't get snippy with me, youngling. You're not even old enough to be a Padawan."

"I'm not a *youngling*," she said. "I'm fourteen."

Rex kept a straight face. "I'm ten," he said, "but I'm tall for my age."

"Anyway, Master Yoda thinks I'm old enough."

"Master Yoda's light-years away, so it's *me* you've got to persuade," Anakin said. "And seeing as I can't ship you back to Coruscant yet, you might as well make yourself useful. Rex, give her an acquaint of the position. And don't take any backchat from her."

Rex checked the charge on his rifle and both sidearms, then gestured to the stairs. "Very good, sir. Come on, youngling."

She followed him without further argument, scowling, but Anakin saw her lips move soundlessly: *Padawan*. She really cared about her status, that one.

"And if Captain Rex gives you an order," Anakin said, "you *take* it, okay?"

Ahsoka narrowed her eyes a fraction. "Yes, Skyguy."

Stang, he didn't have time to play games with a kid. He watched her disappear down the smoke-stained stairwell with Rex before he felt he could breathe again.

Kenobi sat next to the mobile comm station, one ear cocked to the chatter of static thrown up by the solar storm ripping through the upper layers of Christophsis's atmosphere. "Don't you think you're a little hard on her?"

"No. This isn't a game."

"I admit she's not what I expected in terms of self-discipline." Kenobi paused as the white noise seemed to resolve into a clear comm signal, but it vanished again. There was still no window to make contact with Coruscant. "But then neither were you."

"I had a better excuse," said Anakin. "And I didn't play the brat in the middle of a war, either."

"You're not that much older than she is."

"Oh, I *am*, Master," Anakin said quietly. "A lifetime older."

Kenobi just looked at him, one eyebrow slightly raised. There might have been the suggestion of a smile under the beard. Then it faded as he appeared to realize what Anakin meant.

"Yes, I know what war does to you," Kenobi said at last. He didn't ask Anakin to go on, although he must have felt his pain from time to time in the Force. But it was more than the war. Kenobi never asked for any details about what had happened on Tatooine, and whether that was from tact or disinterest, Anakin didn't know. "Well, then, you're old enough to cut her some slack."

You don't know what it is to love, Master. Or to lose. You didn't even know your own mother.

Anakin hadn't yet settled on a consistent view of his former Master—and he still called him Master, and thought of him as such—so that half smile, benign as it was, made him wonder if he was being scolded. Sometimes he felt Kenobi was stability and safety; sometimes he thought he was an overbearing older brother who held him back and even competed with him.

He'd told Padmé that. She'd been taken aback by it.

And he didn't want to take me as a Padawan, did he? He only did it out of duty.

Anakin often found himself ambushed by thoughts he didn't want. It was even worse sometimes than the recurring memory of the Tusken village, because he only had to face its ghosts, but it was harder to handle his sporadic resentments and doubts about a Master he cared for and respected.

"I've got some maintenance to do," Anakin said, grabbing a battered comlink from the makeshift console. "I'll be back soon."

It was his hint that he wanted some space. Kenobi never asked why. Usually, it was to find privacy to comm Padmé or to compose a message to her that he could send when he next got a chance. It was hard to be apart. It was even harder to keep their relationship secret.

No attachments. I know. But I can't live that way, Master.

Anakin found a quiet room two floors beneath the observation level and settled into a corner. The room must once have been an entertainment suite; a large holovid projector jutted from one wall, cables exposed, framed by the pockmarks and scattered black debris from a cannon round that had passed through the room to leave a hole in the far wall. Plush upholstered seats—brilliant green Farus shimmersilk with a close-cut pile—lay tipped on one side, pleekwood legs snapped off, pale stuffing spilling onto the floor in a way that looked distressingly like brain tissue.

Anakin dismantled the comlink almost without thinking, the probes and microspanners as natural in his hands as an extension of his own body. Putting things back together was soothing. It gave him control over events just long enough to calm his thoughts.

Skyguy. I bet she thinks that's cute. It's just juvenile.

Ahsoka *really* annoyed him.

He wasn't sure why, beyond the fact that he didn't relish responsibility for—or power over—others. And she talked too much. And she was far too cocky, in that naive, chirpy, why-can't-we-fix-it way, as if he and the clone troopers had never been in combat before. When it came to battle—well, he'd still take lessons from *them*, thanks. And she could do the same.

The Jedi Council didn't want me, either. Being the Chosen One didn't count for anything. Master Yoda wouldn't train me, or Windu.

Every member of the Jedi Council had had something more pressing to do than help him work out what this terrible, galaxy-changing power of his meant, and how he should live in its shadow.

He still wasn't sure.

Anakin recalled standing there in that grand, polished Jedi Council Chamber, surrounded by what felt like fear, and disdain, and *bewilderment*—who were those Masters to feel bewildered, when *he* was the one uprooted from everything he knew and told he had a destiny?—and feeling that the only person there who cared if he lived or died was Master Qui-Gon Jinn. And they stopped him training the Chosen One.

Qui-Gon hadn't cared what the Jedi Council said. He'd trained him anyway, a Padawan in all but name.

Why am I thinking of all this now? Haven't I put it behind me? Haven't I had enough bad memories since then to take their place? Haven't I vindicated Master Qui-Gon?

If he was consumed by anything, it should have been the death of his mother. Right then, he wasn't even thinking of Padmé.

Anakin realized he'd reassembled the comlink without even being conscious of it. He tested the power switches. It worked the first time. Sometimes the little victories made all the difference.

Maybe she's like me. Maybe nobody else wanted to train her, either.

Anakin didn't want to do it, but he knew how it felt to be rejected. It was time to see if he could repair the rocky start to his relationship with his new Padawan as easily as he'd fixed the comlink.

CENTRAL PLAZA, CRYSTAL CITY

Rex picked his way through the rubble of what had once been a beautiful city square, Skywalker's new Padawan at his side.

He hoped she was grateful for a hasty exit. He wondered if she realized that Skywalker didn't suffer fools gladly, and that if she'd pushed him much further, she'd have learned that the hard way. The men liked Skywalker; he was a soldier's soldier, someone who *understood* the troops, but—no, *and* he had that edge to him. Rex didn't see it as a failing. There was no *but*. It was a necessity in a good officer. You *had* to know who was boss.

Ahsoka paused and looked up at him. "Shouldn't you be wearing your helmet?"

Rex's boots crunched on a shattered marble relief that looked like part of the fountain. "I've got my comm earpiece." He tapped his ear. He thought she wanted to learn SOPs, standard operating procedures. "And we're monitoring for snipers."

"Have you thought about moving that line back?" Ahsoka pointed to the artillery position. "They'd have better cover that way."

Ah. Maybe he was overestimating the scope of the teachable moment. This wasn't a clone kid. She was a know-all, or at least too scared to admit she didn't know much. He had to deal with it, or Skywalker would have his hands full. "Thank you, but General Skywalker thinks they're fine where they are."

"But they need cover."

"They also need range."

"What if I gave you an order to move the cannons? You're a captain, and I'm a Jedi, so I technically outrank you, right?"

"Technically, you're only a youngling."

"Padawan!"

She looked as if she was going to continue, but she stopped of her own accord. Rex didn't need to interrupt her. It was as good a time as any to do what a fellow clone captain called *picturizing*, a lovely mild word for putting someone in their place.

"Look, littl'un," Rex said, "why don't I explain how things are in the real world?"

Ahsoka bristled visibly. Rex had never served with Togrutas before, so he wasn't sure what was normal for their youngsters. But he knew how a Jedi should behave, and she wasn't doing it.

"I still think—"

This time, he *did* interrupt. "Are you scared?"

"No!"

"Well, you should be. Because if you're not scared in a war, then you haven't grasped the severity of your situation." Rex sat down on a chunk of masonry so he was at eye level with her. He preferred training by example, but that would have involved letting her get blown up, and he had to cut her some slack. She was just a kid, full of a kid's weird mix of uncertainty and overconfidence about a brand-new rank, as if it would stop a blaster bolt if she brandished it enough. "I take my orders from General Skywalker. It's called the chain of command, and it *matters*, because we all have to be clear who's in charge, or else we'll be running around like nuna. And you take your orders from him, too, because you're his Padawan. With me so far?"

That defiant jut of her chin had receded a little. "Yes, *Captain*."

"Want to learn the most important things about being a soldier? I mean the things they don't teach you at the Temple."

"How would *you* know what they teach Jedi?"

"By watching *you* . . ."

"Okay." Ahsoka dropped her chin another fraction. "Experience matters."

Rex ratcheted back a few notches. There was no point rubbing a kid's nose in it. You had to climb down *with* them. "One," he said. "*Orders*. You follow orders. They keep you alive. Two, you're part of a *team*. We look out for our buddies—I cover your back, you cover mine. And three, an officer rank doesn't give you automatic respect. You *earn* it. It's not just Skywalker's rank that makes us give him one hundred percent. It's because he treats *us* with respect, and he puts himself on the line with us."

Rex paused to let it sink in. He took a guess that she wanted desperately to be taken seriously, and treated like an adult. She'd grow up all too soon in this war anyway.

Togrutas had head-tails, but unlike Twi'leks, Togrutas had three, much shorter than the twin Twi'lek lekku. Ahsoka's—vividly striped—now hung down in front of her shoulders in a way that made her look crestfallen. "That makes sense," she said at last.

"So . . . are you scared?"

"Yes. Are you?"

"You bet."

"But you're all bred to be fearless."

Rex laughed. "All the same, eh?"

"Well . . . you *are* clones."

Rex sat his helmet on his knee. He couldn't show her the head-up display projected onto the inside of his visor, because the helmet wouldn't fit over her head-tails. But he could transmit something from his database to her 'pad. The lesson was nearly complete. They'd get on just fine after this, he knew it.

"Like Togrutas," he said. "You're all pretty much the same, too."

"What?"

"Take a look at the species database we're given. It says so." Rex slid his hand inside the helmet and activated the link. "Come on—check your 'pad."

Ahsoka grabbed the datapad from her belt and stared at the screen. At first her frown was just one of concentration, but then it deepened into concern. She narrowed her eyes. "Well, that's just *not true*." She started reading aloud. "*Most Togrutas are not independent. Many species are under the impression that Togrutas are venomous . . . Togrutas enjoy eating thiamars, small rodent-like creatures . . .* well, that's not fair. I'm not like that at all."

Rex smiled. *Point made.* Ahsoka met his eyes for a few moments, then nodded in concession.

"Do we have an understanding, Padawan?"

"Yes, Captain." She smiled back, restrained at first, then with a broad grin; yes, Togrutas *did* have the sharp predator's teeth of their ancestors. But the poor kid must have felt terribly alone right then. "There's nothing quite like experience."

"Good. Come on, let's walk the perimeter." Rex stood up and beckoned her to follow. He could hear the local comm traffic in his earpiece; no droid activity, not yet. That worried him more than it comforted him. The tinnies would be back. He ran through the contingency plans in his head, the last-ditch defense they might have to put into operation if they weren't relieved soon. "At least we don't have to worry about civilians. That's the worst thing when you're fighting in an urban area—the risk of civvy casualties. That limits our attack. The tinnies don't have any feelings about killing noncombatants, of course, and they just keep shelling, so we're handicapped by our rules of engagement."

A small creature—nothing Rex could identify—shot out from the rubble and raced away from them. Ahsoka's head jerked around; her eyes never left the creature as she walked, her head eerily steady—unnaturally steady—the whole time. It was a hard-wired reflex reaction to rapid movements. In that moment, Rex saw her for what she was: still a predator, a fast and precise hunter, just as he was the agile, opportunistic, cooperative team animal his ancestors had been. In a war like this, a predator was a great asset.

She's got the right stuff. Let's hope we can keep her from killing herself proving it.

The tiny ball of dark fur darted a few more meters to another vantage point. "Please, not lunch . . . ," Rex said. "At least, not while I'm looking."

"No, rodents give me gas." Ahsoka laughed, and turned her head away from the creature. Then she scanned the horizon slowly, her huge eyes slightly narrowed. Of course; she'd have terrific long-distance vision, a legacy of her predator heritage. Then she pointed, extending her arm slowly. "What's that?"

Rex hadn't noticed it before. From the sudden burst of comm chatter in his ear, the obs post had spotted it at the same time Ahsoka had. It was a huge orange ball, translucent and glowing slightly as it slowly swallowed buildings on the far edge of the city. It was moving.

No; it was *expanding*.

Rex's stomach knotted. "That's going to make things damned near impossible."

"You didn't answer, Rex—*what is it?*"

"It's an energy field," he said, turning back to the battalion's makeshift operating base. "There goes our edge. Cannon won't penetrate that. And we don't have the numbers to keep the droids pinned down. Come on, back to base."

"But you've got a plan, right?"

"We've always got a plan. And another . . . and another. Just have to keep trying until we find one that works, and hope we don't die before that."

She trotted after him and broke into a run. "Master Yoda might get support here in time."

Rex paused to watch the expanding sphere for a few moments, estimating the speed of advance. It would overwhelm them long before anyone flew to the rescue.

"Well, you need experience, littl'un. Here's where you start getting it."

"Don't worry," she said. "I'll watch your back."

Rex didn't doubt it.

"And I'll watch yours," he said.

COMM STATION

The holochart of Crystal City made the Separatists' strategy painfully clear.

Anakin watched the moving points of light that indicated droid troops. They were advancing behind the leading edge of the energy shield, moving back into the center of the city. One column was heading straight for the artillery position in the square. He felt helpless, and he didn't handle helpless well.

Kenobi tilted his head slightly to one side. "It's hard to pin-point the field generator precisely, but it's got to be in this area somewhere. The field's elliptical, which means it's probably within *this* radius." He prodded his forefinger into the meshwork of light and made a loop to indicate the range of positions. "Cannon's not going to make a dent in that, so I say we save our ordnance for later. In the meantime, all we can do is try to engage them in confined spaces."

"We'll draw them into the buildings," Rex said. "They've got to find us to fight us. They can't fire their own cannon from inside the shield, so let's make their defenses work against them."

Ahsoka watched in silence. Anakin wondered what Rex had said to her to subdue her annoying ebullience. She seemed to be calculating, eyes darting from one side of the holochart to the other.

"Why don't we just take out the generator?" she said. She seemed to be asking Rex. "Or is it not that simple?"

"Correct," said Anakin. "It's *not* that simple."

"Suicide mission," Rex said. "Not that I couldn't get plenty of volunteers from the ranks, but we'd probably waste a lot of men getting nowhere, and at least we know we stand a chance if we can pin down the tinnies inside buildings. They're not good at fighting house-to-house."

"I could do it," Ahsoka said. "Let me try, Skyguy."

Rex gave her a look that Anakin couldn't quite read, but it wasn't annoyance. He *felt* it: a kind of sad guilt.

"You don't have to prove anything, littl'un," Rex said quietly.

"I can do it. I *know* I can. I'm small and I'm fast." She lowered her chin slightly. "And where better to use Jedi skills?"

"Very well, Anakin, take Ahsoka and penetrate the Sep lines," said Kenobi. He stabbed his finger into the holochart again. "Rex and I can stage a diversion here, and that should make it easier for you to slip through."

"We'll need to defend the artillery position, sir," Rex said. "But if we can't draw them into the buildings, they'll just roll right down the street into the square and take out our arty pieces, and there'll be very little we can do about it. And then it'll be endex for all of us."

"I can *do* it," Ahsoka said. She shot Anakin a glance. "*We* can do it."

Kenobi didn't comment. He walked away to the comm console to talk to Clone Commander Cody. Ahsoka seemed engrossed in the chart, and increased the magnification to show individual streets as if she was planning a route. Anakin took a few paces and stood in the doorway, then gave Rex a discreet jerk of his head to indicate he wanted to talk to him.

"Don't tell me you can do mind influence, too, Rex," Anakin said quietly. "But it's impressive, whatever it is."

"Okay, I might have overdone the pep talk on how to be a good officer, sir."

"It worked."

"She's desperate to get it right. I'd hate to think I made her feel she has to do something suicidal to earn my respect."

"She's not a passenger, Rex. If she can pull her weight, she has to. She's no less expendable than me or you in this war."

Rex could play deadpan with the best of them, but he couldn't suppress pupil movement. He looked a little awkward for a moment. "Okay, sir."

Anakin turned, walked over to Ahsoka, and caught her by the shoulder. "If we survive this, Snips, you and I are going to have a nice long talk."

"Snips?" she said indignantly.

"That's what you get for being snippy. Got it?"

"Got it, Master. Let's go."

She almost bounced as she walked. He hoped she wasn't excited, as if this were some game, and he tested the eddies in the Force around her to discover her state of mind.

She was scared.

Anakin tried to recall how he'd felt when he walked into hostile situations at her age. It was hard to remember; there were headline events in his past that he recalled all too clearly, because the pain was still there, but that had never gone away, so he hadn't had a chance to forget.

I'm twenty.

It feels like . . . forever.

They worked their way through the abandoned city toward the advancing edge of the shield. Anakin diverted into another tower and made for the twentieth floor. The power was out; no turbolifts. Every time they needed to climb a high point to do a recce, it cost time and energy. Anakin's thigh muscles ached. He longed for air support, or even a single surveillance vessel.

"So what's the plan?" Ahsoka asked.

Anakin scanned the city with his macrobinoculars. The droid army was a lot farther forward now. "I thought you were the one with the plan . . ."

"No, I'm the one with enthusiasm. You're the one with experience. You show, I learn."

He couldn't tell if she was being sincerely naive or sarcastic. At least Rex seemed to have knocked the argument out of her. "Okay, we have to penetrate the shield, and then the line of tanks. Double barrier."

"What about trying to outflank them? Go around the lines."

"It'll take time we don't have."

"Okay, shortest path. Through the middle."

Anakin tried hard to be patient, but the irritation spilled out despite that. "So you can pass yourself off as a droid, can you? Just stroll in, say 'Copy copy,' and hope they don't notice?"

"Okay." Ahsoka seemed resigned. "My first lesson is obviously to keep my mouth shut and wait for you to come up with an answer."

And then it came to him. It was just as well that it did. There was nothing less inspiring in an officer than telling a subordinate to shut up but having no better ideas himself. He wondered why it had taken him so long to think of it.

"You just have to turn the problem upside down," he said. "If we can't cross their lines, we let their lines cross over *us.*"

FIVE

———●———

There is a fine line between neutral and amoral.
In fact, there may be no line there at all.
COUNT DOOKU

REPUBLIC-HELD SECTOR, CRYSTAL CITY

THE STREAM OF CANNON FIRE HIT THE ENERGY SHIELD AND SIM-
ply spilled off it like white-hot liquid. Plasma diffused, vanishing a
few seconds later as if it had never hit its target at all.

Rex lowered his macrobinoculars. He knew it was inevitable.
But it was still as close to being demoralizing as anything ever
came for him.

There was always a Plan B, though.

"It was worth a try," Kenobi said. "Okay, fall back. At least it
makes us look convincing, like we're retreating because we're in
trouble."

"Sir, we look convincing because we *are* in trouble."

Kenobi gave him that look. One day, Rex thought, he'd get a

laugh out of the Jedi. "Just whistling in the dark, Rex. Have we cracked their comm encryption yet?"

With a couple of rapid blinks, Rex switched to an open unencrypted channel on his helmet link. The Seps would hear him as clearly as the Grand Army could. "Fall back! All units, fall back and regroup!" Yeah, that sounded authentic enough. He switched back to a secure channel. "Yes, sir, we have."

He eavesdropped on the voice traffic between the Separatist tank commanders and the battle droid officers. General Whorm Loathsom was being briefed on the clone retreat and seemed flushed with his success. He was ordering his armored column to press forward.

"General Loathsom's given the order to go for our cannon," Rex said. "The shield front will be at this point in around fifteen standard minutes."

Kenobi kept squeezing the hilt of his lightsaber as if he were doing a physio exercise. The man loved a fight. "Do you believe in nominative determinism, Rex?"

"If my name was Whorm Loathsom, I'd prefer not to, sir."

"I'm sure his mother loves him. Now, let's keep our heads down until the shield passes over us. See how much damage we can do once the tanks are committed to a choke point."

There was a crude, easy way to stop an armored advance: knock out the lead and rear tanks, leaving the rest of the column trapped between and unable to maneuver or escape. Rex sized up the exits from the main street, and worked out where to concentrate the anti-armor fire to achieve maximum inconvenience. If only they'd had air support. They could have trapped the Sep forces in the relatively narrow gully of the skyscraper-lined street and just poured down fire from a nice safe altitude. Instead, ground troops would have to pick off tanks and droids one at a time.

Can do—at a price. It's getting harder to define what acceptable losses *means now.*

Rex wondered how far General Skywalker and Ahsoka had progressed. They wouldn't risk opening a comlink. But Jedi have this weird *awareness*, he knew, and maybe Kenobi could detect where they were. Kenobi would certainly sense if they got killed. Rex had seen that working firsthand.

He signaled his men into position and followed Kenobi into the nearest building to wait.

"What if they get captured, General?" Rex asked, letting the welter of data and images on his HUD wash over him. "Ahsoka and General Skywalker, that is."

Kenobi didn't take his eyes off the deserted, rubble-strewn street. The steady *chunk-chunk-chunk* of droid feet and the whining drives of tanks drifted on the air. "If we didn't have the resources to take the shield, then we don't have the resources to extract them, either."

Rex watched for signs of discomfort, awkwardness, even emotion. But Kenobi didn't say another word. He just seemed unnaturally focused on the street.

"I'll volunteer, if the need arises, sir."

"Thank you, Rex. I know he'd do the same for you."

Kenobi's tone was unfathomable. Rex dropped the subject, and wondered at what point he would accept that he had to abandon his general.

We leave nobody behind.

And so far, they hadn't.

CHANCELLOR PALPATINE'S OFFICE, CORUSCANT

Palpatine took a few steadying breaths before answering Jabba's comm. He gazed out onto the skylanes and cityscape beyond the transparisteel wall of his office, head resting against the back of his chair, and then swiveled slowly to face the transmitter on his desk, instantly an icon of benign civic duty.

"Lord Jabba," he said softly. "How are you?"

Jabba's interpreter droid, TC-70, was close by his master's side, and although Palpatine understood Huttese, it suited him to feign ignorance. The droid was a very accurate interpreter, as it turned out.

"Lord Jabba says his son is still missing, and that means he is deeply unhappy, and when he is deeply unhappy, that tends to color his approach to diplomacy."

Quite a tidy warning. I'll give Jabba a point for that. "We might have a lead, Lord Jabba. I have my best operatives on the job. Rest assured we're giving this our utmost attention."

Jabba narrowed his eyes to mere slits and shook slightly. TC-70 listened intently to his rumbling voice.

"Lord Jabba says he notes your current difficulties in moving troops and matériel to the Outer Rim. He wonders if that might hamper your ability to aid the search for his son."

Doing business with the likes of Jabba was actually *enjoyable*. Palpatine relished the chance to lock horns—politely, elegantly, *subtly,* but lock nonetheless—with a being who not only enjoyed his own power but who knew how to exercise it. The politicians of Coruscant were small people with small threats. Jabba might not have been in Palpatine's own league—was anyone?—but the Hutt was a more worthy sparring partner than most, and more subtle than any gave him credit for.

So we both know what's on the table, what we're trading— access to the Outer Rim for his son's safe return. Or, should I say, we both know what I want him to think *is the hidden agenda.*

Palpatine wondered if Jabba assumed the Republic had arranged the kidnapping to put pressure on him, soften him up a little. That would have been his first assumption, had he been the Hutt, except there were layers beneath that, as numerous and finely stacked as a slice through the thousand layers of a nimirot root.

"I admit that being able to route traffic through certain sectors would aid us immensely, Lord Jabba," Palpatine said, with just the right degree of martyred endurance. "But we search, we follow leads, and we *will* find your son."

"Lord Jabba is generous, and will show his gratitude if you succeed."

Palpatine smiled sadly. "We would do it anyway," he lied, knowing Jabba *knew* it was a lie. "No civilized state could ignore a plea to help an innocent youngling. I know how important family is to Hutts."

And how unusual it is for one relative to betray another. My, Ziro's lucky you won't have the chance to blame him.

TC-70 paused to listen to Jabba. "Master Jabba says he's glad you understand him."

Jabba thought he was playing a high-stakes game, that was clear. He was used to it. He hadn't become the unchallenged leader of the most powerful of kadijics by assuming the best of anyone. Palpatine gave him the kind of smile that just *might* have suggested that he knew the Hutt suspected everyone, every time, but that he would keep his end of the bargain anyway.

Yes, Jabba was used to playing deadly games.

But he wasn't used to being one of the pieces. And that, in Palpatine's meticulously planned war in which he controlled both sides for one grand purpose, was all that Jabba was.

He would never know.

SEPARATIST LINES, CRYSTAL CITY, CHRISTOPHSIS

"They're going to notice . . ."

"They're too busy."

"Master, do we still need this thing?"

Anakin came to a halt, the sound of their labored breathing filling the small space. It was hard to navigate under the upturned piece of debris that covered them like the shell of a kasaq mollusk.

Crawl and stop, that was the pattern; they could scuttle only so far down the road before they had to peer out again or try to orient themselves by what they could see beneath them.

Rubble. There was a lot of rubble, and it all looked the same. Under this broken section of conduit, the two Jedi were effectively invisible to battle droids; they were the same temperature and color as their surroundings. Only their movement would give them away—so they darted in random bursts, zigzags, slow crawls.

"Okay . . . ready, Ahsoka? In three . . . two . . . *go*."

They edged a few meters farther and stopped again.

Anakin caught his breath. His neck ached from the strain of holding it at an unnatural angle with the weight of both the shell and the strap of his satchel on it. He heard the faint hum of the energy field coming closer; the air tingled with it, making the hairs stand up on his arms and nape. The enemy line was—obligingly—passing over them.

"Ugh. . . . ," Ahsoka said, shuddering.

"Nearly there."

"It's like having someone walk on your grave."

"What happened to chirpy and positive?"

She didn't reply. Maybe the frequencies irritated something in the Togruta nervous system that humans didn't have. In a few moments, the tingling stopped and Anakin felt he could breathe properly again.

"That's it," Anakin said. "We're in. Now let's locate that generator." He was pretty sure he could find it by a combination of his Force senses and the odd infrasonics he was picking up as he got closer to it. "Be careful."

"My legs are going to give out," Ahsoka said. "I have to stand up."

"I said, *be careful*—"

Bang. They hit something. Anakin thought they might have run into a lump of masonry, but as the shell of conduit tipped and they fell over, he found his field of vision full of a curve of jointed metal.

The metal sphere uncoiled. Side panels snapped open. Servos whirred.

"It's a droideka!" Anakin yelled, scrambling to his feet. He drew his lightsaber and flicked the blue blade into life. *"Run!"*

The destroyer droid's metal casing lifted to expose its center-mounted laser cannon. It didn't seem to be able to work out what to do with them for a moment; maybe they were too close for it to get a firing solution. Ahsoka was rooted to the spot, and Anakin thought she was simply too scared to move until he looked and saw the lightsaber in her hand, and the look on her face.

"Jedi don't run!" she snarled. "We stand and fight!"

The droideka had worked out its targeting. It scuttled back a meter or two on its yobcrab legs. Its cannon clicked into position. They were going to be two dead Jedi pretty soon if they didn't make a run for it.

"No, you *run*!" Anakin barked, and grabbed her shoulder as he sprinted. She broke into a run, stumbling a few paces, and the droideka opened fire. "Zigzag—don't let it lock on. Run!"

They dodged and jinked, leaping into the air, spinning around to deflect cannon fire with their lightsabers. The droideka couldn't get a lock. They were out of its effective range when it coiled up again to pursue them, rolling after them like a ball. This was their chance. It couldn't fight and move at the same time. Anakin gestured wildly at Ahsoka.

"Stop dead when I say," he yelled. " 'Saber ready."

"You said—"

"Just follow a stanging order, will you?" He ran as hard as he could. The droideka sped along at their heels. If he could fool it into thinking they'd keep up this speed, it wouldn't have time to uncoil before he drew his weapon. "In three . . . two . . . *stop!*"

Ahsoka skidded to a halt and the droid rolled between her and

Anakin for one critical fraction of a second too long. They were both on it in a heartbeat before it could unroll and deploy, slashing it to pieces with their lightsabers.

A smooth, polished section of casing rolled to a standstill a couple of meters away. They stared at each other for a moment, breathless.

Anakin couldn't have taught her a better lesson if he'd planned this. "*Now* you understand why you have to follow orders. Think twice, and you'll be *dead*."

"Orders keep you alive," Ahsoka said, as if she was repeating a lesson. It sounded awfully like Rex's wisdom. "And we watch each other's back."

Yeah, that was Rex, all right. Well, she'd learned the hard way now. Anakin gave her a rough pat on the back.

"You got it in one, Snips," he said. "Now let's find that generator."

SIX

The Jedi didn't give a second thought to my world and its suffering. The only Jedi who ever did was my poor late Master, Ky Narec. The Republic and its lickspittle Jedi parasites left him to fight and die alone. And now the fine, decent, oh-so-moral Republic wonders why it's made so many enemies.

ASAJJ VENTRESS OF RATTATAK,
Force-user and sworn enemy of the Jedi

FRONT LINE, CRYSTAL CITY

THE FORWARD EDGE OF THE SEPARATIST SHIELD PASSED OVER REX and Kenobi as they crouched beside the shattered wall, making Rex's scalp tingle.

"Now, let's do some proper *damage*," Kenobi said.

He drew his lightsaber and plunged into the first rank of spider droids, slashing at their extended cannons and managing to deflect fire at the same time. Rex didn't see much of him after that. As the clone captain opened up with both sidearms at nearly point-blank range, he was aware only of the shrapnel flying in front of him, almost in slow motion, and rattling against his helmet and chest plate. Liquid spattered on his visor; he fought a reflex to wipe it away, because it would turn into an oily smear and blind him.

The battle droids behind the spiders slowed for a moment, trying to step over the barrier the fallen shells had created. Rex seized the moment to find cover around the corner of the comm post building. He heard the missile coming even before he saw the blip on his HUD sensors. He had just enough time to whip his head around and see something streak overhead before he threw himself flat and masonry rained down on him. A chunk hit him square in the back, winding him. By the time he got to his knees, he could see that it was the comm post that had taken the impact, and two walls and the roof were gone. Astonishingly, a couple of clone gunners were still operating a repeating blaster in the debris, laying down fire. How they'd survived the blast Rex would never know.

There was white plastoid armor everywhere. Rex didn't have time to check, but he counted the scattered helmets as KIAs. A mix of anger at the deaths and a guilty flicker of relief—*I'm still alive, I'm still moving*—washed over him. Then he snapped straight back to training so ingrained that it was instinct, pure muscle memory.

"Get out of there!" he yelled, gesturing furiously at the gunners to clear the area. "You crazy or something? Fall back! Get to the arty pieces!"

They ran as ordered, joining the general retreat. Battle droids swarmed after the troopers. One grabbed a gunner and lifted him by the throat. Rex turned to help, but before he'd even aimed, Kenobi appeared from nowhere and sliced through the droid's arm, missing the trooper's head by a hair. The battle droid fell back as if punched by an invisible fist—Rex knew the Force in action when he saw it—but it swung its cannon arm at the general, and by then Rex had aimed his blaster. He poured his entire clip into it. Metal flew everywhere.

Kenobi spun around. "Thanks, Rex." He hauled the injured trooper clear. Just being grabbed with a metal fist like that did a lot of damage. "Get your men out. Get back to the artillery position."

"We're stuffed, sir. Unless we let the shield overtake the cannon, that is."

"Fire cannon *within* the shield?"

"I know it'll direct the blast and the overpressure will cream us, but we're dead either way unless Skywalker can kill that shield generator. Might as well take as many tinnies down with us as we can."

Kenobi shoved him away in the direction of the artillery. "It's not a suicide mission yet, Rex. Not on my watch. Get your men out and defend those cannons. I'll slow these clankers down."

"Sir, with respect, you're crazy."

"No, I'm your general, and it's an order. Get clear."

I don't leave any man behind.

But Rex did, because it *was* an order, and the smart automatic soldier part of his brain, trained and drilled and honed to respond, reminded him that orders were there for a reason. His body was moving away at speed while he was still arguing with himself. He gathered troopers as he ran, but he couldn't resist looking back, and the last thing he saw before he ran for the cannons was Kenobi slashing a battle droid in half at the waist before a Separatist tank crashed through the last remains of a wall.

SEPARATIST-HELD SECTOR, CRYSTAL CITY

Anakin worked out the general direction of the generator from the graduating intensity of the field. The orange glow was brighter the closer he got to the infrasonic hum that was making his throat and inner ear itch; it was just a matter of using his senses.

"There it is," Ahsoka said.

She pointed ahead. Across an expanse of open ground, a temporary building—the snap-assembly kind common on construction sites across the galaxy—stood conspicuously new and unweathered. And as they edged closer, the energy field felt stronger.

"I do believe you're right," Anakin said. "I'd have thought they'd hide it, but maybe they're getting lazy or—hey, where are you going? *Wait!*"

Ahsoka broke into a loping run as if hunting down prey, head lowered. Then she stumbled; and Anakin could see why. All across the ground, small projections were just visible above the soil— antennae. *Oh, stang.* She'd run into a droid minefield. That was all they needed. He'd hold the ugly record of getting his Padawan killed faster than any other Jedi, not even seeing out the first full day.

"Stand still!" he called. He couldn't even stop to worry now about who might see them. "Don't move. Stay right where you are . . . I'm coming . . . stand absolutely *still*, youngling . . ."

But she lost her balance. She fell back and landed right on top of one of the antennae. Anakin braced for an explosion. But nothing happened.

The next two seconds were long and silent and terrible.

He held his breath, but his relief was short-lived because he realized why there had been no catastrophic detonation.

The ground shivered.

Nothing explosive, nothing dramatic for a few more seconds— just a kind of slow eruption, like massive seeds germinating in a hurry and breaking through the soil. Orange shapes pushed up to the surface and shook off the dirt, dozens of them.

"Droids!" he called. "Ahsoka, they're sentry droids! You've set off an alarm. Forget them—set the charges, *run!*"

"Sorry, Master!" She drew her lightsaber and sliced the head from one of the droids, then Force-pushed another away from her like a shock-ball. It hit the antennae of slumbering sentries and more popped up from the ground. "Oh, no . . ."

Anakin waded in with his lightsaber to tackle the droids while she sprinted for the generator and slapped hemispherical magnetic charges on the flat surfaces. She scaled the structure and laid charges on the roof; and he was surrounded, standing in an orange sea of droids. He had to buy her more time. She *had* to get as much ordnance on that generator as possible, every last charge, be- cause—as the clones often said—the formula for calculating a detonation was P for plenty, to go for certain overkill, obliteration, rather than risk not taking out the target first time.

Kenobi, Rex, and the troops wouldn't get a second chance if Ahsoka didn't get it right the first time.

The Force was with him: the droids were pretty dim. They responded to his provocation rather than identifying Ahsoka as the priority threat. More of them erupted from the ground, massing around him and driving him back toward a single crumbling wall on the perimeter, the last remnant of a bombed building. His focus was on Ahsoka. Would she make it? If she didn't, that was too bad, but he had to kill that generator one way or another.

I can think that so easily. I can think that I might have to die.

The odd thing was that it was happening to another Anakin, not him, and he carried on regardless, drawing the droids away from his Padawan. He disconnected, trance-like.

Who's expendable? All of us? None?

He batted away an orange droid, kicked another off its legs and cut it in half as it fell. He was pressed against the wall now. Anyone who thought Jedi never got themselves in tight corners— well, he was human, Force abilities or not.

And I can die like any man.

"Ready!" Ahsoka yelled. "All primed!"

Anakin looked away from the droids for a second. The mass of charges he and Ahsoka had carried all this way, much of that distance on their hands and knees, formed a mesh of lights blinking in synchrony. A faint *beep-beep-beep* carried on the air.

Whatever happened now, the shield would—*had* to—be destroyed. The moment of triumph was slapped down hard by a different kind of adrenal rush, the realization that he now had to get them both out of there alive. The droids were relatively compact, not hulking SBDs, but in these numbers their persistence would eventually overwhelm even a Jedi who wanted very badly to *live*.

Ahsoka cut and slashed her way toward him. He wanted to tell her to save herself, to run and not stop running until she was back with Kenobi and Rex. And he'd have expected her to run just as he told her; not because she'd follow orders, but because he felt that, in the end, nobody would save him in the way he so desperately wanted to save them.

But he didn't get a chance to find out. She stopped dead in the crowd of droids and stared up past him at the wall.

It wasn't until she reached out her hand and he felt what she was doing that his stomach lurched.

She was Force-pulling the wall down on top of him.

"Don't move, Skyguy . . ."

"Don't!"

"Trust me. Don't move a muscle."

"No! *No!*"

He was plunged into rumbling shadow. His instinct made him duck and cover his head, still clutching his lightsaber. A *whump* like an explosion hit him and he couldn't breathe; he was sucking in choking dust. Something hit him in the leg. Grit peppered his face. He spat and coughed, trying to gulp in clean air, but there wasn't any. The sun had vanished. He struggled in a gray, smothering fog.

I'm dead, I'm dead, what a stupid way to go—

It took him a few moments to realize that the wall hadn't crushed him. He found himself squatting in a well of clear ground a little wider than his shoulders, surrounded by rubble and metal. A droid's arm was flailing, making a repetitive *urr-urr-urr* noise as its servos struggled. He spat and gasped. He felt as if he'd inhaled every scrap of pulverized permacrete on the planet.

"Are you okay, Master? Come on, we can't hang around."

Anakin looked up to see an outline of a small figure with headtails. His eyelashes were caked with dust. Something scratched his eyeball. He spat on his finger instinctively to wipe his eye clear, but doing that just ground more debris into it.

But he wasn't dead. The kinetic force of the collapsing wall

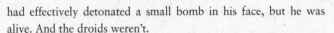

had effectively detonated a small bomb in his face, but he was alive. And the droids weren't.

"How the—"

"*Window,*" she said. "I could see there was a gap where a window had been. *Come on.*"

"You could have killed me!"

"No, I knew exactly what I was doing." Her tone was faintly offended—Anakin could hear it despite the ringing in his ears. "I'm a Togruta. We've got much better visuospatial awareness than humans. I knew the window gap would clear you . . . as long as you stood still, anyway." She peered down at him. He could see her better now. His eyes were running with tears from the irritating grit. "We've got to get clear before I can detonate the charges."

Anakin felt both angry and churlishly ungrateful at once. She'd saved his life. How many times had he calculated a lightsaber sweep so finely that it almost shaved an ally to take out an enemy?

Did he really need rescuing by a green Padawan who'd landed only a few hours ago?

She reached down into the pit and extended an arm. "Come on, Skyguy," she said. "Rex is counting on us."

GRAND ARMY CANNON BATTERY, CRYSTAL CITY

Rex hadn't ordered the gunners to open fire with the main cannon yet, but he couldn't leave it much longer.

Men were falling around him. The medics were at full stretch. The last platoons of troopers had dragged twisted railings into place to block the droid advance, filling the gaps with chunks of SBD casings and anything they could lay their hands on. They'd excavated a crude trench in front of it with grenades, wide and deep enough to stop the clankers from overrunning them for a few more minutes, and filled it with liquid fuel before setting it alight.

And that was all they had left. Rex stared through the flames and the shimmering heat haze at an approaching wall of droids and tanks that simply would not stop.

"I'm out of ideas, sir," said Sergeant Coric. He gestured to one of the artillery pieces behind them. "Other than making them come and get it."

Rex calculated a final firing solution that would cause maximum destruction of the armored column and droids. If they placed a few rounds just so, set them to cook off at chest height rather than on impact, the explosion would flatten anything standing and the shrapnel from the droids would kill any organics standing in the blast radius.

"Let's do that, Sergeant," he said. "Because I don't do surrenders."

He looked up at the orange glow of the shield overhead and reloaded. It was too late. Where the stang was Kenobi? Rex hadn't given up, but it was a close-run thing, and he never counted on holovid-style miracles. Just his Deece—his DC-15 rifle—and his buddies.

In the end, that was all any soldier had.

"Sir, *sir,* comlink! Sep channel!" One of the troopers tapped urgently on the side of his own helmet to indicate to Rex to switch channels. "Kenobi!"

Rex stopped dead, forgetting the plasma bolts scorching the air above his head for a moment. He cut into the Sep chatter and listened.

"Surrender . . . Kenobi wants to talk terms . . ."

No, not the general.

". . . having a drink with Loathsom . . ."

Definitely not. Kenobi wouldn't surrender, at least not without warning Rex, but if he'd been captured . . . no, Kenobi was pulling a stunt on Loathsom, stalling for time.

He obviously wasn't dead. And that meant he was still reassuringly dangerous.

"You reckon that's genuine, sir, or a Sep trick to demoralize us?"

Rex indicated the chaos and destruction all around them with a jerk of his thumb. "No, *that's* the demoralizing stuff." He turned to his handful of troopers. "And has it worked?"

"No, *sir!*"

"Come on then, tinny boys, do your worst," Rex muttered, and reloaded for a final stand before resorting to the cannon barrage. But he really didn't want to die just yet. "And bring your Kerko buddies, too."

He raised the rifle. In a way, it didn't matter any longer where he aimed, but he sighted up on a Kerkoiden tank commander with his head sticking out the top turret. The reticle settled on the Kerkoiden's face. Rex's finger contracted slowly on the trigger, he held his breath for a moment, and—

He heard the explosion from clear across the city. It was a distant *boomp* more than a bang; and then the sky changed color.

It was smoke-smeared blue again, not orange.

"Shield down!" Coric yelled. "They've lost their shields."

Thank you thank you thank you . . .

Rex squeezed off one shot anyway, from sheer relief, just as the tank commander looked up in horror at the absence of a shield. He was an *ex*–tank commander now. "Gunner? *Take take take!*"

The battered remnant of the 501st contingent was more ludicrously outnumbered than ever, but it had cannon, and the tide had turned. Fire ripped into the droid ranks and blew the hatches off tanks. Flame ripped from every weld, seam, and aperture. Rex allowed himself to feel it personally now, all his dead men, all the lives snuffed out, and he jumped through the flames billowing from the defensive trench to empty clip after clip into the stalled Separatist advance.

For a moment he couldn't work out why an army that still outnumbered them hundreds to one didn't just roll over their position, shield or no shield, but then the static and crackle in his helmet comlink gave him the answer. Republic ships, inbound; he heard Admiral Yularen trying to raise Kenobi. LAAT/i gunships were coming. He could hear them now, and so could the Seps. The distinctive sound of the larty's drive meant life and hope.

A pilot's voice interrupted their helmet comm circuit. "Five-oh-first, keep your heads down while we do some housecleaning . . ."

"Loathsom's ordered a surrender," said the trooper monitoring the Sep voice traffic. "The blockade's broken, sir. General Yoda's here."

"And there was I thinking it was our persuasive artillery and manly demeanor." Rex waved his men out of the larty's path. Two skimmed overhead and a staccato burst of fire sent a line of pluming smoke and flame ripping through the droid tanks. "Hey, we've got at least two men still alive out there. Check your HUDs."

Despite the warning from the pilot, Rex and Coric picked their way through the rubble, responding to the lifesigns transmitted automatically by each man's armor-mounted monitors. It took some time. One set of lifesigns stopped while they were moving rubble.

If only you'd showed up an hour or two earlier, Admiral.

Rex shook away the resentful thought as soon as it formed. This was the reality of the victory, if a victory was what this was.

SEVEN

*Yes, I did sit down and talk surrender terms with Loathsom,
over a cup of tarine tea. He became most ungentlemanly when he
realized it was his surrender we were talking about. Have these people
no manners? He didn't even offer me a sweet-sand cookie.*

GENERAL KENOBI, explaining his "surrender"

HANGAR DECK, JEDI CRUISER

AHSOKA STOOD IN FRONT OF A GROUP OF CLONE TROOPERS,
making expressive arm movements, head-tails bobbing as she
talked. They sat on the ammo crates, helmets stacked on the deck,
watching her with studied concentration.

Anakin caught only the words *wall* and *droids* as he crossed
the deck. The troopers burst out laughing.

"You *never*, ma'am," one of them said. "That must have made
the general's day."

Anakin sighed. "Rex, I'm never going to live that down, am I?"

"Give her a moment to enjoy it, sir." The captain strode beside
him. "It's all part of winding down after you've been scared witless
and survived to tell the tale. The boys know that. She did pretty
well, you have to admit."

Ahsoka didn't seem to sense him coming up behind her. The clone troopers saw him, though, and stood to attention. She paused in midsentence and turned.

"Humility is a requirement for a Jedi," Anakin said quietly.

She looked stricken. "I was—"

One of the troopers interrupted. "Apologies, sir, but we asked questions. Padawan Tano was *debriefing*, not bragging."

There was a telling second as Anakin saw Ahsoka's eye movement to her impromptu audience, a kind of surprised gratitude. Rex slapped his gloves together with a clap that made her flinch.

"Come on, you lot," he barked at the troopers. "You haven't got time to warm those crates with your backsides. What are you trying to do, hatch something? Get back to work."

They scattered. Face was saved; Rex was good at that kind of thing. Anakin seized the respite and steered Ahsoka to one side, while Rex stood a tactful five paces from the conversation, both there and *not* there.

"I was just keeping up their morale," Ahsoka said. "They need to know we take the same risks that they do. That we'll sit down and talk to them, and know their names, instead of just snapping our fingers and calling them *clone*. Nobody likes being treated as if they don't matter."

For all her bluster, she had her very adult, perceptive moments. Anakin knew how it felt not to matter. "Well . . . they seem to like you. That's good."

"They've lost so many of their friends. Can't you feel their pain?"

"They're soldiers," Anakin said. "It's the job."

"It's yours, too, but *you* hurt all the time."

Anakin didn't look at Rex, and Rex didn't look at him, but the captain took a few slow paces and put a little more distance between them, appearing engrossed in something via his helmet comlink. He was obviously anxious to avoid hanging around for what threatened to be a very personal exchange.

"You're right, Padawan," Anakin said. She was, and he didn't want to discuss it; agreeing with her served both purposes. "We all handle our loss in our own way. Thank you for thinking of the men's welfare."

Ahsoka had been looking directly into his face, but then her gaze darted again to something behind him. She didn't just have keen focus. Her peripheral vision was exceptional too. Anakin turned to see Kenobi walking slowly toward him, deep in conversation with Master Yoda. He decided to meet them halfway.

"Master Obi-Wan," he said, bowing. "Master Yoda."

Yoda fixed him with a critical stare. "Trouble you have with your new Padawan, I hear."

"I was explaining the situation to Master Yoda," Kenobi said.

"If not ready for the responsibility of a Padawan you are, then perhaps to Obi-Wan she should go . . ."

Anakin didn't take kindly to those kinds of psychological games, not even from Master Yoda—*especially* from him.

Remember me, Master? The Chosen One? The one you *didn't want to train?*

"There are no problems, Master," he said calmly. "Who could possibly make such a far-reaching judgment about a youngling's future in such a short time, anyway? That would be rash. Unfair, even. It's our duty to nurture talent and support it."

If Yoda felt the barbs in Anakin's comment, he didn't show any reaction. "Mature your judgment is becoming. Perhaps teach *you* she will, as much as you teach her."

Anakin bit back a riposte, because he would *not* rise to the bait. He bowed instead. "I shall do my utmost, Master."

"Then go with you she will, to the Teth system."

Anakin felt he was walking into something set up for him. *Did you know this was coming, Obi-Wan?* No, he wouldn't show dissent. "Has the fighting spread that far? I didn't think the Separatist army had any presence there."

"No army. But kidnapped, Jabba the Hutt's son has been."

It took a couple of seconds to sink in. He couldn't hide his disgust, not completely anyway. "You want me to rescue a *Hutt*?"

It was a test. It had to be. However much it rankled, Anakin was determined to pass it.

Kenobi dived in immediately. "We need Jabba's backing to fight this war, Anakin. If we can't use Hutt-controlled routes, we can't fight in the Outer Rim. It's that simple. I'm going to negotiate with Jabba while you retrieve the hostage."

"Hostage . . ."

"His baby son. Rotta."

Anakin wondered whether it was expedience, simple logic—both he and Kenobi spoke Huttese and were experienced in covert missions—or some exercise in character building. Yoda knew Anakin's past, that he and his mother had been slaves of a Hutt. Jabba raked off a cut from the slave trade, too, so he was personally connected to Anakin's boyhood misery, and even his mother's ultimate fate. *Callous* didn't begin to cover it.

Anakin's instinctive reaction would have been to tell Jabba that it was too bad and that people you loved got killed all the time.

But the bit about the need to get Jabba on their side—*that* made sense. Anakin swallowed his hatred and did what he knew he had to, because he had to be *better* than this.

Ahsoka seemed to realize the tension wasn't about her. She took a pace back and stood beside Rex, who'd followed discreetly. "I'll get the troops organized," she said. "Ready when you are, Master."

"I'd better get under way," Kenobi said. "Mustn't keep Jabba waiting."

Anakin bowed and walked away with as much serenity as he could muster. He didn't want the Masters knowing the task had hit a raw nerve. He slipped into a machinery space off the docking bay for a little privacy, sent a message to Padmé to let her know he was fine and that he missed her—no mention of close calls with col-lapsing walls, or crazy Padawans—and centered himself again.

I'm not a kid. I shouldn't be feeling like this. It's not the Jedi way. Maybe Yoda was right; I was too old to train. I can't be like them, all serene and unfeeling.

He was the Chosen One, they told him. He was supposed to bring balance to the Force. Anakin thought that some little extra support might go with being the Chosen One, a helping hand or at least some understanding from the Jedi Council, but instead he was passed around like an unwelcome burden, ending up with Qui-Gon Jinn and then Kenobi because nobody else would have him.

His chosen status meant less than nothing; it felt more like a stigma. And they wondered why he was *difficult* at times. Maybe they didn't want balance, whatever that was. Maybe nobody liked a Jedi who was *that* different. He felt like an embarrassment to them.

I do everything you ask of me. I try so hard. When is it going to be enough? When are you going to say, "Okay, Anakin Skywalker, you're good enough"?

The hatch swung open. "What's wrong, Skyguy?" Ahsoka fixed him with that you-can't-avoid-me stare. "It took me ages to find you. We're ready to roll."

"Have you heard of knocking?" *Don't do this to her. You know how it feels to be invisible to the grownups, a nuisance.* "I'm just thinking, that's all."

"Worried about helping Jabba? Don't worry, everyone else is, too."

Anakin could never answer her. He tried not to think about it, but the thought was like a corris weevil, eating away at his resolve. The Jedi had never tried to rescue his mother or buy her out of slavery. Instead, they had taken him, given him this new life, but left her behind on Tatooine. He had just accepted it at the time, but now . . . now he knew how much power Jedi had, and all he could wonder is why *she* hadn't been worth their time and trouble, too, if only to keep him happy.

Not even Qui-Gon Jinn had cast a backward glance at Shmi Skywalker. As the months and years wore on, the question would *not* leave Anakin alone.

He didn't want to let resentment eat away at his fond memories of his old Master, but he couldn't stop it sometimes.

"Skyguy . . . ? *Skyguy!* Are you listening?"

The Jedi Council had credits. Real wealth. Would it really have been beyond them to buy his mother out of slavery?

Anakin accepted that some things had to be learned from the cradle. He was already full of attachment and emotion, too set in his ways of being a messy, ordinary human to adopt the aloof serenity—the unloving detachment, the arm's-length and measured compassion—a Jedi needed.

He did his best.

Why wasn't my mother worth saving?

Jabba grew fat on the misery of beings like Anakin's mother. He'd probably taken a percentage of the very transactions that had kept Shmi Skywalker in slavery.

And still I have to save his son. Because we need his goodwill. His space lanes.

The idea stuck in Anakin's throat like a splintered nuna bone. The pain was palpable. He didn't know if it was grief for his mother, or guilty anger at Qui-Gon Jinn, or just the vague simmering discontent that told him he needed to have more control over his life.

"It's got to be done," Anakin said at last. "I don't *feel* anything about it. Only *think* how we're going to do it."

Ahsoka considered him for a while as if there were something projected on a holoscreen slightly to one side of him. Could she *see*? Could she see he'd slaughtered those Tusken Raiders? Was it etched in the Force around him? Did she know he'd committed an atrocity to avenge the death of his mother?

If she did, she wasn't sensing his guilt.

He didn't feel guilt about it at all.

"Let's go," he said.

JABBA'S PALACE, TATOOINE

Jabba didn't have to feign contemptuous anger to cover his fears for Rotta this time. He *was* enraged. He rounded on TC-70.

"Clear the chamber." He looked around at the cowering dancers and the Nikto guards, who didn't seem sure if the command applied to them. "Get out! Leave us!" The throne chamber emptied as if on fire. "Someone will *pay* for this. Who is even *capable* of slaughtering my employees like nerfs?"

The heads of the bounty hunters he'd sent to Teth had been returned to him in a neat, anonymous, flimsiplast-lined crate. Nothing else; just the heads. He stared at it, furious. This was all that remained of the finest bounty hunters creds could hire. These were tough operators, exceptionally hard to evade, let alone capture and kill. Jabba tried hard to think of any assassins who might be tougher, and who they might work for.

He came up blank. He knew every being who wielded power, both sides of the law, and there was nobody he could imagine who would or could do this. It was bad enough to find he had so underestimated an unseen enemy that his own son could be kidnapped. Having his top bounty hunters sent back in butchered pieces was beyond an insult. It rocked his world.

"The Jedi is here, Lord Jabba," said the droid. "He seems most anxious."

"And so he should be. It'll be *his* head if he doesn't get results fast." Jabba let his anger escape in a rumbling hiss, and settled back on his dais into as dignified a pose as he could manage. "Show the Jedi in."

Jabba treated Jedi with caution. The mystic side of them made him wary, because he could never get the measure of their physical limits. But they were, for the most part, humans or similar bipedal species—and they could be killed, Jedi or not. They were not immortal, and any living being had something that it needed and would trade advantages to obtain.

Jabba would do whatever it took to get Rotta back unharmed. After that—if he needed to exact revenge, and he *would*—he would reconsider his position. He'd been maneuvered. He didn't care much for that.

Obi-Wan Kenobi was a general in their army, a bearded human with unkempt hair and loose robes. He walked in, stood before the dais, and bowed.

"Mighty Jabba, I'm come personally to report on our efforts to find your son." He seemed to speak Huttese fluently. That was unusual for someone who moved in the more genteel circles of the Republic's power elite. "We know where he is, and we've sent one of our most powerful Jedi to rescue him."

Jabba gestured to TC-70. He indicated the crate of decapitated heads. TC-70, who knew the drill by now and the impression that needed making, tipped the crate over, spilling the heads on the tiles. Most of them rolled out. One hit the floor with an odd crack like porceplast breaking.

"*That,*" said Jabba, "is what befell the last experts who were looking for my son."

Kenobi studied the severed heads impassively, then raised one eyebrow. He didn't seem shockable. Maybe he was just a good actor. But either way, he must have understood the stakes.

"I think our man will be harder to separate from his head," Kenobi said at last. "We won't let you down."

"You'll find Rotta and return him to me," Jabba said. "And there's an extra condition if the Republic wants free passage through my space lanes. Bring me the scum who kidnapped my son."

Kenobi didn't blink. "Dead or alive, Lord Jabba?"

"Either," Jabba said. "But alive would give me greater satisfaction, for reasons I probably don't need to explain to you."

"I understand, Lord Jabba."

"See that you do." Jabba paused, knowing that timing was everything when making a point to humans. "Because if you can't do the job, then Count Dooku and his droid army will."

He had to hand it to the Jedi. The man didn't grovel or flatter, like Palpatine; he seemed to stop and calculate instead.

"We'll do it," Kenobi said.

"You have one planetary rotation to finish the job." Jabba gestured to TC-70 to collect the heads. "A Tatooine rotation."

"It will be done, Lord Jabba. Now, in anticipation of that, may we discuss terms?"

Kenobi was nothing if not cool. He managed to be respectful without showing fear. Normally, Jabba would have treated that as showing insufficient deference, but he needed the Jedi's cooperation for the time being.

"We may," he said.

REPUBLIC GUNSHIP, INBOUND FOR TETH

Anakin stared back at the blue hologram of Kenobi in the crew bay of the gunship.

"One day to find the kid and get him back home," he said at last.

"That's right, Anakin."

"We'll do it, Master." He was aware of Ahsoka, Rex, and the squad of troopers tasked with inserting on Teth sitting with their backs against the bulkhead in silence. "You just sweet-talk Jabba. I think you have the harder duty . . ."

"We really don't know who's holding his son. I'm uneasy, to say the least. Whoever it is managed to kill a complete team of bounty hunters. That's not your average criminal scum."

"And we're not the average hostage-extraction team."

"I'll rendezvous with you as soon as I've concluded negotiations."

"Don't worry about us, Master."

The hologram vanished. Anakin turned to the team. "This won't be an unopposed insertion, but then I think we expected that. Everyone ready?"

"Ready, sir."

"Ready, Master."

The lead gunship streaked low over an ocean, three or four meters above the waves, giving Anakin the impression of moving above an undulating runway when he glanced out of the open hatch. Behind the LAAT/i, more gunships flew line astern, hugging the same contours and occasionally tracking diagonally in case an enemy was trying to get a lock on them. But they were alone on a remote planet for the time being, and they probably wouldn't encounter resistance in the form of anti-air cannon until they reached the coast. Anakin checked the rear and then leaned into the cockpit. "Picking up anything, Lieutenant Hawk?"

The pilot indicated the console. His screen showed red and green icons. "Long range shows a heavily defended target, sir. Laser-cannon emplacements, at the very least. We won't be undetected now, you do know that, don't you, sir? I'll drop below the tree canopy as soon as I get a clear run."

"Good, then bang out as soon as we're down. I need you standing by for extraction."

"Will do, sir."

The sea gave way to glittering turquoise shallows speckled with dark masses of weed and then dense emerald jungle. The trees were wreathed in mist. It looked like a nice, ordinary day in a pleasant, unspoiled place. Anakin knew the illusion wouldn't last long.

"Buckets on," Rex said, and snapped his helmet into place.

The squad followed suit. Then all of them went through the ritual of checking charge levels on their rifle and sidearms, tugging at carabiners on their rappel kit, and flexing their hands. Without the complex helmet the clone troopers wore, Anakin was shut out of their data-laden world. He couldn't see what they saw, or receive the welter of information—images, text, sensor readings—or hear the constant comm chatter on a dozen frequencies. He took a guess that Rex was now transmitting last-minute orders to the gunships in the squadron. He'd never know for sure.

Some things had to be known and quantified rather than felt in the Force.

The audio system in the crew bay crackled into life. "Sir, estimated time on target—five standard minutes. Better assume they've seen us. I'm sealing the blast hatches now."

"Copy that, Hawk," said Anakin.

The crew bay dimmed and the sunlight was replaced by red emergency illumination. He looked down at Ahsoka. He'd almost grown used to her being so small, but in the crowded compartment, dwarfed by troopers hanging on to overhead rails, she looked as if she'd boarded the wrong flight.

Even with the hatches sealed, Anakin heard the first stuttering rounds of laser cannon.

"Taking fire, sir," Hawk said. "I'll drop below their range, but stand by for a bumpy ride when we hit the forest."

"Thirty seconds," Rex said quietly.

Once they hit the ground—*if* they hit the ground, *if* they made it in one piece—then their task had only just started. Their objective was a monastery on top of a plateau surrounded by dense jungle.

They'd tackled worse.

Anakin tightened his belt and felt for his lightsaber. They *had* to pull this off. His feelings about Hutts didn't matter. It wasn't about the kid; it was about his men, the Grand Army, about getting the war won and over with. He focused on that. The troopers were now lined up at both hatches.

The gunship shook as it took a direct hit, but the armor plating held. Anakin closed his eyes for a moment. Then the deck seemed to fall beneath his boots, random thuds echoed through the airframe—the gunship was hitting something on its descent, not taking fire now—and then there was a distinct lurch as Hawk set the LAAT/i down. The jump lights showed green and both hatches lifted. Moist, hot, tree-scented air flooded into the crew bay.

How Hawk had found a landing area in this dense forest without shearing off a gun pod, Anakin had no idea.

"Go!" Rex said, slapping the first trooper in line on the shoulder. "Go, go, *go!*"

Anakin reached out and grabbed Ahsoka's wrist to make sure she was right next to him. Then, watching the white outline of a trooper vanish into a sea of branches and glossy green foliage, he jumped clear.

EIGHT

One day, I must thank Master Yoda and the Jedi Council for contributing so generously to our cause. You would think they would take better care of their Chosen One. But all they seem to do, from what I hear—and I hear a great deal—is to frustrate and alienate young Skywalker. I believe they're storing up trouble for themselves.

DARTH SIDIOUS, better known as
Chancellor Palpatine, to Count Dooku

RV POINT ON THE FOREST FLOOR

BENEATH THE ABANDONED MONASTERY, TETH

THE DROIDS COULDN'T GET A VISUAL ON THE GAR FORCES through the thick foliage, but that didn't stop them pouring down fire.

"Something tells me the residents have given up a contemplative life of prayer," Rex said. A burst of laserfire crashed through the tree canopy, bringing down branches and vines. He wiped something wet, sticky, and dismembered from his forearm plate. "There goes their tax-exempt status."

Ahsoka spun and deflected a stray bolt with her lightsaber. "I don't even want to think what happened to the monks. What do you know about tax, anyway?"

"Everything HNE bulletins taught me." It was his window on

a world he wasn't part of, but he was used to absorbing information that way. Flash-training had formed a large part of his early life, and it often diverged from the real world, but he could fill in the gaps—most of the time, anyway. "Now, it's at times like this that I wish all we had to do was blow that castle to pieces from orbit."

Rex stared up the sheer cliff of the granite plateau that rose from the jungle floor like an island covered in a frozen waterfall of fleshy vines. There was only one way to insert: the hard way. He calculated the height precisely with his visor's inbuilt telemetry system.

"Got enough cable?" Ahsoka asked.

"Just about."

He could hear the grinding *whee-umpp-whee-umpp* sound of the AT-TE armored vehicle as it picked its way between the trees on sturdy mechanical legs. Skywalker came jogging ahead of it, gesturing to stand clear. The machine slowed to a halt, and its cannon turrets elevated.

"Here's our covering fire." Rex switched to the AT-TE crew's comm circuit. They were getting a sensor fix on a parapet running the length of the castle wall so they could fire through the canopy unseen. "Stick close to General Skywalker."

"That's what he keeps saying, too."

"Smart advice, obviously." Rex tapped the top of his helmet to get his squad to form up on him, and reinforced the command with a quick comm burst. "Stand by. We'll ascend behind the fire line."

The AT-TE had a firing solution. He could see it on one of his HUD icons. But as he waited for the barrage to start, something heavy came crashing down through the branches overhead, dislodging chunks of stone and vine.

Rex ducked instinctively, thinking it was an explosive device; if he'd been up there defending that position, he'd have been rolling lateral-blast ordnance down the cliff to detonate a meter above ground level and disintegrate everything—and everyone—in a five-hundred-meter radius. But they weren't him. And what had fallen from the plateau wasn't ordnance, but a battle droid commander.

It hit the ground with a crash. Rex pulled his sidearm and put a burst of fire through its head without thinking. It wasn't armed, but he ran a hand sensor over it to make sure it wasn't booby-trapped.

"They don't bounce much, do they?" He looked up the cliff wall again, then glanced back at Skywalker. Ahsoka stood at his side as if bolted there. "Ready when you are, sir."

Skywalker had a distracted look on his face that Rex had seen before. It was like a brief trance; maybe it was Jedi meditation of some kind. Whatever it was, Rex read it as the moment when Skywalker tussled with himself, trying to overcome something within, or psyching himself up, or something where two elements of him pulled in different directions; because whatever it achieved, he came out of it in what Rex thought of as his killing-machine mode. He was unstoppable, all lethal movement, cutting down everything he came into contact with.

"A-tee," Skywalker said, "return fire."

He started climbing the vine.

A stream of blue-white bolts seared upward through the trees, vaporizing branches. From that moment, the forest was all deafening mechanical noise, and Rex's helmet activated buffers to protect his hearing. He could have switched off the audio completely and fought in soundproofed peace, but he needed to hear something of the battle environment around him to get a gut feel for what was happening. The shapes and icons in his HUD were just detail now. AT-TEs thundered and wheezed as they moved up to scale the cliff face, firing as they went.

The armored walkers, tanks in six heavy jointed legs, were built for horizontal terrain, however uneven, and perfect for it.

They *could* climb, but it limited their effectiveness and made them very vulnerable. Using them to scale a vertical cliff was as near to a last-resort deployment as he'd seen so far in this war.

But they didn't have time to do it by the book. They had one day.

Because some jumped-up gangster of a Hutt says so.

He put it out of his mind. All flesh and blood could do was concentrate on what was immediately in front. Rex fired his rappel line almost vertically through the tree canopy, feeling the grappling hook bite into something solid. Then he let the powered winch lift him. He became one man in a curtain of white-armored troopers ascending the steep rock face. He could see himself as a sitting target hanging in midair, or as a fast-moving weapons platform conserving his energy for the battle that was certain to be waiting at the top of the ascent. He chose the latter.

Rocks, burning fragments of droid casing, and chunks of vine as thick as a man's waist fell past him. He batted away what he could, but there was little room for maneuver on the end of a winch line.

He glanced down to see where Ahsoka was. She'd been scrambling up a vine, face set in grim, wide-eyed determination. No sign of her: his gut lurched, fearing the worst. But then he looked to his side, spotting one of the AT-TE walkers lurching its way up the vertical face like a manakur climbing a fruit tree, and there was Ahsoka, clinging to the deckhead plate of the armored walker with her gaze fixed firmly above her.

She was a smart kid. But then so were his boys, and plenty of them wouldn't be returning to barracks after this assault. War didn't care much about *smart* or *nice* or *deserving to survive*.

Rex stopped thinking about it. Another droid plummeted past him trailing smoke, and struck a trooper on one shoulder. The man swung helpless on his line for a moment, but hung on. If he was lucky, his armor would have dissipated the impact and he wouldn't have a fracture.

The next falling object, though, was an AT-TE.

Rex felt the shock wave from a blast above him. The next impression he had was of falling from a building and watching the walls streak by. But it was the armored walker: he hung relatively motionless to its rapid fall, senses telling him he was the moving object. He managed to swing to one side by kicking out from the cliff wall. The stricken AT-TE tumbled. It had no other route down than through the troopers ascending the cliff.

Rex couldn't divert his eyes from horror any more than the next human being could. There was always that one terrible moment when a death in all its unexpected detail grabbed his attention, and wouldn't let go for what felt like hours until he jerked his eyes away the next second. Then there was the desperate relief at not being dead, followed rapidly by equally desperate scenarios about how the guys below *could* have survived if . . . if . . . if . . .

Rex couldn't let himself dwell on it. He could hear something else, a sound his helmet systems recognized and identified as a droid STAP fighter.

And another.

And *another*.

They were fragile aerial platforms just big enough to carry a battle droid, not proper airframes, with narrow profiles that made them hard moving targets to hit. Their blasterfire punched into the cliff face. White blurs fell in his peripheral vision.

If any of his 501st company reached the top of this plateau, it would be a miracle. And then they still had to fight their way into the monastery.

Rex went back to concentrating on surviving the next moment, a second at a time, and hung from his rappel line spraying blasterfire at the strafing STAP fighters.

ANAKIN HAD NO CHOICE; he jumped.

Plummeting down a cliff face now infested with spider droids, he landed briefly on the AT-TE below, narrowly missing Ahsoka, and then launched himself at the first STAP fighter in the formation.

It was mainly blind instinct that made him do it. He could get killed like anyone else, he knew. But once his body had taken control like this, his brain was just along for the ride, unable to step in. As he hit the tiny platform, barely big enough to take a droid's metal feet, he smashed the battle droid pilot squarely in the chest, sending it tumbling hundreds of meters into a blurred green sea of treetops, then leaped again, onto the next STAP. The sheer inertia of his body sent the droid plummeting. He didn't even need to draw his lightsaber. Now he was fully mobile in a way that not even his Force powers could match: he could *fly*, not just glide.

And that meant he could stand off from the vertical rock face far enough to make a difference. The other droid STAP pilots were now in disarray, seeming not to know how to deal with an organic that could leap from fighter to fighter, and that confusion gave Anakin the edge he needed.

He checked the cliff below, *felt* where there were fewest of his men, where he might safely bring down tons of droid and debris, and opened up with the STAP's laser cannon. A path of pluming, flame-filled smoke ripped up the cliff face to the top, blazing a clear path. Anakin dived closer. Now he could see exactly where to place fire to clear the way for individual troopers or provide suppressing fire for an AT-TE to get a better foothold.

One simple STAP platform shouldn't have been enough to make that much difference, but he was Anakin Skywalker, and he knew without even thinking how to hit an enemy where it hurt most, and strike fear into them.

Droids *did* feel fear. He could see it now. They reacted to threats like a living being. They avoided damage and destruction wherever they could. *That* was all fear was; a safety mechanism, whether it was organic adrenaline or a computer program. The battle droids on the top of the plateau, peering down onto the GAR assault, seemed to be in chaos. Anakin swept a dozen of them aside with a raw surge of Force power. Could Rex see the path? Could *any* of the troopers, clinging so close to the cliff? They had no overview.

Yes, Rex *could* see it.

Anakin picked him out by his traditional *kama*, the leather half kilt worn over his armor. He was waving troops toward the smoking line. It was almost as good as a beacon. And they were close enough to the top now to use the vines rather than hang passively on the rappel winches. Anakin could do no more here. He swooped for the line of droids forming up on the plateau.

He jumped off the STAP onto the parapet, leaving the fighter to crash into the droid line. As he regained his balance, a battle droid commander stepped forward and raised its rifle.

"Surrender, Jedi."

"Bad time to ask me," Anakin said, more to himself than anything, and plunged into the droid ranks with his lightsaber. "*Bad* time."

There was nothing in his mind beyond his troops and that only he could save them. *Save;* he did so much *saving* now but it would never be enough to make him whole. He felt his lightsaber blade slice through metal—there was always a slight kick on contact, like a drill hitting a hard spot—but he craved more. He craved destruction, not to prove to himself that he had such huge *power,* but simply to hold the chaos at bay.

I didn't save my mother.

He had the strength and skill to wipe out legions of droids, but he hadn't used it for the person who mattered most.

Anakin tore into droid after droid, killing on upstroke and downstroke, spinning to take out droids rushing him from behind, rolling to scythe his way through their legs. Hot hydraulic fluid spattered on his face like blood.

Why didn't I go back for my mother, when I could have done this, *and* this, *and* this?

As the surge of Force power almost squeezed the air from his lungs in his all-out effort to crush the next rank of droids, he felt suddenly light-headed, and in that second's pause he became aware of troopers fighting furiously to his right—smashing metal skulls with butts of rifles, ramming vibroblades into weak points— but he couldn't see Ahsoka.

She'd been clinging to an AT-TE. He didn't know where she was. He couldn't even sense her in the maelstrom of Force disturbances churned up by desperate combat, and when the last battle droid crashed to its knees, he steadied himself to look for her.

He was never going to lose someone he cared about again. If anyone so much as looked at Padmé the wrong way, he'd make them regret the day they were born.

You can't think those things. You're a Jedi.

But I can. And I do.

Then three destroyer droids rolled through the battle debris, unfurled themselves and raised their shields. Anakin, exhausted by jungle heat and a hard ascent, raised his lightsaber two-handed, muscles screaming for rest. One droid rocked back a fraction on its gyros to fire.

I promised Obi-Wan we'd wrap this up inside a day.

I promised Ahsoka I'd look out for her.

Anakin steadied himself for a split second that lasted forever, choosing between lunging forward or waiting to block the cannon round, and then the lead droid exploded in a white-hot shower of shrapnel that made him duck to shield himself with the Force. The plateau echoed as the blast bounced back off the monastery's high walls.

When he jumped up, ready to fight to the death, he was staring at an AT-TE as it clunked its way forward from the monastery walls. One cannon was still trained on the smoking spot where the destroyer droids had paused.

"Did you get hit?" Ahsoka called. She was standing on top of the armored walker, looking breathless. "Sorry."

"No, I'm fine." His legs shook with fading adrenaline. It was always like this for a few moments when the fighting stopped. "I told you to stay close, so I can't complain, can I?"

"Just watching your back, Master."

The plateau was silent now, and the remnant of 501st Torrent Company were spread out, securing a perimeter. Anakin did a quick head count. He'd lost nearly half his men.

All for a kriffing Hutt. This had better be worth my men's lives.

Rex jogged over to them, lifting off his helmet. He obviously thought the situation was under control to do that. Anakin could sense no immediate danger. Rex's HUD sensors must have given him similar reassurance.

"Fifteen wounded, sir." He didn't mention the KIAs. He wiped the palm of his gauntlet across his shaven head, looking oddly exhilarated—odd, because while his face was flushed and he was breathing harder than usual, his eyes looked distant and anguished. "I've called in one larty to casevac the injured. I didn't wait for your order, sir . . ."

"Fine by me, Rex. I don't want to spend one more life on this Hutt than I have to." Anakin didn't look at Ahsoka, but he could feel her gaze boring into him, tinged with dismay. A Jedi was entitled to be less than saintly sometimes; sooner or later, she had to learn that it could be a dirty job. "Judging by the number of droids, I'd say this is an official Separatist operation, not a spot of freelance hobby extortion."

"Agreed. It's got Dooku's fingerprints all over it, sir. Explains the dead bounty hunters, too."

Ahsoka edged her way between the two men and looked up expectantly. "But the hard bit's over, right? I mean, we just crawled up a cliff under fire and wiped out a battalion of droids or something."

" 'Fraid not, littl'un," Rex said, patting her on the head. "The hard bit isn't over until we put our boots down on Republic soil again, preferably with one Huttlet on board."

Anakin kicked through the carpet of shattered droid components like fallen leaves. Some chunks of debris were still smoking. His boots came away oily and dark.

"Yes, it's definitely Dooku," he said. "Expect the worse."

UPPER LEVEL, TETH MONASTERY

Jedi were so predictable.

Asajj Ventress stood one pace back from the narrow slit of a window, but she could see the aftermath of the battle. Everything was going according to plan. Skywalker would think he'd won a magnificent victory rather than that he'd been duped. He'd encountered just enough resistance to make it look like more than a token defense, without the droids getting lucky and actually killing the Jedi. The things couldn't *act*. She'd had to balance the battle carefully.

I need you and your little Padawan in one piece, Skywalker.

The Jedi Council could spare the resources to drop everything for a Hutt they despised, when there was something in it for them. But Rattatak—her homeworld—could drown in blood for all they cared.

It had.

"What would you make of all this, Ky?" she said aloud. Ky Narec was long dead, and maybe that was just as well. He wouldn't want to see what the Jedi had become now. "Or me, maybe. But you'd understand why it had to be done, I know."

"Ma'am?" said 4A-7. The droid watched from the window too. "Who's Ky?"

"Nothing you need to know." She pulled the hood back and let it slide from her smoothly polished scalp. Her twin lightsabers hung from her belt. She was ready. "The battle droids have done their duty. Now it's your turn. Be *convincing*."

"That's my programming, ma'am."

The spy droid slipped away. Ventress ran through her mental

checklist. All she needed was that one incriminating holocam sequence of the Jedi with Rotta the Huttlet, anything that would convince Jabba that the Jedi were behind the kidnapping to force Jabba's cooperation with the Republic—handling Rotta roughly, making him cry, anything plausible. The slug cried a lot; that wasn't going to be hard. But there would be many ways to explain that away as innocent circumstance unless she could then deliver the Huttlet to Jabba.

I still think it would be better to have the Jedi framed with a dead Huttlet. Inarguable. Case proven.

If the situation demanded it, then that was how it would have to be, and Dooku could rage at her later. All that mattered was that the Jedi be denied access to Outer Rim space lanes, and that Jabba throw his considerable weight behind the Confederacy of Independent Systems.

So I'd kill a youngling, would I?

Ventress was sometimes surprised by what she would consider doing these days, but it would have been a routine event on Rattatak; not even a minor headline, as it would have been on tidy, civilized Coruscant. Many youngsters died in the constant battles between the rival warlords. She could have been one of them. Her parents had died violently, just two more bystanders in the endless gang wars. Life was cheap on Rattatak.

It had no strategic importance for the Republic. It didn't matter to Coruscant, and no Jedi stepped in to right wrongs.

Except Ky Nerac. I'd be dead now, without him.

Yes, she could kill a youngling, if she had to. She could kill the offspring of a criminal who made part of his fortune from slavery, if it meant putting an end to the Jedi, because Rattatak knew too much about slavers, too. Jedi kept a corrupt government in power. *Anything* was justified. Their massive power required exceptional countermeasures. They would not concede without a fight to the death.

Fine. I'm more than ready.

The holoreceiver flickered to life, and Count Dooku appeared as a blue ghost, elegantly cadaverous.

"Yes, Asajj?" Dooku said. "Progress?"

"It's under way, Master." Ventress snapped her two lightsabers together into one weapon, interlocking the hilts. She clutched the extended handgrip like a parade baton. "Skywalker and his party are about to enter the monastery. The droid will intercept them and make sure they perform to order."

"Be careful. They'll realize by now that this isn't a routine criminal kidnapping."

"Does that matter?"

"Not if the incriminating evidence is forthcoming, and their secret dies with them."

"I could take them now and fabricate very good evidence, Master. The longer we give them to play, the greater the risk of their escape."

Dooku considered her in silence for a few moments, stroking his fingertip down the center of his beard, apparently distracted.

"They're not going to escape, Asajj," he said at last. "You're going to deliver the evidence I need, and rescue the Huttlet. Not because you fear my disapproval, or what I might do if you fail, but because you know why the Jedi and the Republic must be stopped. You know better than anyone what the stakes are. Better than me, in some ways."

Dooku was right; she wasn't afraid of him. There was no pain he could cause her, no physical threat he could hold over her, because Rattatak had broken her long, long before she met him.

"You're right, Master," she said. "I died a long time ago. So did everything I cared about. It's only the likes of me, with nothing to lose, who'll really be prepared to tear the galaxy down and start over."

Dooku smiled. It was actually a sympathetic smile as far as she could see; he had his reasons, too, and she knew they weren't about expense accounts and feeding in the rich waters of government. Both of them had a vision of a fairer society.

"The galaxy will be torn apart by orphans," Dooku said at last. "I think that everyone I know who has the potential to bring down empires has been robbed of parents." He seemed to be talking to himself. "Carry on, then, Asajj. I'll wait to hear from you. And look out for Kenobi. He may yet show up."

"I'll be ready for him," she said. "For *all* of them."

Asajj Ventress waited for the hologram to vanish, then took her jointed lightsaber in both hands and snapped it back into two lethal blades.

That was how she would snap Skywalker's neck when he finally stood in her way.

NINE

The Jedi Order's problem is Yoda. No being can wield that kind of power for centuries without becoming complacent at best or corrupt at worst. He has no idea that it's overtaken him; he no longer sees all the little cumulative evils that the Republic tolerates and fosters, from slavery to endless wars, and he never asks, "Why are we not acting to stop this?" Live alongside corruption for too long, and you no longer notice the stench. The Jedi cannot help the slaves of Tatooine, but they can help the slavemasters.

DOOKU, Yoda's former Padawan, to Darth Sidious

MONASTERY ENTRANCE, TETH

THE ARMORED DOOR OPENED WITH AN OMINOUS RUMBLE LIKE A bantha's gut and a faint smell of decay. Rex sighted up, checking out the long corridor in his rifle's optics.

Yeah, he thought. *We picked the wrong end of the bantha again.*

He flicked on his helmet spot lamp, throwing a blue-white disk of light on the far wall. The four troopers with him—Coric, Vaize, Ayar, and Lunn—followed suit. Dense black pools marked the alcoves spaced at regular intervals along the full length of the passage, and where there were blind spots, there were potential ambushes.

It was like one of the nightmarish house clearance exercises the

GAR instructors on Kamino would run as part of training. They liked to show you just how many ways you could get yourself killed if you didn't have eyes in your backside and didn't treat every shadow as hostile.

Standing on a nice open battlefield with good honest laser rounds raining down was actually comforting by comparison. Rex put his finger to his lips and signaled his squad to do a forward overlap maneuver, checking and clearing each section of the tunnel before moving on.

"Kill the lights unless we make enemy contact," Rex said. "Night-vision visor and infrared." He turned to Skywalker. "You can see okay, can't you, sir?"

"I can sense my way," Anakin said.

Ahsoka's boots crunched on something. "I'm fine. Togrutas have good low-light vision."

"No snacking on the local rodent life, littl'un." He was glad she could take a joke. That was a big plus. "But unless it's wearing a diaper, shoot it. No chances."

"Is that fair?" Ahsoka asked. The two Jedi crept along the passage behind him. Rex hoped their Force sense of danger was working.

"In hostage extraction, you don't have the luxury of checking ID. You slot them before they slot you. The only ones you give the benefit of the doubt are those you've already identified positively as hostages. Everyone else is a hostile until proven otherwise."

"Wow," she said. "What if—"

"I think *hostile* is a given here, Ahsoka," Skywalker said. "Do what Rex says."

They edged down the passage, waiting for the worst. Rex tried to get an idea of the layout of the monastery, planning a search pattern in his head. It was going to take time.

And it's going to have some Dooku surprises along the way. The general knows it. I know it.

Something a few meters ahead showed up in Rex's night vision, an unnaturally smooth surface that appeared as a green smear. It moved. Rex raised his rifle. Coric and Lunn, five meters ahead, slammed it against the wall and put their Deeces to its head just as Skywalker lunged forward with his lightsaber drawn.

It was a droid—not a battle droid, just a regular domestic clanker—and it was lucky it wasn't already a smoking pile of scrap.

"Who are you?" Skywalker demanded. His blue blade lit up its face.

"I am the caretaker of this holy place, sir. Four-A-Seven. You have liberated me from those battle droids." The droid froze. Coric and Lunn didn't stand down. "Thank you."

Skywalker didn't look inclined to shut down his lightsaber either. "Where's the Hutt?"

"The battle droids kept their prisoners on the detention level."

"*Kept.*" Skywalker's grip on his weapon didn't relax one bit. "So they've all left, have they?"

"I appear to be alone here, yes."

It didn't matter if Four-A believed that or not. Rex didn't, and it was obvious that Skywalker didn't either. "So where's the detention level?"

"Down those stairs, sir. They lead to the storage cellars, which were turned into cells by the heathens who defiled this place."

Rex gestured to Coric and Lunn to let the droid go on its way, but he kept an eye on it as it left. And he didn't like the sound of *cellars* and *stairs*. Both presented their own security issues. Skywalker motioned Ahsoka ahead and turned to Rex.

"Yes, I know—but you stay here and secure the exit, Captain."

"Yes, sir. You must be psychic."

"No, just as suspicious as you are."

Skywalker vanished into the gloom, Ahsoka at his side. Coric flicked on his helmet spot lamp and tracked Four-A up and down the passage as the droid went about its business, which seemed to consist of flicking pieces of debris from ledges and muttering to itself.

Rex switched to a secure comm circuit that linked him to his squad and nobody else. "Trust is a virtue, Sergeant." He stood at the doorway to scan the courtyard outside for devices and droid activity. "Like patience."

"I must have been at the back of the line when they handed those out, then, sir."

"Me too."

"He knows he's walking into trouble, doesn't he?"

"Yes."

"I have this nagging feeling we ought to be down there with him."

"Don't worry, Sergeant." Rex activated a few more HUD icons with rapid blinks. He knew the coordinates of every gunship, each sergeant. "If the general comes back with any broken bones . . . they won't be his."

DETENTION LEVEL, TETH MONASTERY

Anakin couldn't sense droids as entities in the same way that he could *feel* organic beings, but his Force sense of danger knew something was wrong.

He also had a brain that worked just fine, and it told him that no Sep commander in his—or her—right mind would kidnap a strategic hostage, put up a token fight, and then run away.

Count Dooku certainly wouldn't.

"Master, you do know you're walking us into a trap, don't you?" Ahsoka whispered.

Anakin crept carefully along the flagstones, ready for booby traps and ambushes. Something moved in his peripheral vision. "I do."

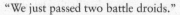

"We just passed two battle droids."

"I know."

"Can I just take care of them?"

"If it makes you feel better. They obviously don't want to kill us."

Ahsoka fell back. Anakin heard the *vzzzm* of her lightsaber, saw a bloom of green light reflected from the slick layer of condensation on the wall, and waited for the sound of destruction. Metal clattered; Ahsoka grunted a couple of times. Then she was at his side again, but he hadn't heard even a single footstep. She really could be a silent hunter.

"Why did you say they don't want to kill us?" she whispered. "You think they weren't *trying*? They were pretty serious about it from where *I* was standing."

Then again, maybe she hadn't caught on to the whole stealth thing. "Can we have this conversation later?"

"Won't that be *too* late?"

"It's a trap. And if it's Dooku's, then it won't be a simple case of *gotcha*."

The whole monastery smelled of decay and ancient dampness. But on top of that aroma wafted something distinctive, a scent firmly embedded in Anakin's memory. Smell was the most evocative of senses for a human, the most primal, even for a Jedi; and this smell went back to before conscious memory, to his earliest childhood.

It was . . . ammonia. That was the nearest thing Anakin could compare it to. It had that sinus-searing quality, but it was also laced with sulfur and other compounds that made him gag.

Hutt.

It was a scent he'd somehow grown up with on Tatooine. At a time when he was trying hard to suppress emotionally painful memories and concentrate on doing his duty, however much that duty stuck in his craw, he didn't need his buttons pressed by things that whispered to the buried primal self deep within.

"He's down *here*." He broke into a faster walk, still alert and ready for a fight. "I can sense him. Cover me."

When he looked back at Ahsoka, she was sniffing the scent too, inhaling with her lips slightly parted as if tasting the air. The more he looked at her, the more he saw not this gawky child desperate to be taken seriously and treated as an adult, but the legacy of a species that could bare its claws and rip apart its prey without a second thought when need arose.

Anakin knew what it was to be dismissed as just a pushy kid when there was *so much* that he could do.

"*Eugh,* that's pretty rank." She inhaled like a Corellian wine taster, sucking in the air in a long, slow sigh. Droids moved in the shadows, and Anakin half watched them, waiting. "Not just scent glands . . . something ickier. I don't think Dooku's minions know how to take care of kids. Like changing diapers."

"They all smell like that. He's a Hutt." Anakin's revulsion just slipped out, or maybe he wanted it to. Ahsoka was attuned enough to sense his emotional struggle anyway. "I hate them."

"I can tell, Master. So why are you doing this?"

"Because duty is about doing what's right, about keeping your word, not just doing what you feel like doing."

"And this isn't about helping Jabba but about defeating Separatists."

"We won't be able to destroy them if we don't grab his kid. It's that simple."

"I think that must be the hardest part of being a Jedi." She put her hand on the door of the cell. The stench of ammonia and sulfur was like a flashing sign saying THE HUTT'S IN HERE. "I think I can hear him."

Anakin strained to hear. The door to the cell looked almost like a cube that had been rammed into the aperture, so massively heavy that it was as good as soundproofing. "Stand back."

Ahsoka snapped her lightsaber to life and stood to one side of the door. Anakin eased it open with a Force push to leave his hands free for whatever might try to rush him on the other side. But as the creaking slab of wood swung inward, what hit him wasn't a fist or a blaster bolt, but a wall of noise, and a smell that he could have sliced with a blade.

The Huttlet was crying—screaming—on a mattress in the middle of the floor. Ahsoka rushed in and knelt down beside him.

"Oh, he's just a baby!" Her expression was part pity, part dismay. "I was expecting him to be older."

"Yeah, and then we wouldn't have been able to lift him . . ." Anakin was still waiting for the trap to be sprung, but the baby needed moving. "Come on. Let's get him out of here."

The Huttlet was screaming himself into a frenzy. Ahsoka tried to soothe him. "It's okay, Rotta, you're going home. You're going home to Daddy. Come on, Rotta, stop crying . . . Master, do you know any Huttese?"

Oh yes, I most certainly do. I grew up speaking it. I never wanted to speak it again.

"Rotta," Anakin said quietly. "*Rotta, pedunkee, da bunk dunko. Sala. Sala.*"

He was a slug. A baby slug, a helpless one, but Anakin knew what he'd grow into. When Rotta sobbed himself to a gulping standstill and squirmed to see where the voice was coming from, Anakin couldn't quite reconcile his feelings.

How can I hate a youngling? He's just a victim. He doesn't know what his father is. He just loves him and wants to go home.

And Anakin understood that simple hunger better than any Jedi he knew.

"Wow," Ahsoka said, "I don't know if he understood you, or if you stunned him into silence, but he's calmed down. He's so cute. He's just like a little toy!"

"You just volunteered to carry him, Snips . . ."

"Fine." She squatted down and scooped Rotta up in her arms,

but Anakin saw the surprise on her face as she realized he was a lot heavier than he looked. "How did you learn Huttese? Or were you just making that up?"

"You pick up all kinds of things as a Jedi." Ahsoka wasn't stupid. She knew there was something eating away at him, and he hoped she'd think it was just a dislike of Hutts. It wouldn't make Anakin unique, that was for sure. Hutts didn't inspire affection. "Let's go. Rex, this is Skywalker, over. All clear?"

Rex's voice carried over the comlink. "All secure here, sir. Got him?"

"Safe and sound. We're coming now."

"I'll send Coric back to make sure the droids don't get ideas. Can't risk any accidents with the kid now."

"Good point, Captain." Anakin sized up the Huttlet with a practiced eye. "Ask Coric to fetch a backpack, too. Rotta's heavy cargo."

"Copy that, sir."

It was nearly done. Anakin waited, defending the door until Coric showed. Ahsoka did her best to keep Rotta calm, rocking him. Nobody could ever accuse her of giving less than a hundred percent; cuddling a Hutt was beyond the call of duty, because she'd be in the 'freshers for a week scrubbing the smell off herself.

So the Jedi Council can pull out all the stops for a Hutt criminal when it suits them.

And they send me.

Is Master Yoda trying to teach me a lesson about submission to the will of the Force? Does he even remember how I came to be a Jedi?

Anakin wondered just how good, how clever, how brave he'd have to be to get any acknowledgment from the Jedi Masters. He didn't serve for prizes; he served because Qui-Gon Jinn believed he had a destiny, and he needed to know what that was to make sense of the pain and loss in his life. But he knew as surely as he knew anything that his troops liked him and cared if he lived or died, and that Kenobi did his best to make up for the sheer . . . *dislocation* Anakin felt at being absorbed into this Jedi world of no families, no loves, and no passions.

But I've got Padmé, and nobody can take her from me. Not your rules, not your traditions, not your disapproval. I have to find my own way, Masters.

"You okay, Skyguy?" Ahsoka asked. "You look worried. You know I only call you that to get you to lighten up, don't you?"

"Yeah . . ."

"You worried that this has been too easy?"

"Not with half my men lying dead, no. Not easy."

"Sorry."

Boots thudded in the passage outside. Coric entered with a backpack in both hands, and almost screeched to a halt as if he'd hit a wall. Anakin couldn't see his face, but the jerk of his head showed he had his helmet filters open and had inhaled Rotta's distinctive aroma.

"Sir, permission to speak freely?" Coric held the backpack out to Ahsoka. "That kriffing Hutt is *honking*, sir. His dad must need a decomposing nerf as an air freshener. Can we stow him in the cargo bay?"

"My sentiments entirely, Sergeant. Let's go."

"Awwww," Ahsoka said. Her sympathetic noise turned into a grunt of exertion as she heaved the laden backpack onto her shoulders. "He probably thinks we stink, too."

"I bet you wish you had a helmet with filters right now, ma'am . . ." Coric adjusted the breather unit of his helmet and stood back to let the two Jedi exit the cell. "The captain's got a larty on standby, sir. You got everything you need?"

"Yes, let's get out before I change my mind about the Hutt."

"He doesn't mean it, Rotta," Ahsoka said, jiggling the backpack and trying to glance over her shoulder. "We need you to get your daddy to let us use his space lanes." She paused, dropping her voice. "And I think you're adorable."

Anakin made his way back to the exit, checking every alcove for Dooku's real trap. There had to be one. Separatists made mistakes and lost battles, but not like this, not this blatantly. He saw daylight ahead and Rex silhouetted against it, *kama* swinging as he turned repeatedly to check something outside in the courtyard, and he tried to work out what could possibly go wrong in these final minutes.

An attack once we're airborne.

Hawk was the best pilot of a brilliant squadron, and the LAAT/i could take a serious pounding.

They couldn't possibly have booby-trapped a baby . . .

Seps would try anything, but there weren't many places to strap an explosive on a baby Hutt.

I don't get it. I just don't get it. Not yet.

"Skyguy . . ."

Anakin didn't look around. His gaze darted everywhere in the shadows ahead. Coric had their six. "Don't tell me, the Hutt's thrown up on you."

"No, but I think something's wrong."

Here we go.

"*How* wrong?" Anakin slowed, ready to swing his lightsaber. He was prepared to believe that a Togruta could detect things that even he couldn't. "Can you sense something?"

"I think I know why he was screaming. And then why he went quiet."

"What? Spit it out, Snips."

Ahsoka did a turn so that Anakin could peer into the backpack. "Look at him. He's making awful noises. Does he look okay to you? I think he's ill. *Really* ill."

Anakin couldn't recall seeing a baby Hutt on Tatooine, but he didn't have to be a doctor to see that Ahsoka's fears were justified.

Rotta the Hutt, his vengeful father's pride and joy, was dull-eyed, tongue lolling, struggling for breath.

He was ill, all right. They now faced the prospect of handing back Jabba's kidnapped heir in a body bag.

Now, that's some trap.

Dooku was much, *much* subtler than even Anakin had imagined.

JABBA'S PALACE, TATOOINE

As soon as the Jedi Kenobi left, satisfied that he had a deal, Count Dooku arrived.

Jabba had long since decided they were both in this for the same thing, both of them from the same nest—arrogant *ootmian*, offworlders from the Core who thought that he was some ignorant Outer Rim peasant *shag* who couldn't see the bigger picture or the political game they were playing.

One of them had probably set up the other. Jabba just didn't know which. Maybe the Jedi wasn't that devious—*maybe*, although Jabba would never bet on it—but he served politicians, and the Senate was *not* Jabba's kind of scum. They were beneath contempt. They bribed, lied, cheated, defrauded, stole, and murdered. Jabba did quite a few of those things too, but he never claimed otherwise, nor was what he did against Hutt law and custom. Republic Senators, though . . . they paraded one morality in public, but lived another in private.

Hypocrisy wasn't the Hutt way. Jabba was ashamed of nothing.

"Show Dooku in," he growled at TC-70.

Dooku was stiffly formal, a much older man than Kenobi. They said he was incredibly wealthy, from an old dynasty, but Jabba had never seen or heard the slightest rumor about how he spent that wealth—if he did anything with it at all. And a business like Jabba's ran on good intelligence about the market and the needs of the rich.

I hate beings who can't be bought. Credits are clean and simple. Other motives . . . are too messy.

"Lord Jabba, I have urgent news about your son," Dooku said. "You were right, he *was* taken to Teth. This will anger you greatly, but I have to tell you—the Jedi are behind this."

Well, you would say that, wouldn't you?

Jabba played the game that Dooku seemed to expect. "If you know so much, tell me how he is!" he bellowed. "Is he dead? Is he alive? How is my son?"

"He's alive, Lord Jabba."

"He'd better be. Why should I believe you, though? You know the Jedi came to me to negotiate. You want the same thing from me, so you would say anything to get it."

"I'm disappointed you feel that way, Lord Jabba."

"Well? Convince me. Tell me how you know."

He couldn't. Jabba watched him clasp his hands slowly, and wondered what he might lever out of the Separatists by turning the tables on Dooku.

"It would be wrong for me to reveal my sources, because it would put my agents at risk, but I have evidence."

Jabba stared at Dooku in complete silence. It was a tactic that always worked, sooner or later, and it was less trouble than strapping him to a thermal detonator with a ticking timer.

Dooku took a visible breath. "Lord Jabba, I have footage from a security holocam on Teth that shows your son being held hostage by Jedi, and . . . I'm sorry, there's no easy way to tell you this, but the recording also shows that they're planning to destroy you."

Jabba hadn't been expecting *that.*

But Rotta was alive. Now Jabba had some control over the situation again, real hope, the kind that set him thinking what revenge he might exact on the guilty parties—beyond denying them the access they needed. But he had no intention of begging for crumbs.

"This is an outrage—show me!"

Dooku held up his hand. "One of my agents is risking her life right now to get your son back from the Jedi. She has the recording and is due to transmit it very soon—a matter of minutes."

Jabba leaned on one elbow and disguised the kind of desperate hope and relief that didn't look at all becoming on a kajidic lord.

"Then I will wait," he said. *"Minutes."*

TEN

General Kenobi, you're clear to land, Docking Bay Five.
Ready to proceed to Teth on your order.
AIR GROUP CONTROL, Jedi cruiser *Spirit of the Republic*,
Tatooine space

MONASTERY BUILDING, TETH

ASAJJ VENTRESS HAD TAKEN SOME YEARS TO FULLY UNDERSTAND
that information was as much a weapon in war as the lightsabers
on her belt.

She understood it fully now as she watched the espionage
droid 4A-7 edit the holocam record of events in the Huttlet's cell.

"This," said 4A-7, "is elegant proof of a saying they have at
HNE News."

"How do *you* know anything about HoloNet news?"

"The media are an integral part of *intelligence*, ma'am,
whether they know it or not. Sometimes very *helpful*, too."

"Whether they know it or not . . ."

"Indeed. Feed them convincing information, and they do our
job for free."

Ventress studied the recording intently, keeping an eye on the chrono. She didn't have long to put this evidence together. She knew the sections of hologram she needed, and now it was just a matter of editing them together in such a way that they appeared to be one continuous event. "So what *is* this saying they have, then?"

"That every audio receiver is a *live* audio receiver." 4A-7 paused the recording and magnified the image; the little Togruta Jedi was frozen with Rotta the Hutt in her arms. "Meaning that you should assume anything you say is being recorded to be used in the most inconvenient way. They catch many unwary Senators that way, I gather. They chatter too candidly when they think the audio recorder is switched off."

Ventress suspected that 4A-7 *enjoyed* his calling. She didn't feel that her conditioning to want something very badly—justice, a different kind of galaxy, some way of putting her terrible memories to rest—was all that different from whatever lines of code controlled this droid's motivation. "Any innocent conversation can be edited to look less innocent than it is."

"But if the speaker is especially careless . . ." 4A-7's manipulators moved at lightning speed and tapped codes onto a small keyboard. "See if *this* is the effect you wanted. If this is satisfactory, I'll adjust the edit points so that the recording appears seamless. Just a matter of blurring the transitions so that there are no embarrassing *jump cuts*."

Yes, he was as pleased with himself as any droid could be. Ventress watched the edited sequence and understood why.

Anakin Skywalker and the Togruta child Ahsoka stood outside the cell, seen from an angle just above their heads. The security holocam image had a frame at the bottom with a record of the local time, moving forward by seconds. Skywalker's tone was surly: "They all smell like that. He's a Hutt. I hate them . . . we won't be able to destroy them if we don't grab his kid." The two

Jedi walked into the cell, disappearing from vision for a moment until the next holocam inside the cell picked them up, with a screaming, obviously terrified baby. The time code had jumped. "Come on. Let's get him out of here." The Togruta bent over Rotta and picked him up. Then a clone trooper walked into the cell. "That kriffing Hutt is *honking*, sir. His dad must need a decomposing nerf as an air freshener. Can we stow him in the cargo bay?" The Togruta put the baby in a military backpack with some difficulty; then Skywalker turned and walked out first, face not visible but voice clearly audible. "Yes, let's get out before I change my mind." The holocam angle then switched to the exterior passage again, as the Togruta carried the now immobile baby in the backpack on her shoulders, she was heard saying, "We need you to get your daddy to let us use his space lanes."

Ventress had to smile. It was *very* clever. But then the Jedi had inadvertently given them such wonderful raw material.

The droid turned his head to focus his photoreceptors on her. "It's not perfect, but once I fill the timeline gaps with a little image extension, and match up the light and audio levels, it'll look like one continuous event in real time. I have enough images of Skywalker with his face turned away from the lens to put any audio of his voice over it, suitably spliced. No need to synchronize with lip movement. Then I blur the whole sequence with a little haze from signal interference, insert a bogus time code that makes it look as if nothing has been edited out, and nobody knows the difference."

Brilliant. Ventress checked the chrono again. "You've got three minutes."

"I'll do it in two," said 4A-7.

And he did. His manipulators moved faster than she could follow. She leaned over his shoulder, mesmerized, and she watched reality bent out of shape and remolded into a new and equally convincing record of events.

Truth was a flexible thing at the best of times. In the hands of technology, though, it became utterly fluid to the point of having no meaning. Truth—reality—was whatever you wanted or needed it to be. She might have been distorting the facts, and that troubled her because she had never thought of herself as dishonest; but if the detail of the event was distorted, the reality for her had not been compromised. The Jedi did the Republic's bidding, and the Republic was self-serving and corrupt. The larger truth was still *true*.

Ventress inspected the short but eloquent holorecording. "Perfect."

"Thank you, ma'am."

Ventress opened her comlink and turned to the holoreceiver. An image of Dooku appeared instantly. He was impatient, waiting, stalling an equally impatient Jabba.

"I'm transmitting the recording now, my lord." She didn't smile. She was long past smiling, and the elation of success had lasted only a moment. It gave way now to grim satisfaction, because no technical skill could edit the past and bring the dead back to life, and all she could do was work for a different future. "It'll achieve the desired outcome. Stand by."

She gestured to 4A-7 to transmit the footage. Then she watched Dooku's expression as his gaze dropped to the datapad in his hand.

Dooku wasn't one of life's smilers either. His eyebrows twitched, though.

"Excellent, Asajj," he said softly. "Mission accomplished. Now you have another."

"Yes, my lord?"

"Retrieve the Huttlet alive and well. Don't let Skywalker leave with him."

Ventress gave Dooku a stiffly formal nod. "Consider it done, my lord."

JABBA'S PALACE, TATOOINE

"You took your time," Jabba growled as Dooku swept back into the throne chamber.

"I wanted to be certain, Lord Jabba," Dooku said. "Even I was surprised by this."

He set the holoprojector on the nearest table, and waited a couple of seconds to make sure the weight of what was to unfold hit home. Jabba sat almost alone—no decorative dancers or musicians, or even his menagerie of exotic species that might or might not have been fully sentient, just two Nikto bodyguards.

The edited evidence flickered to life. Jabba, to his credit, waited until the he'd heard the offending phrase before exploding into fury. The slit pupils of his eyes widened and he bellowed insults and threats that even Dooku's grasp of Huttese couldn't fully follow. It was a more complex and vividly expressive language than non-Hutts gave it credit for. By the time Jabba had settled into the more familiar vocabulary of what he would have done with Skywalker had he still been a slave here, and what Jabba would do to him anyway when he finally caught him, and what would happen to any Jedi *poodoo* who dared enter Hutt space, Dooku was satisfied that a wedge the size of Coruscant had been rammed between Jabba and the Republic.

"My son!" Jabba slowed into outraged disbelief. "Did you hear his screams? They treated him like an *animal*!"

Dooku had wondered if Jabba's rages were all part of keeping up his image of a dangerous enemy to make—as if that needed emphasis—but he felt no hint of a bravura performance now.

"I'm sorry you had to see that, Lord Jabba, but it was necessary. I've taken the liberty of deploying my droid troops and agents to rescue Rotta, and they're engaging Skywalker's forces now."

"His welfare," Jabba said, almost hissing with frustration, "is paramount. No mistakes. He must *not* be harmed."

"You have my word."

"And?"

"I'm afraid I don't understand, Lord Jabba." Dooku didn't, not for a moment anyway. "And what?"

"What do you want in exchange for this help? Because it will cost you troops, and nobody does anything in this galaxy for nothing. Even the pious Jedi have a price, as we've seen."

"Very well, I'll ask for something that's of mutual advantage."

"How much?"

Dooku waved away the suggestion. Credits meant nothing. It was what they could buy when it was unbuyable that mattered, and what he wanted was the weight of a galaxy-spanning operation that even the Republic couldn't shut down when it wanted to.

"I want your support, Lord Jabba," Dooku said. He wasn't going to lie to him—well, not over anything this fundamental. The doctored holorecording was a necessary evil. What he said now was something he believed, and believed in, with every fiber of his being; he was prepared to die for it. He certainly wasn't in this to grow wealthier. "The galaxy needs to clear house. Support the Confederacy of Independent Systems, Lord Jabba. The Republic's become a disease, and the Jedi are keeping it in power for their own ends, so help the systems that are breaking away to end that dictatorship once and for all. Because it *is* a dictatorship. Planets do things the Republic's way, or not at all. Otherwise, why not just let them cede from the alliance?"

"Hutt worlds aren't part of the Republic." Jabba wasn't bargaining now, that was clear. It seemed as if he hadn't seen things that way before. "We're separate already."

"But if the Republic wins this war, and forces unwilling worlds to submit, do you seriously think they'll leave *you* alone forever?"

Jabba's eyes narrowed for a moment. "You'll have full access to Hutt space, and the Republic will not. Now get my son back."

Dooku bowed and left, following a Nikto guard to the exit. The palace was unnaturally quiet, as if all Jabba's motley entourage were hiding in their rooms in terrified silence, waiting for his rage to erupt and engulf them. The corridors echoed, and Dooku emerged into the blinding midday of Tatooine's twin suns.

"Thank you," he said to the Nikto. "I can make my own way from here."

The sand sucked at Dooku's boots as he walked to his swoop bike, concealed in a cave in the sandstone cliffs.

Nearly done. Nearly won. But just one more battle in the longer war.

He had never expected Jabba to take up arms and rush to the barricades in a frenzy of revolutionary fervor, so simply sowing more seeds of dissent was a bonus. He had what he needed; the Separatist forces would be able to move at will in the Outer Rim, and the Republic would not.

The one thing he needed to be certain of now was the safe return of the Huttlet.

After that, he would give consideration to which of his various contingency plans for Jabba's uncle Ziro he would put into effect.

Ziro wasn't going to get the chance to take over Jabba's empire now, and he'd be disappointed in the emphatic and troublesome way that only a Hutt could. If Ziro had any sense, he'd keep his mouth shut about their deal when he finally found out that his leverage over Jabba was gone.

Dooku pondered. *More convenient surveillance footage showing Ziro arranging to frame me? A tragic accident? A shoot-out with a rival kajidic or Black Sun gang which ends—also tragically—in Ziro's death?*

There were many ways to make sure Ziro treated the change of plans as a character-forming experience that nobody else ever needed to know about.

"You would have reneged on our deal in time if the Republic had offered you more," Dooku said to himself. "Wouldn't you?"

Now he'd never know for sure. And he would lose no sleep over that.

COURTYARD, TETH MONASTERY

Anakin's Delta starfighter dropped into the courtyard and R2-D2 hopped out of the astromech housing mounted on the wing. The droid swiveled his dome to focus on Rotta, whistling mournfully.

"Yeah, he's not well at all, Artoo." Anakin peered into the backpack. "But at least we have him. Is General Kenobi on his way?"

R2-D2 projected a hologram of Kenobi in midair in front of him. "I am," Kenobi said. "With reinforcements, too. Have you found Jabba's son?"

"If holomessaging transmitted smell, you'd know already. Yes, we have him. But . . ."

"But what?"

"He's really ill. We need to get him to a specialist medic soon. Hutts just don't get sick, so this is serious."

Kenobi ran his hand over his beard, not in that considered I'm-pondering-mighty-issues way, but fast, as if he was stifling a groan of despair.

"That's the last thing we need right now, Anakin."

"I think I worked that out, Master. And I'm pretty sure that this is a sting by Dooku. The whole situation stinks worse than the Huttlet."

"He's set us up to alienate Jabba, then. To stop us from getting access to Hutt routes."

"I realized something was wrong after I lost half my men in breaching the monastery, and then we were allowed to just stroll in unopposed and get the kid." The adrenaline had now ebbed enough for Anakin to start wondering how he could have seen this coming and avoided the bait. "I was waiting for the ambush, but maybe this is it—he's literally left us holding the baby. And it might end up being a *dead* baby."

Kenobi leaned out of the range of his transmitter, looking as if he was checking something. "You think Dooku has poisoned the youngling?"

"No idea. But the timing and circumstance make me wonder."

"Let's make sure Rotta survives, then."

"I'm sorry, Master. Maybe I should have seen this coming. But it was a bad idea to deal with the Hutts. You can never win with them. You can only choose how badly you lose."

"Anakin, if we'd refused Jabba's request for help, we'd never have been granted access to those routes anyway. We had no choice."

"You think he's colluding with Dooku? That he maneuvered us? It was *very* unlike Jabba to ask for Republic help."

"I don't know, but one thing we *can't* do is play into Separatist hands by letting anything happen to the baby. Top priority. We return it in one piece."

Ahsoka had been completely silent up to that point, rocking the Huttlet by bouncing a little at the knee as she stood there, but Anakin heard her rumble at the back of her throat. It was an oddly feral noise that made the hair stand up on his nape.

"Okay, Master," Anakin said, ignoring her. "Understood. We—oh, great . . ."

That was as far as he got.

"Down! Everybody down! Enemy fighters, incoming!"

The next thing he knew Rex was yelling at everyone to take cover, and Ahsoka was running for the shelter of the monastery doors. Flashes of brilliant light blinded him as he instinctively looked up at the sky. Something rumbled and thundered. It wasn't a storm; it was a massive Separatist landing ship escorted by at least one squadron of droid vulture fighters. R2-D2 stood his ground, still transmitting Kenobi's message.

"Master, we're under attack. Got to go. And hurry up . . ."

"Anakin?" Kenobi's transmission was breaking up. *"Anakin!"*

And then it was gone, and the rising whine of a fighter diving to attack sent Anakin scrambling to the monastery wall with R2-D2. Vulture droids swooped. There was no option but to retreat into the monastery.

"Ahsoka! Are you okay?" Anakin couldn't see her. A fighter strafed the monastery, ripping up ancient flagstones in a dead straight line and scattering chunks of stone like shrapnel. R2-D2 rolled up beside him. "Talk to me, Snips!"

"I'm okay, Master." Her voice came from behind him, muffled by something. She must have had her face buried in the backpack against her chest, shielding Rotta the hard way. For all the sheer terror of the attack, Anakin could think only of the fact that she was inhaling concentrated essence of Hutt. *Now, that takes guts.* "I've got Rotta. I think he's too sick to notice what's going on, poor kid."

"It's okay. Keep your head down. And his," Anakin gestured to the droid. "Artoo, get over there with her."

"Sorry, Skyguy," Ahsoka called. "I ran instead of sticking with you."

"Rotta's *got* to stay alive. You did right, Snips." Callous as it seemed, Anakin was also relieved that he didn't have an alert, panic-stricken Huttlet screaming blue murder as the laser rounds tore up the ground around him. "Getting shot when you don't have to isn't heroic, it's dumb."

Rex, skidding to a crouch beside him, slammed his hand down on top of Anakin's raised head. Laser rounds punched a shower of brick dust and rubble out of the wall above them. "Yes, sir, it *is.* Keep your kriffing head down."

"I can sense rounds coming, Rex."

"Okay, then do it to humor me."

It was gestures like that—real concern, however abruptly worded—that made Anakin feel he could tackle anything. He relished the heady comradeship born in desperate situations. Even cornered and outgunned like this, he knew someone was watching his back—not because he was the Chosen One or an officer, but because the soldier next to him was a comrade. And Anakin would do the same for him.

It wasn't quite the serene acceptance that Kenobi had tried to instill in him, but Qui-Gon Jinn would have understood.

"So what's it to be, sir?" Rex asked. His voice was almost drowned out by the hammer of laserfire. "Stall them until General Kenobi gets here, or slug it out?"

"You know what they say about discretion and valor. Can we land a larty?" Sometimes Anakin longed for a helmet like his clone troopers', something that would give him hard data. Right then he needed to see real-time sensor information. "Can we get Ahsoka off this rock with the Huttlet?"

"Negative, sir. Even if the larty isn't pounded to pieces when it sets down, not even Hawk could guarantee getting past the Sep ships in one piece, and he couldn't outrun them. We're stuck."

"Okay, then we dig in. Fall back and hold the monastery. Just concentrate on keeping that Hutt alive."

"Got it, sir." Rex fell silent for a moment, head lowered as if talking on another circuit. Anakin saw troopers dart back through the gates just before something smashed into the wooden supports and left them splintered and smoking. "They could turn this whole plateau to molten slag from the air if they wanted to."

"Not if they want the Hutt alive."

"Okay, a picture is forming now . . ."

"If Dooku set this up, then he needs to be the one to hand Rotta back to Jabba."

"What I wouldn't give for air cover."

"Twice in a row. Next time—we pack a squadron of Delta in-tercepters."

Rex froze for a moment as if listening, then trained his rifle on the massive gates that had stood untouched for centuries.

"Here they come," he said. "Coric, Hez—covering fire. A-tee, get to that gate and block those tinnies. Everyone else—inside, *now!*"

"That means you, Ahsoka!" Anakin yelled. But when he glanced over his shoulder, she was already running for the doors, clutching the pack to her chest, with R2-D2 at her heels like a herding akk dog.

"Steady, boys . . . ," Rex whispered. "Make every round count."

The first of the battle droids pushed through the remains of the gate as the last AT-TE plodded toward them, laying down suppressing fire. The front rank was cut down into a flurry of metal shredded so thoroughly that for a moment it hung in the air like decoy chaff. Anakin crouched with his lightsaber held horizontally over his head in a backhand grip and backed toward the main monastery doors. Troopers ran past him, vanishing into the passage.

"How many men still out there, Captain?"

Rex paused to reload. The AT-TE pounded at a target beyond the gate that Anakin couldn't see. "Nobody outside the walls. Courtyard—the A-tee, Coric's squad, and Hez's squad."

"Okay, pull them out now."

"The A-tee can't walk through doors, sir. The crew will have to dismount."

And they'd be cut down the moment they opened the hatches. Anakin struggled with that same sense of comradeship that had so buoyed him up minutes earlier.

No. I will not *slam the doors on my men.*

Officers were supposed to accept those losses. But Anakin wouldn't, not as long as he had a lightsaber in his hands. "Then I'll cover them."

He didn't wait for Rex's answer. He sprang to his feet and raced forward, batting away droid blasterfire and trusting his Force senses to steer him between the strafing runs of the vulture fighters. He was almost at the feet of the AT-TE, wondering if Rex was giving them an order to dismount or if he'd have to hammer on the belly hatch, when a pack of spider droids scuttled into the courtyard and opened fire on the armored walker.

The walker took multiple hits as Anakin lunged forward to get to the belly hatch. The next round caught it in one of the forward turrets, and the explosion threw Anakin flat. As he struggled to his feet, he could see the smoke and flames belching from two hatches. The walker tottered, then collapsed on its front legs before crashing onto its side.

The belly hatch flew open. Anakin let instinct take over and he was instantly between the stricken AT-TE and the advancing droids, using the fallen vehicle for cover while he deflected small cannon rounds. From the corner of his eye, he saw four white shapes stagger clear, two of them dragging another man. *Five.* The turret gunner was vaporized. That left one of the crew. Flames now licked from the hatch.

"Sir—"

"Run. I'll hold them. Anyone alive inside?" *Dumb question, but I need to know.*

"Negative, sir."

"Get going. Count of three."

Anakin bobbed up from behind the walker and was greeted by a hail of blasterfire.

"Three!" he yelled, swinging at the bolts.

The men sprinted for the door, plunging into the acrid black smoke that now filled the courtyard. It was some kind of cover for a few seconds. Anakin saw the droids, hampered by their own debris, and his eyes went to the blazing carcass of the AT-TE.

Just do it.

Adrenaline fueled him. He sent the wreckage skidding across the ground with a massive Force push. The kinetic force of the impact and the sheet of flame released when it slammed into the droid ranks had the effect of a bomb going off. Then another explosion—the walker's magazine, probably—sent a fireball soaring into the air.

Anakin found he wanted to wade in and cut down whatever was still standing when the flame died, but common sense told him to get out. He ran full tilt for the monastery door, leaping over debris, masonry, and downed droids. The door, a solid portcullis, still hung open. Rex stood outside with his rifle aimed past Anakin. They'd never lock the door down before the droids reached them if they didn't start closing it right *now*.

Anakin bellowed at the top of his voice. "Rex, get inside! Seal the door!"

"With respect, sir, no."

Rex let loose with a couple of anti-armor rounds that skimmed to Anakin's left. Their distinctive *husshhh-ump* sound as they passed him was swallowed by a blast that kicked him forward.

The sound of running metal feet hammered behind him. He didn't dare turn and look. "I said *shut the kriffing door*."

Rex stood motionless for a moment; then—as if he'd been counting—he spun around and fired a round into the controls just inside the door. The heavy slab fell.

It wasn't a controlled closure.

Anakin focused on the gap. Nothing else existed.

The last thing he saw before he dropped onto his right ankle to skid the last few meters was Rex ducking under the falling door almost alongside him. For a split second, Anakin looked up and was sure the door was going to slice clean through his skull.

It crashed down behind him, close enough and hard enough to blow his hair over his eyes. The passage was plunged into darkness.

Nothing moved; Anakin looked at his clenched fist and breathed a silent sigh of relief that he'd shut off the lightsaber in it instinctively. The silence was broken only by the clacking of armor plates in the darkness, and then the faint sounds of droids massing on the other side of the door. Helmet spot lamps began lighting up like a cautious sunrise.

So I got you into this. So I'll get you out. Anakin rose to his feet, gearing up to deploy the men for a last-ditch defensive action.

"Sir," said one of the troopers, "I think I left my lunchbox outside. Want to go and collect it for me?"

The remnant of Torrent Company burst out laughing, and so did Anakin. It was that moment of life-or-death desperation that flipped instantly into the black humor of sheer relief at finding your lungs were still working.

"Rex, how many casualties?" Anakin asked. Ahead, he could see R2-D2's array of lights and panels winking in the gloom. "How many medics made it?"

"Forty-two men remaining, sir, three medic-trained. Six walking wounded, one seriously injured and immobile."

The last point was visibly obvious. Three troopers clustered around the injured AT-TE crewman, whose armor plates and helmet had been placed to one side while they tried to stabilize him with hemostats and a plasma line.

Three-quarters of my men dead. For a Hutt. "Okay, you know what to do, Captain. We'll hole up in the least accessible cell we can find and if they get past you, then they'll still have to get past me and Ahsoka. And Artoo."

"Understood, sir."

There were some things clone troopers did that made Anakin realize that their relentless training from infancy was both like his and also utterly alien. At a single gesture from Rex, no audible command given, the troopers split into groups. One party began stripping anything that was removable from walls and alcoves, and stacking it against the door. Another group laid ordnance out on the floor and seemed to be assembling booby traps; three men ran down the passage and started setting up a first-aid position. One trooper pressed a thin wire into the gaps between the flagstones from one side of the passage to the other. Others—it took Anakin a few moments to work it out, but they were wiring themselves, packing ordnance into their backpacks.

No droid was getting through except over their dead bodies, and maybe not even then. The message was clear.

Anakin said nothing, but walked among the troopers, tapping his palm against the hand of every man he could reach. Some returned the gesture. Nothing *needed* saying. Rex was last; Anakin clapped his hand on the captain's backplate as he passed, and Rex just gave him a deceptively relaxed pat on the shoulder in return. Anakin jogged down the passage, collecting Ahsoka and R2-D2 on the way, and headed into the bowels of the monastery.

It wasn't like this in the holovids. Anakin wasn't sure how he would ever describe it to Padmé, or if he'd want to. *I haven't even thought about her since the battle started.* He felt briefly guilty about that. And, unbidden, another little voice nagged in his head: *Yoda still won't give you any genuine praise if you save the day, you know . . .*

But that was the other Anakin's voice. Now the resentment against everyone who wouldn't let him have his head, the pendulum that swung between seeing Kenobi as the big brother he needed and the older sibling who just held him back, was silenced. Something in him switched on—his older, battle-hardened self.

The innermost sanctum had been a Hutt throne room, judging by the overblown decor. What it had been before—Anakin couldn't guess.

But now it was sanctuary. He shut the doors, and prepared for a siege.

ELEVEN

I haven't heard from Dooku. What's he doing with Jabba's son?
I hear worrying rumors from my spies on Tatooine.
But then there are always rumors.
ZIRO THE HUTT, to a trusted aide

COURTYARD, TETH MONASTERY

THE RANKS OF BATTLE DROIDS PARTED, AND ASAJJ VENTRESS walked slowly through their line to pause at the entrance to the monastery.

White armor jutted from the rubble. The Jedi were running out of slaves to take the blaster bolts for them.

"Skywalker!" Ventress suspected he wouldn't hear, but she wanted to say it anyway. "You've got nowhere to run. Just choose how fast you want to die."

The battle droid commander trotted up to her. "They've barricaded themselves in. The door controls have been destroyed, and we heard activity behind it that suggest the Republic troops are reinforcing it."

"Then get them *out.*"

"Permission to use explosives for rapid entry, ma'am."

Ventress took a few steps back, hands on hips, twin lightsabers swinging from her belt. She didn't have forever, but neither did the Jedi. The baby slug—Hutts were hard to kill even if you tried, but this wasn't the time to find out that she was wrong.

"Denied. Use cutters. Take no chances around the Huttlet—I don't want a scratch on him, do you hear? No explosives unless you confirm he's not in the blast area. Got it?"

"Yes, ma'am."

She withdrew to a meter-high wall that had managed to survive the assault and leaped onto it to survey the progress. Droids ferried cutting equipment to the doors. When they began lasering the surface, smoke curled off the ancient panels—was it metal, composite, or some ultra-hard wood?—and the droids seemed agitated.

Whatever it was made from, it was going to take some time to breach.

"We could demand a surrender and offer them terms, ma'am," said the droid commander.

"A waste of time," Ventress said. "They won't accept. This is the Grand Army—and the Five-oh-first, at that, Skywalker's own men. Every indication we have is that they're not just good little loyal clones, they're *personally* loyal to him. If he orders them to die for him, they will. Fools. I hope for their sakes that they realize what the Jedi are before they die in the proverbial ditch to save their miserable skins."

"That's a negative, then, ma'am."

Droids weren't capable of sarcasm. Ventress went back to watching the progress of the cutting tools. "Skywalker got a message out to the Republic. We'll have armed company sooner or later. Stay alert. I want vultures and spider droids patrolling the whole complex."

"Copy that."

Ventress didn't like heroism. She didn't disrespect heroes; she just knew that sacrifice was seldom rewarded, and always exploited. Narec's heroic efforts for the people of Rattatak hadn't meant a thing to Mace Windu. It was the Jedi Master who had abandoned Narec—her mentor, her only friend—to die.

I wish you hadn't told me that, Dooku. But we all need a focus.

Narec had been expendable, just like those clones behind that door. There was no point thinking too hard about their plight, though. It would weaken her resolve. There was only one outcome if you tried to help a mistreated akk dog; it would still rip out your well-meaning, sympathetic throat, because its master had made it dangerous and it knew no other response.

She waited, locking and unlocking the hilts of her twin lightsabers.

ABANDONED THRONE ROOM, TETH MONASTERY

R2-D2 always had the air of a droid with a mission, driven by something Anakin couldn't detect even when he overhauled him. As soon as R2-D2 oriented himself in the vault, he made a straight line for an alcove and plugged himself into a computer hub.

The terminal flickered to life. R2-D2 whistled happily to himself as he sliced through security interfaces.

"I refuse to believe a place like this hasn't got plenty of alternative exits," Anakin said, peering over the droid's dome to look at the screen. "If it didn't have any to start with, I bet the Hutt who moved in added a few. Right, Artoo?"

R2-D2 bleeped in agreement. Ahsoka laid the backpack down on the floor and examined Rotta.

"He's asleep," she said. "Or unconscious."

Anakin checked the Huttlet, too. "He's breathing. That can only be good."

"But he's burning up." Ahsoka had no fear of slime, it seemed. She put her hand flat on Rotta's head. "Kids can run fevers, have fits, and then be right as rain in an hour. Well, *human* children can. Can't they?"

"Where'd you learn that?"

"Same way you learned Huttese, probably. Jedi pick up stuff."

Anakin wasn't sure if she was being sarcastic or defensive, but he suspected the latter. "You're doing all anyone can, Snips. Don't beat yourself up."

"If anything happens to him, it'll be my fault."

"No it won't. What are you trying to prove, anyway?"

"That I'm not too young to be your Padawan."

"Oh, that? Have I sent you back to the Temple yet? No. Have I stopped you fighting? No. So I must think you're old enough."

Ahsoka didn't reply. But she managed a smile and went on fussing over Rotta. He really did look bad, even for a Hutt. His eyes weren't completely shut, even though he wasn't responding to anything, and Anakin could see a hint of the glistening membrane under his eyelids. The smell—he'd forgotten it. The last few hours had been so numbing that the stench had just ceased to register on him.

"Got anything, Artoo?"

The droid burbled to himself for a while, then let out a long, low whistle. He was slicing as fast as he could, he said.

"Okay, I'll be patient." Anakin rummaged in the small satchel attached to his belt. "Snips, when did you last drink some fluid? Come to that, when did our fragrant little precious?" He held out his water flask. "Come on. Dehydration makes you confused, and then it kills you."

He should have known better by now. Ahsoka reached out, took the flask with a grimly determined smile—she would *not* let the side down by showing discomfort—and then dribbled a little of the water into Rotta's mouth.

There was no way Anakin was placing that flask near his own

mouth again, if he could help it. Ahsoka moistened the baby's lips again. An oversized slimy tongue darted out and Rotta slurped.

"Oh, that's good! Good boy! Come on, stinky, drink some more for Mama . . ."

"I don't think Hutts *have* mothers . . ." Anakin watched, listening for trouble outside and trying to sense the degree of danger at the front door. There was something malevolent and dark lurking at a distance; it didn't feel like Dooku, though. Anakin would place it eventually. "If you're not careful, he'll bond with you."

"Do they do that?" Ahsoka took a swig from the bottle without wiping the neck. Anakin's stomach rolled a little. Maybe if you snacked on rodents, Hutt dribble didn't seem so offensive. She wrinkled her nose, though. "I don't want to confuse the poor little guy."

"When he's all grown up and he's a two-ton crime lord, you'll have a devoted friend for life."

"Talking of loyalty—Rex and his men . . ."

"I know. I *know*." The job had to be done. It didn't mean Anakin had to like it, though. "This is one of the worst lessons you'll ever have to learn, Snips. Command means being prepared to get troops killed."

"They'd do anything for you."

"And I won't throw their lives away."

"Is it better not to get to know them?"

"No. It's not. It's shirking your responsibility, and it's disrespectful. Get to know them, and then you fully understand the price you're asking them to pay."

"With any luck," she said, "General Kenobi will arrive before then."

Kenobi was pretty good at showing up when needed most. But Anakin had the feeling he'd be too late for what was left of Torrent Company.

R2-D2 trilled triumphantly. It was a merciful distraction for Anakin.

"Found it, Artoo?"

The droid spun ninety degrees. He'd found plans of the drains, he said, and those might do in a pinch. But where there were drainage plans, there might also be construction schematics. He'd carry on drilling down.

"Drill faster, buddy," Anakin said.

ENTRANCE TO THE TETH MONASTERY

"Can't you work any faster?"

Ventress jumped down from the wall and strode up to the door. Cutting was taking far too long. The droids were opening a square section in the door, which was unsatisfactory enough given how much it would limit their rate of entry, but at this pace it would take the rest of the day.

She needed to get that Huttlet back to Jabba fast. The longer he fretted, the worse it got.

"Ma'am, this isn't as simple as it looks," the commander said, trotting ahead of her and trying to look back at the same time. "The door is massive, and you said no rapid entry using charges."

"I didn't tell you to work your way through with a manicure file, either . . ."

Two droids were working on the external controls, tinkering with colored wires. No wonder the Republic chose to use cloned humans. Ventress watched in dismay for a few moments as they debated over which wires to reattach, the red ones or the blue ones.

"You're not defusing a *bomb*, you fools!" she snapped. "Try each combination and see what works. There aren't that many, are there?"

"Ma'am, the Republic troops fused the interior controls by—"

"So you can't open it."

"We can, but we have to isolate the circuit above the point where the damage occurred."

Ventress sized up the panels that surrounded the door. In the time the droids had taken to get this far, the clones inside would have prepared any number of traps and countermeasures to slow them down. *She* certainly would have. She'd have excavated a pit just inside the door, for a start; she'd have rigged charges in the joists and supports to bring the roof of the passage crashing down the moment the bulk of the droid assault force was inside. She'd have made finding a rear exit a priority.

She estimated that Skywalker had maybe forty or fifty troops left, but it was impossible to know how much ordnance they had or if they'd taken any special equipment in with them.

"Stand aside," she said.

At least droids didn't argue. They let her inspect the controls. She could see wires protruding from a metal conduit buried in the doorframe, but the frame was so thick that the internal mechanism was embedded too far inside for her to see it or reach it. There was a quick, one-way solution, though. She motioned the droids away from the frame, drew both lightsabers, and turned to face the ranks of battle droids waiting to begin the assault.

"When I give the order," she said, "you will storm the entrance, because the door will be open. The troops inside will have the initial advantage, because you have to negotiate a choke point which will negate your numbers, but you have vastly superior numbers, and you will simply press on until you overwhelm them. It's that simple. You will neutralize the Republic forces, but you will not proceed farther until I tell you to do so, because I must have that Huttlet alive and well. Is that clear?"

The droids listened intently. They should have been programmed to do this, but she liked to be certain that they were on the same page of the manual that she was. Lateral thinking was not their forte.

The battle droids responded in one synchronized chorus. "Copy copy!"

Ventress raised her right arm, igniting one red lightsaber blade and twirling the hilt in a stab grip. "Stand by."

She brought the blade down in a fast arc and gouged clean through the frame and the metal conduit, shorting out the entire system in a pyrotechnic display of blue-white sparks. Most doors were designed to fail in the fully open position for safety reasons, and had been made that way for centuries; the monastery door was no exception. The slab of material rocketed to the lintel, opening a dark maw that spewed blue blasterfire and anti-armor rounds. The first two lines of droids fell, and Ventress stepped calmly to one side as the ranks behind them marched through the shattered debris of their comrades to press into the entrance.

They would keep marching, and marching, and marching. Eventually—very soon, in fact—Skywalker would run out of troops before she ran out of droids.

As she waited, she wondered briefly what she might have done if the door had failed in the closed position.

It didn't matter. She was a thorough planner, like her master, Count Dooku.

She already knew where the exits were, and had them covered.

And this was the day those lives finally ended.

His helmet could dampen the decibels from external sources, but as long as he was on the comlink circuit, he couldn't shut out the cries and panting breathlessness and screams of his men.

A wave of battle droids caught the trip wire that Ged had laid a few paces from the door. Thermal detonators taped on both walls blew inward and buried what was left of the droids in rubble. *We should have done that first. We should have collapsed the first ten meters of the passage and made them dig us out.* But it was too late for that now, and super battle droids poured in after the smaller battle droids, blaster arms extended and firing. Spider droids rushed ahead of them and opened up with laser cannon. The bolts passed close enough to Rex for his damage sensors to detect the fizz and crackle of superheated air before smashing into something behind him.

Something. My boys.

Every detonation was more lethal for being in a confined space. The smoke was now so thick that Rex was relying on thermal imaging in his HUD. He glanced up at the huge beams supporting the ceiling, the vaulted section behind that, and knew he didn't have the firepower to bring it down on the tinnies. All he could do was aim and fire at whatever was coming at him.

Rex saw Ged fall, then Hez and three of his squad. A trooper who hit a tinny at point-bank range was decapitated by a razor-sharp slice of shrapnel that flew from the thing. Coric, caught on a reload, swung his Deece sideways like a club, and Rex broke off from laying down fire to put a stream of bolts into the droid. If it saved Coric's life, he didn't see; the next thing he knew he was on his back, knocked flat by something much heavier than himself, and his hardwired reaction was to draw one of his sidearms and empty the clip into the dark shape bearing down on him.

Events were moving so fast that he had no time to do anything more than let his body react, and yet—as always—what he could see was unfolding in slow motion, some detail so intense that he would never forget it, everything else a blur.

The hot flare in his infrared told him he'd hit something at close range. Then every bit of breath was knocked out of him. He felt a crushing weight on his chest, followed by an intense pain like a blade in the ribs. No, that was wrong; he'd been stabbed before, and it felt like a punch, not sharp at all. Why the stang was he thinking stupid stuff like this? He was dying. This wasn't how he thought it would be.

"Coric!" he called. "Coric?"

If Coric could hear him, he didn't answer. His helmet filled with muffled silence, and try as he did to move, he felt pinned down.

No, it wasn't how he thought it would be at all.

ABANDONED THRONE ROOM, DEEP INSIDE THE MONASTERY

The noise of the explosions made Anakin start, even in these buried vaults. He had no hard data, but he felt death, pain, and fear rip through the fabric of the Force, and that only could come from living beings snuffed out of existence, not droids.

I'm sorry, Rex. I'm so sorry.

"The droids have broken through," he said. "Artoo, get a move on. We still have an objective to achieve. Ahsoka, are you ready to evacuate?"

She snatched up the backpack and struggled into the straps. Rotta seemed to wake, blinking, and gurgled.

"Hey, you back with us, Stinky?" Ahsoka craned her neck to look around at him. "Little nap do you good?"

"Just don't die on us," Anakin said. He'd probably lost an entire company just to save this slug. He wondered if the Outer Rim routes were really that critical, and if a little more strategic thought could have circumvented the supply-chain problem. It was all too late now. "The sooner we can get rid of you, the better."

Ahsoka frowned slightly. "I know you probably have good reasons for hating Hutts, just like everyone else, but what can Rotta possibly have done? He's a baby. He's only guilty of being a slug."

"I'm sure he'll make up for that when he gets older." Anakin wasn't in the mood to debate speciesism. The Huttlet was still alive, but most of his troops weren't. *Maybe none of them.* The worst thing about the pressure easing for a moment was that all the other ugly thoughts and memories flooded back in. "Look, I do my duty, but I reserve the right to think what I like about whether it's worth the sweat and blood or not."

"If it means we can fight more effectively, doesn't that save lives?"

"If we get chummy with organized crime, and turn a blind eye to our allies making a living from slavery, drug running, extortion, and murder, what exactly are we fighting for?"

Ahsoka stared at him, wide-eyed. "Is this a test?"

"No, it's just me getting angry."

R2-D2 beeped frantically. He was triumphant. He'd found what he was looking for. Anakin's train of thought was broken—mercifully—and he concentrated on the holographic plan that appeared from the astromech droid's projector.

It showed a network of passages leading out of the monastery. But even better than that was a landing platform jutting out of the sheer side of the cliff, set a little way from the top, and approached from the rear.

"That's a great place to land a larty," Anakin said. "Artoo, you're the navigator—lead us down there and I'll call for extraction."

"You're going home, Stinky," Ahsoka whispered to the Hutt. "Hang in there. You'll be back with your daddy soon."

"Lucky slug," Anakin said sourly.

It wasn't the way a general should have behaved, he knew; it was a poor example to set for a Padawan. But Anakin was twenty, having lived through things most kids his age hadn't, and he'd had few of the carefree times that young men his age took for granted.

And Rex and his men had even less. I've at least got Padmé. What am I griping about?

It was too bad. He was the Chosen One, a Jedi, and he wasn't the one doing the choosing. He had a destiny. But sometimes it was very hard to take it in his stride without anger, frustration, and a growing list of unanswered questions.

"Get going, Artoo," he said. "Next stop, Tatooine."

MONASTERY ENTRANCE PASSAGE

Rex wasn't sure when the weight on his chest lifted, but it had, and he could breathe again.

He flicked his visor back to normal light vision with a couple of blinks. Either he was dead, and being dead was an awful lot like being alive, or he'd survived. It took some moments to work out that he was propped against the wall on a carpet of wreckage.

Biosign icons blinked in his HUD; five of his men were still alive.

Yeah, I'm alive. I really am. You should have finished me off when you had the chance, tinnies . . .

But he couldn't spring up and get on with the fight. He needed to assess the situation.

"Nobody move," he said. In the privacy of his helmet, he could speak with his men undetected. "Report in if you can hear me."

"Receiving, sir."

"Yes, sir."

"I hear you, sir."

"Got you, sir." *Coric.* He'd made it. "Just a few bruises."

"And me, sir."

"CT-nine-nine-three-two, sir."

Rex felt he'd taken back control of the situation, no matter how many droids were still out there. "Anyone not capable of moving or using a weapon, speak up now." There was just the sound of breathing in his audio circuit. "Okay, time for dynamic risk assessment. Follow my lead. When we get the chance to make a run for it, we head for the courtyard, grab any spare weapons, and rappel back down onto the jungle floor."

There was a chorused mumble of agreement. He could make it sound so simple. As he lay slumped, he saw a pair of boots and the swinging hem of a robe coming toward him at a leisurely pace, accompanied by a pair of droid legs. The range of vision in his HUD gave him a panoramic view without him moving his head if he needed it. Playing dead, he adjusted the view with a few blinks and saw a battle droid in commander's livery, and a severe-looking, shaven-headed woman in a black costume, with what looked like a lightsaber grasped in one hand.

Nice choice of hairstyle, sweetheart, but something tells me you're not a Jedi.

He knew who she was. His HUD database held a rogues' gallery of Separatists, and Asajj Ventress, Dooku's assassin, was one of the easiest of the scumbags to identify.

"Stand by," he whispered.

Rex took a chance that the rest of the droids had moved on. He reached slowly for his sidearm. Droid first, or Ventress? He opted for the droid, aimed his sidearm and blew its head off, then swung onto Ventress—

He really should have picked her off first.

She ignited her lightsaber and batted the fire away in the fraction of a second it took him to shift his aim. The next he knew, his weapon was jerked out of his fist by an unseen force, and he was lifted bodily by his throat. The rim of his helmet took most of the stress, and if it hadn't he was certain that it would have snapped his neck.

Ventress had grabbed his throat in a stranglehold. She didn't even need to touch him.

I won't make that mistake again. Now, nobody else move . . . keep your nerve . . .

"Captain," Ventress said. "What a miraculous return from the dead. Where's your general?"

"Which one?"

"Don't get smart with me. You know who. *Skywalker.* I know he's here."

"I haven't seen him since the shooting started."

"At least you're not lying."

"I'm not talking, either . . ."

She gave a little surprised snort. "Why do you bother to waste your lives for these Jedi scum?" Her Force grip tightened, not enough to choke him into unconsciousness, but hard enough to let him know she could rip out his trachea. "They don't care what happens to you. They don't care about anything except themselves and their nice, comfortable, Coruscant lives." She loosened her grip a fraction. "You're less than an animal to them. A piece of equipment. So tell me where Skywalker and the Hutt are. I've got no personal grievance with you or your men."

There was only one answer he was obliged to give as a prisoner of war. "Rex, Captain, Five-oh-first Legion, number CC-seven-five-six-seven."

Ventress tightened her grip a notch. "They don't deserve your loyalty, soldier. When are you going to realize that?"

"Rex, Captain." He was trained to resist interrogation. He focused on that, shutting out her threats and cajoling exactly as he'd been taught. "Five-oh-first Legion, number CC-seven-five-six-seven."

"When you've served your purpose, they'll leave you to rot

and die like they left my Master. And he was one of their own, a Jedi. How much do you think Skywalker cares about a chattel like *you*? When you're too broken to use, he can get another one just like you right away."

"Rex, Captain, Five-oh-first Legion, number CC-seven-five-six-seven."

He tried to look past Ventress and fix on a point in the wall behind her, to escape mentally to another place. He focused on getting out alive. He focused on getting his remaining men out alive. He focused on everything except the words coming out of her mouth, because those were her real weapons, a far greater danger than her lightsabers or violent Force powers. When he accidentally caught her eyes, they were disturbingly pale, blue, *obsessed.*

She loathed the Republic, and Jedi in particular. It was written all over her face. She meant every word. She *hurt* deep down. They'd made a devoted enemy of her somehow. She wasn't an opportunistic criminal, she was—

No, stop. That's all part of her game.

"They'll leave you when it suits them, clone." Her voice was now softer, conspiratorial. "We're all the same to them, you see. Even those of us with Force powers. We're all expendable when it suits them. Help me crush them now, before they end up getting you all killed."

Rex jerked his eyes from hers. Part of him was playing his own game to buy some time, but part of him was disturbed by the way her words somehow struck an unwelcome chord.

Jedi can do this. Seen it done. Mind influence. Only works on the weak-minded, they say. Well, I ain't, and I'm ready for you, sister . . .

"Rex, Captain, Five-oh-first Legion, number CC-seven-five-six-seven."

Ventress leaned in. Her nose was a hand's breadth from his. His throat felt bruised and raw, but on the inside rather than the outside. "You will contact Skywalker now. You will tell him you've held the droids. You will ask for his position."

Rex could do that slight defocus and clear his mind. It was just a basic concentration technique for getting him through a tough time, but it convinced Ventress well enough that he was a naive, trusting, *suggestible* pawn.

And, of course, she didn't know how he normally spoke to his general.

She slackened her grip on him, and he tapped the comlink control on his forearm plate, still apparently in that calm, unresisting state.

"Anakin, come in," he said, putting on his best I'm-not-Rex-at-all voice. "We've held the droids, sir. What is your location?"

THIRTEEN

Republic reinforcements are going to be in Teth orbit shortly, ma'am.
We must make our move.

BATTLE DROID COMMANDER, to Asajj Ventress,
on detecting a Republic cruiser dropping out of hyperspace

ABANDONED THRONE ROOM

ANAKIN TIGHTENED THE STRAPS ON AHSOKA'S BACKPACK. ROTTA
squealed in protest, fixing Anakin with those unsettling yellow
eyes that he preferred to avoid.

"Yes, I know it's tight, but you're going to slip out if we have
to do any jumping around, aren't you?" Anakin said. "You're a
slippery customer. And you'll be even more slimy and slippery
when you grow up."

"He doesn't understand," Ahsoka said. "All he knows is that
you're being mean to him."

"Yeah." Compassion in a Jedi was essential, but Ahsoka could
take it too far. "Now let's get moving. Those droids will be all over
us before we know it."

R2-D2 headed for the exit. Ahsoka trotted after him, Anakin defending the rear.

"Don't you remember what it was like to be a kid?"

If only you knew, Snips. "A pain in the neck, you mean?"

"No, being treated as if you're inconvenient, deaf, and stupid by adults who ought to know better."

Ouch. That was a real smack around the head, and Anakin couldn't actually argue with it. It pretty well described his relationship with the Jedi Council. He didn't have a smart answer to fire back, and found himself interrupted by wondering how long it was going to be before this numbness wore off and reality slammed him against the wall, screaming: *Why didn't you save Rex? Why can't you save anyone who matters? What's the point of being the Chosen One if you can't save people you care about?*

He was in the doorway, checking down the passage behind them, when his comlink crackled.

"Anakin, come in."

Ahsoka stopped dead. "Who's that?"

"Anakin, come in."

Anakin knew the voice, but not the strangely flat, mild tone. It was all he could do not to respond. Rex: *Rex is still alive, thank the Force.* Anakin wanted to pour out his relief and ask how the rest of the men had fared, and just tell his captain that he was glad he was okay. But something was wrong.

Rex would never call him *Anakin.*

"We've held the droids, sir."

No, you haven't. I know it. I feel it. I heard it.

"What is your location?"

Ahsoka walked back to Anakin. He hadn't pressed the transmit key, but he put his finger to his lips. *Not a word.* He strained to hear clues in the background. Rex was clearly not alone, and he was under duress. He was warning them. Anakin wanted badly to tell him he'd understood, and to hang on because he'd rescue him,

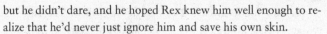

but he didn't dare, and he hoped Rex knew him well enough to re-alize that he'd never just ignore him and save his own skin.

Anakin closed the link.

"Skyguy, what's going on? That was *Rex*. He said—"

"I know what he said." Anakin turned her by her shoulder and pushed her gently on her way. "He was warning me that we've got trouble."

"Was that some code? Look, he's *alive*, and—"

"Rex would never call me Anakin, he never talks like a dumb droid, and he knows perfectly well that I can tell from disturbances in the Force that our guys were *slaughtered* up there." Anakin didn't have time for this. "He's being held, and I bet I know who's trying to use him as bait."

"*Who?*"

It had to be one of Dooku's minions, of course. And it wasn't always possible to identify other Force-users simply from the impression they left in the Force, only that they were around, but some—some just *announced* who they were so clearly that they might as well have stood there in the flesh.

Asajj Ventress.

Anakin knew that raging pain, that absolutely obsessive ha-tred, a focus so harsh and clean in its dark way that it was like looking into the heart of a diamond.

"Dooku's assassin," he said. "Ventress. I bet she thought she could mind-influence Rex to trap us. Fat chance. You have to have a weak-minded subject, or do it very subtly. Maybe she's getting sloppy in her desperation."

"What do you think she wants?"

Anakin was certain where this was heading now. "She's here to kill the Hutt and blame it on us."

"And kill *us*, too . . ."

Yes, that was a given. "We're here solely to get that Huttlet home. Everything else, Snips, will just be detail in the final report."

As they followed R2-D2's unerring path down the twisting passages that snaked close to the foundations of monastery, Anakin was amending his plan to take account of the changing situation. Plans were just a hope, something to start from and try to follow until the enemy came along, poured reality on it, and threw the whole thing in the trash.

Call in a larty.

Transfer the Hutt.

Send the larty back to the ship and tell them to stand by with medics.

Go back for Rex. Call for evac.

Extract Rex and other survivors.

Once Rotta was safely on board that LAAT/i gunship, the primary mission would be out of his hands, and he would then have the time to concentrate on his troops.

Should I send Ahsoka back with the Hutt? She'd be safer. Come to that, should I stay with the Hutt at all times, and leave Rex?

No, that wasn't an option. And even if Anakin boarded the LAAT/i with the Hutt, the gunship was as prey to getting shot down as it would be if he hadn't been there. It was down to luck and good piloting in the end.

Wow, these tunnels stink worse than that Huttlet. They must have broken sewage pipes down here.

R2-D2 whistled in his told-you-so way. There was a door at the end of the passage, exactly as on the holoplans. It opened—a little stiffly, but it opened—and an inrush of hot, damp air hit Anakin in the face like a wet washcloth. They were standing on a platform jutting out over a sheer drop. The trees beneath were still hazy with mist. Ahsoka inhaled deeply, and even the sickly Rotta whined with apparent relief at relatively fresh air. As Anakin assessed the approach to the platform, he saw huge insects soaring on thermals, glittering like gems, and they had to have wingspan of three meters or more to be visible from here. He'd warn the gunship about those. They'd make a mess of a drive intake: FOD, they called it, foreign object damage.

Anakin raised his comlink to his mouth. "Skywalker to 501st air support, anyone receiving? I say again, Skywalker here, we require evac and a medic—"

"Skywalker, this is larty three-niner receiving, please give your position."

"Transmitting coordinates now."

"Copy that, sir. On my way. Estimate six standard minutes. Injury?"

"Negative, but the hostage is sick and will require treatment. Better get someone looking through the species pharma database. And look out for FOD—three-meter flying insects."

"Already fried a few of them in the drives, sir—they're attracted by the noise and seem to think we're a prospective mate. We've lowered the intake filters to stop them fouling the propulsion units completely."

"Romance really is dead, then. Standing by, three-niner."

Anakin didn't know where the gunship had been standing off, or even if it was the last one left. He wondered what it was like for those pilots to have to listen to the comm chatter, and know they had to wait rather than fly in and extract comrades in trouble.

All for a Hutt.

And they never said a word about how they felt.

"Give me the backpack," he said. "Have a rest while you can. Stay close to the wall—when the larty lands, it kicks up a lot of grit. And we don't know who else is airborne."

Rotta seemed to be twice the weight he was when Anakin had first picked him up. He was still looking rough, even by Hutt standards. Once Anakin slung the pack on his back, though, he didn't have to look at the thing.

And he turned into the wind to take the smell of Hutt away. The stench still took him back to a time and a place he preferred to forget, when he and his mother were the property of a Hutt called

Gardulla. They were used to settle a gambling debt, like a table or any other object that didn't matter or have an opinion.

You're not worth Rex's life, slugs. None of you.

Ahsoka, with her hunter's hearing, jerked her head up even before Anakin detected anything. As he concentrated, he heard the distinctive sound of a LAAT/i's drives. He knew now why it had such a galvanizing effect on clone troopers waiting for extraction. Just hearing it, knowing that solid help was close at hand, made Anakin's spirits soar. The gunship appeared suddenly from beneath the platform level and swung its tail one-eighty degrees to set down with its port side hatch open. Its downdraft kicked grit into Anakin's face even this far back. He didn't care. It was the finest sight he'd seen in forever, even covered in bug-spatter and fragments of giant insect wings. Ahsoka shielded her face with one hand.

"Sir!" The winchman leaned out, one hand extended, the other hanging on to his safety line. "Let's get going. We've got Sep craft all over the place."

"Just take the Hutt." Anakin started to slide the pack off his back, feeling stupid for not doing that first so that he had the backpack ready to hand over as soon as the hatch opened. "We're going back for Captain Rex and the others."

The winchman didn't say a word and Anakin couldn't see his expression behind the visor.

Run. That was all he had to do, run the few meters across the landing platform, hand over the Hutt, and run back while the LAAT/i got out as fast as it could.

He saw the winchman whip around to look back into the cabin; he heard the sensors sounding a cockpit alarm.

He was ten strides out from the wall when the shadow fell across the platform, dark and fast, with the whining note of a diving fighter.

The LAAT/i exploded in a ball of flame.

Metal and duraplast fragments flew out from the blast. Anakin was knocked flat and the last he saw of the gunship was a burning, twisted frame teetering on the edge of the platform before plunging into the jungle below. *Seconds*. Just seconds separated elation from total despair. Black smoke rose in a column high into the air.

"Master!" Ahsoka ran to him. The pack on his back made him struggle to right himself. "Master—"

"The Hutt's okay," he heard himself saying. "Get back. Get under cover."

As he got to his feet, the shadow fell again. It wasn't smoke. It was a vulture droid. It landed right in front of them, barring their path back to the safety of the door, and both of them drew their lightsabers. For a moment Anakin thought it had come to take the Hutt and so wouldn't open fire and risk killing its quarry, but he was wrong, *totally* wrong.

The thing rotated its wings to become sharp-edged legs, then opened up with laserfire. Anakin darted from side to side, batting away bolts, trying to keep facing the vulture so that Rotta was protected by his body. Ahsoka tried to draw it off. R2-D2 beeped loudly and rumbled forward as if he was going to join in.

"Artoo!" Anakin snapped. The Hutt was slowing him down, but he couldn't stop now and stow it somewhere safe while the vulture waited politely for the match to resume. He tried to calculate if R2-D2 could get close enough to grab Rotta from the backpack and get him to safety. *No, I tightened the kriffing straps too much, didn't I?* The astromech droid started to roll forward at his master's summons. "No, Artoo, no, get inside! I need you in one piece!"

Ahsoka lunged again and made the vulture spin ninety degrees to face her, but then it seemed to learn her ploy and ignored her, swiveling one cannon to blast at her while its main fire was directed at Anakin. Didn't these piles of junk *ever* run out of power like the intel said?

But he'd never call them dumb again.

It had worked out how to rush him and get inside the arc of his lightsaber. The vulture darted forward, stabbing at him with the sharp points of wingtips that had become its feet and legs. It forced Anakin back. And he had no choice but to *face* it. He didn't dare turn his back to it even for a heartbeat. That limited his ability to spin, to somersault, to do things that a Jedi could and a heap of metal couldn't.

So this is how regular beings have to fight.

Fine.

Rotta squealed and grizzled. Anakin was sure he'd thrown up during the savage shaking he was getting, and he couldn't face the idea of winning the fight but ending up killing the hostage. But Rotta was a Hutt, and they were far tougher than any puny human.

"Come on, you useless piece of wreckage . . ." Anakin edged backward, knowing exactly where the edge of the platform was without looking, and trying to factor in the shifted center of gravity caused by a backpack full of Hutt. "Show me what you've got."

It did. It ran at him. But as he backed away, it came to a dead halt and started firing, leaving him wrong-footed for a crucial moment. A living opponent could be sensed and gauged in the Force, but a droid . . . a really smart one could give a Jedi a serious run for their creds. Anakin fended off the laserfire, spraying ricochets of energy. Then it turned its fourth cannon—the one that had been keeping Ahsoka busy—and started a random firing pattern with all four cannons that Anakin struggled to block.

He was close to beaten. He felt it. He was losing. He reached for one strap, ready to start loosening the pack to throw Rotta to the safety of Ahsoka's arms—she'd catch him easily with that predator's flawless coordination—and throw himself on the vulture.

Ahsoka was suddenly close in, *way* too close. "Hey, trashcan!" she yelled, and swung her lightsaber.

She wasn't close enough to hit the vulture, but she got its attention, probably because she triggered its complex threat analysis

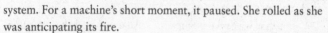

system. For a machine's short moment, it paused. She rolled as she was anticipating its fire.

She rolled too far.

Had she skidded on a pool of Hutt vomit? Her lightsaber went spinning from her hand and she went clear off the edge of the platform.

No, no, no—

"Ahsoka!"

The vulture abandoned its attack on Anakin and clattered toward the point where she'd fallen. Anakin thought it was checking where she'd fallen until he saw it raise one leg in a stabbing motion. By then, he was right behind it, almost on its back. *He heard her voice.* He saw her fingertips—just her fingertips—clinging to the edge of the permacrete, completely white with the pressure of the grip.

"I'm okay," she gasped. "I'm okay."

No, she *wasn't*: she was about to lose her arms to a droid and plummet to her death, Jedi or not. Anakin went for the vulture, lightsaber whirling. It swiveled and poured laser fire back at him. In the seconds he distracted it, Ahsoka swung back onto the platform purely on her fingertips, throwing one leg high like a gymnast and pivoting at the hip to hurl her body forward. Then she reached out to bring her lightsaber spinning back into her hand with a Force pull.

Anakin was so close to the vulture now that the sheer light output of its laserfire was almost blinding him as he deflected it with his blade. Then it lurched to one side. He thought it was a feint and leaped onto it in that split second, driving his lightsaber deep between its visual sensors, but then he realized it had lost half a leg, and that Ahsoka had sliced through it.

He let himself fall back and landed heavily on his feet just as the vulture lost stability and tipped over the edge of platform.

It didn't have fingers. It couldn't grab and save itself. And its leg was its wing, and so it couldn't even fly again.

It fell, and fell, and *fell*.

"Oh, that was *smart*, Snips . . ." Anakin heard the sob of exhausted relief in his own voice. He straightened up. *Hey, I've still got a Hutt on board. I almost forgot.* "I thought I'd lost you for good."

Ahsoka's head-tails had taken on a slightly more vivid striping. Maybe it was the Togruta equivalent of being red in the face. She smiled, not her usual polite smile, but a feral baring of her sharp teeth that was pure triumph at catching her prey.

"I really didn't want to find out if it was true that we Togrutas always land on our feet," she said.

"Good distraction, though."

"Maybe I meant to do it," she said, mock-gravely, "and maybe I didn't."

It took all sorts to be a Jedi. Her way worked fine as far as he was concerned.

But the relief was short-lived. Rotta wailed pitifully in Anakin's ear. Rex and his men—he *had* to think some had survived—were still held by that fanatic Ventress. He tried not to dwell on what she might be doing to them. Anakin still had a few fights ahead.

He shrugged his shoulders to ease the ache from the backpack and opened his comlink.

"Master Kenobi, can you hear me? Master—are you in range yet?"

The comlink rattled with static. Anakin waited.

JABBA'S PALACE, TATOOINE

TC-70 almost pushed Dooku along the passage to the throne room.

It was just a brief touch in the small of the back, the subtlest of shepherding movements, but from a protocol droid it was the equivalent of grabbing a guest by the scruff of his neck and drag-

ging him. It warned Dooku of the rage to come when he stood before Jabba.

TC-70 showed all the signs of a droid that had been threatened
and *made afraid*.

That intrigued Dooku. It almost distracted him from the crisis
that faced him now, but as the knowledge might come in useful
one day, he made a mental note to return to it and gently pry the
story out of TC-70. Motivating the reluctant was often Dooku's
task. He collected the finer points of the skill.

The doors parted and Dooku walked into the throne chamber,
now littered with Jabba's entourage. They sat or stood in silence,
looking not at one another but at the floor. It was silent in the way
that a kitchen with a sealed steam-pot about to explode on the
range was *silent*. Rage simmered on the dais.

Jabba obviously needed his displeasure to be seen. Dooku had
now gained the measure of Hutt power displays.

TC-70 began his preamble. "Glorious Jabba is losing patience,
and he demands—"

"Thank you, Tee-see," Dooku said. "I'll address Lord Jabba
directly, to better show my respect for his culture and language."

"*My son*," Jabba spat. "My son is *still missing*. I demand to
know what your useless minions are doing about it. You should
execute them and buy better ones. I wouldn't tolerate such incom-
petence in *my* servants."

Ventress wouldn't have liked that comparison. Dooku lowered
his head slightly. Deferential postures worked wonders.

"My droid army is about to capture Skywalker and rescue
your heir. This would have been over by now, but I gave strict in-
structions that nothing was to be done that would cause the slightest harm or distress to little Lord Rotta. So the operation is being
handled *delicately*. This is not some Republic hostage extraction
where the security forces go in with all blasters blazing and end up
killing hostages."

That wouldn't be lost on Jabba. The Republic had seen a run

of botched hostage rescues lately. And Dooku wasn't lying; a dead Rotta would do him no good now. It had to be handled with care.

Jabba hadn't calmed down, but he hadn't blown his top either. Dooku could still retrieve the situation. "My son looked *ill* when Skywalker seized him. Is he even still alive? Because if he isn't, then I will—"

"He's alive, Lord Jabba. I have reliable and current intelligence. Skywalker tried to escape from Teth with your son, but he was stopped, with no harm to Rotta. He's now trapped, he has no army, and he has nowhere to run."

Jabba leaned forward a little. "Count Dooku," he said, "you're no fool, and neither am I. Do you think that once I knew my son was on Teth, that I wouldn't monitor the sector? I have my sources. And my sources say that Republic forces are on their way to support Skywalker."

Yes, Dooku should have guessed that much. He affected a tired patience, as if Jabba was stating the obvious.

"Not that I'm complacent, Lord Jabba, but Skywalker and a company of his elite infantry failed to deal with my army. Their fleet, if they have a fleet, will be easily neutralized. I have more firepower in orbit around Teth than the Republic can muster."

"I asked myself a question," said Jabba, changing tack in a worrying way. "I asked why Skywalker would kidnap my child."

"Jedi have a bad habit of seizing children, my lord. They're all taken from their families."

Jabba swept over the point, oblivious. "Why would Skywalker not realize that taking Rotta would only get my cooperation until I had my son back, and that I'd do everything I could to destroy the Jedi, the Republic, and anyone who so much as smiled in their direction? Did he think he could hold him hostage *forever*?"

Dooku was fascinated by the way beings seldom asked the most obvious questions right away. Jabba was now getting too curious. Dooku had to steer him back to outrage. "You saw the recording, Lord Jabba . . . he loathes Hutts, and I suspect pure hatred of your people was as much a factor as underestimating your resolve."

"Yes, and he'll die for his disrespect. But he—or Palpatine—must be insane to think I'm some cringing human who'd cave in to their blackmail without striking back as soon as I could." He reared up slowly, and Dooku had to admit that it *was* physically intimidating. "I am a kajidic *lorda*. I have a *duty* to my people to show that nobody gets away with an outrage like this. If we let such outrages go unpunished, what would happen to our *civilization*?"

He repeated the word *outrage*—*chomma*—and Dooku suddenly realized that the word had a different shade of meaning from what he'd thought. In all his dealings with Hutts, he'd thought a *chomma* was just a terrible insult to someone. But it was a threat to the social order, and so to the smooth running of Hutt society.

Chomma was a uniquely Huttese crime.

And human crimes had no meaning for Hutts. It was why all Hutts seemed to be criminals to the Republic. There was no common ground on morality. It was yet another area where the Republic thought its rules were the natural and obvious way for the entire galaxy and a million sentient species to behave.

I can use this as another lever.

"They don't understand Hutts," Dooku said. He wasn't so sure that *he* knew as much as he thought he did, either. "The Republic and the Jedi are very much cozy *human* organizations, and they think every being reacts as they do. And they're both completely arrogant. It comes from having held easy power for too many centuries."

"I must have Skywalker's head," Jabba said. His tone was suddenly neutral, as if this were some administrative detail rather than a raging threat. "Rotta will use his skull for a toy. Lessons will be learned."

"If my army leaves enough recognizable parts of him, you shall have it." Dooku would have to comm Ventress and see that it happened. "Now, Lord Jabba, while we wait, may we begin negotiating the treaty between the Hutt kajidics and the Confederacy of Independent Systems?"

Jabba took a long draw on his pipe. "I will negotiate *nothing* until my son is back, alive and unharmed. Humans might not understand Hutts, but Hutts understand humans *very* well . . ."

Dooku had set himself up for that, but it was no bad thing. Jabba had to be *seen* to win—and Dooku had to look at that not as some egocentric personal failing, but as part of what kept Hutt society running: complete confidence in a leader who would never be pushed around by *ootmian*, outlanders. It wasn't just about loss of face, but about letting Hutts know that the boss of bosses was still in charge, and all was right with their world.

Accepting that would help Dooku deal better with Ziro when the difficult time came.

"As you wish, Lord Jabba," Dooku said, and backed out of the chamber with his head still bowed.

He returned to his ship and commed Ventress. She was slow to respond. When her hologram image appeared in front of him, she was standing with her boots planted firmly at shoulder width, a lightsaber in each fist, and a murderous expression. He guessed that she had stopped in midbattle and rounded on a nearby droid to pick up the comm channel.

"I'd ask how things are progressing," Dooku said. "But I think I can work that out."

"Master, Skywalker is trapped on a landing platform. We're cutting through the door, and then I shall cut through his *neck*."

"See that you do. Jabba actually *wants* his head. Literally."

"And you still want the Huttlet alive."

"If there was ever any doubt in your mind, Asajj, I'd be disappointed. Do not fail me. Skywalker is already discredited, so there'll be no help for the Republic from the Hutts, but to get Jabba to the negotiating table, the baby has to be returned intact. Do I make myself clear? Take no risks with him."

"Yes, my lord."

"Call me when you succeed."

Dooku closed the link. He wondered if Skywalker would work out that killing the child would cut the Republic's losses, because then neither side would get Jabba's blessing to use his routes. If he *had*—would he do it?

Dooku knew Jedi who would turn a blind eye to carelessness even if they wouldn't do the deed themselves. Interestingly, they weren't the disillusioned Jedi who'd now joined him.

He thought of contacting Darth Sidious and bringing him up to date with events, but then decided it would be better not to trouble his Master with detail until he could tell him the task was complete.

It wasn't just Hutt lords who had their image to keep intact.

COURTYARD ENTRANCE, TETH MONASTERY

"Sir?"

"I hear you, Coric."

"Just checking you're still with us."

Rex hadn't moved since the mad-eyed Sep female had finished with him. His chance would come, and he'd know when he saw it. He lay where Ventress had finally thrown him, slumped against a wall, working his way through all the comm channels he could access from his helmet systems, then starting again, in case he happened to find one that wasn't being blocked at that moment. As soon as the GAR comm center neutralized a Sep jamming signal, the Seps would rush to change it again. If he kept trying, he might get lucky and find a window.

"I'm fine, Sergeant," he said. He suspected she'd broken his ribs. When he breathed, it hurt enough to make him bite his lip. "I've never hit a woman, but she'll be the first when I get a chance."

"I've never been called a *lickspittle Jedi lackey* before."

"I rather liked *naive cannon fodder* myself."

Droids didn't seem to realize that clone helmets were sound-proofed when sealed, so he could chat freely with his men. Maybe droids judged by their own limitations. He'd never worked out why droids needed to talk aloud instead of just silently transmitting machine code to one another, but that probably said more about the beings who built them than the droids. Funny: one side in this war was making droids more like men, and the other was making men more like droids.

"I thought she'd like you, what with the same haircut and everything," Coric said.

"Maybe I should have taken my helmet off and shown her."

"So she's a Jedi of some kind?"

"Sith, or a dark adept. Red lightsaber is a giveaway, apparently."

"What's the difference?"

"Membership subscription, maybe. It all hurts the same, though." Rex was more interested in pragmatic issues. "I'm still not getting any clear comm channels."

"Me neither, sir."

Rex began at the top of the frequency list again, lingering on each for a moment and straining to hear some stable audio before moving on. As he listened, he watched droids clearing a path through the debris from the door. Four others stood nearby in the courtyard itself, making a token effort to guard all that was left of Torrent Company. The scale of Rex's losses was threatening to gnaw away at him if he didn't channel that anger into leveling the score.

The comm frequencies were still white noise and bursts of static.

What use are we going to be to them?

He had a pretty good idea what Ventress was going to do to them, if only to vent her spleen because she couldn't get her hands on a Jedi. Boy, whatever they'd done to her buddy had *really* bent her out of shape. He'd already made up his mind that he'd rather die fighting than wait for her to kill him slowly, and he wasn't going to let her get his men, either. He'd shoot them himself before he'd let that happen.

The tinnies had taken their weapons, but *that* wasn't going to stop him. The debris was still littered with DC-15s and sidearms.

They hadn't found his vibroblade, either . . .

Rex bided his time.

He'd been careful not to show any external signs of talking— moving his head, his hands, any of the little unconscious movements people make when they are speaking. He didn't want to alert the droids. He was sure he'd covered every security angle.

And then his wrist comlink bleeped, and the droid nearest to him looked around.

Stang. He hadn't diverted the kriffing thing to his helmet.

"Rex, are you receiving? This is Skywalker."

Yes, the droids had heard. Another turned.

Rex stayed on his internal comm circuit, completely still. "Here we go, gentlemen. Stand by."

The droids weren't exactly fast thinkers. Two were debating their course of action. One clunked over to him and tilted its head down to look at the source of the sound. It peered at his wrist. The comlink crackled with static again.

"Rex, if you can't respond—tap the receiver or something."

The droid leaned a little farther. Rex raised his arm very slowly, the back of his wrist turned outward, and steeled himself to ignore the pain he was going to be in very soon. He heard the swallowing and general sounds of his men getting ready to make a move.

"Want to see how it works, clanker?"

Rex stabbed his fingers over the edge of the droid's breastplate and held it as he drove his other fist under its jawline to send its head cracking upward vertically with its neck, ripping its control cables from their connectors. He didn't even need to give an order.

Each of his five troopers sprang to their feet. Coric snatched the rifle from the crippled droid as it tottered backward; Nax grabbed a lump of masonry and battered another droid until its head caved in. Rex ejected the vibroblade from his forearm plate and jumped onto a droid, tipping it off balance and gouging out its photoreceptors. As it flailed blindly, he severed all the control cables to its head.

The six clones sprinted across the courtyard and took cover behind a fallen AT-TE. There were enough charged rifles—Deeces and Sep weapons—within easy reach to keep the tinnies at bay for a while. Rex took a single-use painkiller sharp from his belt medpac and injected it into the back of his hand before taking aim. The firefight began.

Tinnies seemed to be okay with standing up and firing. It was all the other business of soldiering—stabbing, strangling, gouging, all the up-close and personal stuff—that left them baffled. They weren't much good on anything other than level terrain, either.

"I *enjoyed* that," Nax said, almost to himself. "Really got some tension out of my system."

"Well, relax with a few of *those*," Rex said. Some SBDs had shown up. No heads to batter in or rip off: the spider droids would be along soon, too. Rex indicated the edge of the plateau. They could take their chances in the jungle. "Everyone got their rappel lines primed, just in case?"

"Yes, sir."

It was another option. Meanwhile, they had weapons and personal scores to settle.

"Rex, respond!"

Skywalker hadn't given up on him, then. "Receiving, General. We're pinned down in the courtyard—me and five men . . ."

"Need assistance?"

". . . and a Hutt-load of tinnies." He squeezed off a few more plasma rounds. The noise of blasterfire was magnified by the courtyard walls. "Make that a Hutt-load minus one."

"I'll take that as a yes, Captain. On our way."

The carcass of the dead AT-TE shook as SBD fire punched into its flank. Nax lay flat and peered into a gaping hole, then reached in. When he pulled out, he had a pair of bolt cutters in one hand.

"Toolbox," he said, making the jaws of the cutter snap open and shut. "Here tinny, here *nice* tinny . . ."

Rex sighted up again, and decided that was another thing that made a human clone a far better soldier than any droid.

They weren't just inventive.

They had brothers they needed to avenge.

"Save a live one for me," he said.

FOURTEEN

*War is a vile thing, and it brings out the worst in beings.
But it also brings out their best—courage, sacrifice, resourcefulness,
tenacity, comradeship, genius, even humor. Would that we could
achieve that enlightened state without shedding blood first.*
MENTOR PEET SIEBEN, Jal Shey philosopher

LANDING PLATFORM

ANAKIN STRODE BACK TOWARD THE DOOR, WORKING OUT HOW best to extract Rex and the troopers from the courtyard.

He'd never get a gunship down in one piece even if any were left. Depending on where the Sep forces were, he might be able to divert the droids, trap them, or just keep them busy until Kenobi arrived.

"Master!" Ahsoka ran after him. "Master, Stinky's still in a bad way. Our mission's to get him back alive, remember?"

"So what are you saying?" Anakin knew anyway. He walked on. "That we leave our men to die?"

"Doesn't the mission come first?"

"Answer the question, Snips. This is a man you know. Whatever happened to covering one another's backs?"

"Whatever happened, Master, to *command means being prepared to get troops killed*?"

"Okay, I said that, but *prepared* doesn't mean leaving them before you've exhausted all the options."

"If saving Rex means Stinky dies, doesn't that make the death of every trooper we lost a senseless waste?"

"What if the slug dies anyway?"

Anakin would have swapped every Hutt in the galaxy for one trooper. Ahsoka seemed to be rethinking the position.

"Rex won't thank you for it."

"Okay, Snips, open your comlink and tell him."

"What, me?"

"Yes. Comm Rex and say you've made me change my mind, because you've convinced me that neither he nor his men are important enough to save."

"Master . . ."

"If you want to make a tough decision that costs men their lives, you better be prepared to look them in the eye and tell them why."

He bet she wouldn't. He was worried that she would, though, just to prove she was grown-up enough to be his Padawan. And then she'd quote it back at him.

"Besides," he said, "Rex can help us find a ship. Get us out."

"Master, that's not very convincing."

"Okay, I'm not leaving him while we still have a chance of getting the Hutt out *and* the troopers. He wouldn't abandon me. He wouldn't abandon *you*. That's what holds an army together. Break that unspoken promise, and we might as well surrender now."

They were fifty meters into the corridor when Artoo whistled a warning. Anakin heard a sound he dreaded: the steady hum of destroyer droids. Movement caught his eye, and he saw two of the things rolling down the corridor toward them, readying cannons. They opened fire and the two Jedi were forced back.

"Only one way to go," Anakin said, blocking laser bolts as he backed away. "Artoo, get ready to bar the door."

They retreated to the landing platform. Just before R2-D2 rolled in to shut the door and lock it, Anakin saw a humanoid form striding in the wake of the Destroyers, a shaven-headed woman. R2-D2 thrust his interface arm into the lock. The door sealed with a hiss.

"It's Ventress," Anakin said. "At least they're sending the management to kill us now."

The door vibrated for a moment. Two hot spots appeared in the metal plate: Anakin took a guess that Ventress had thrust her lightsabers into the door. He watched, and then realized she was cutting with both of them simultaneously, sawing a circle like a workshop laser cutter.

"Time to retreat," he said. "There's a lot of jungle to hide in."

Ahsoka looked over the edge. "There's a lot of *things* in the jungle, too, carnivorous and poisonous things . . . oh, and spider droids."

Anakin darted to the platform perimeter and looked down. The droids were clambering up the shroud of vines that draped the whole plateau. Several paused to fire into the platform. Anakin felt the shock wave under his boots.

"Well . . . the choice is to have the platform shot out from under us, or stand here and wait for Ventress, or go over the side and meet the spider droids."

Ahsoka's gaze was darting everywhere, as if she was sizing up distances and options. "Can I answer *none of the above*, Master?"

Rotta was wailing intermittently now. Anakin recalled the hasty battlefield first-aid training he'd been given before he was deployed with troops—a noisy casualty was less concern than a quiet one. As long as they were screaming, they were conscious. It was the silent, unconscious ones who were in the most trouble.

"Carry on complaining, my smelly friend," Anakin said over

his shoulder. Rotta switched to a new sound, a coo of surprise repeated over and over. "Well, a change is good as a rest."

"What's he pointing at?" Ahsoka asked.

"He's pointing?"

"Over there."

Anakin turned to look, and Rotta wailed. Ahsoka scanned the trees, eyes narrowed.

"How did we miss it? I never spotted that before." she said. "Over there. Another plateau. And look what's on it!"

"*What?* I can't see."

Anakin reached into his satchel for the electrobinoculars. The flat-topped peaks dotted like stepping stones through the jungle were ancient volcanic plugs, so there might have been a chain of them across the landscape on a fault line. With Ventress hacking her way onto the platform and spider droids firing from below, his mind wasn't on a geology lesson. All he could see was the thick haze above the trees and a group of those huge insect-like creatures the size of speeders. They looked like a ketes, or even a Kashyyyk can-cell; long bodies, two pairs of rapidly beating gauzy wings, and a bulbous head. They circled the plateaus, diving and snatching at invisible prey.

"Look at the thing that's glittering," Ahsoka said.

"It's—hey, you're right." It was a vessel on a landing platform much like the structure they were standing on now. It made sense; how else could anyone get around this terrain? "It's a ship. But we're here, and it's there. I make that . . . two klicks away. Three."

"Yeah . . . I know. It was just a thought."

R2-D2 warbled frantically. Anakin turned to the door. Ventress's twin lightsabers were making better progress than he'd expected. In a matter of minutes, she'd break through. And they'd be trapped.

The platform shook from another cannon barrage. It couldn't withstand much more of that.

And we'll be plunging to the forest floor, too . . .

Then the word *Kashyyyk* hit him squarely between the eyes. It was one of those moments that Master Qui-Gon used to call *intuitive association*. Anakin groped for the link, and then he saw the answer his subconscious had laid out for him. Kashyyyk also had dense forest, impassable terrain, huge flying insects, and . . . those insects *could be ridden*. Can-cells—Aleenan scouts and sometimes even humans rode them. They were also drawn to the sound of fliers' drives, just as the giant insects here had buzzed the LAAT/i.

"Artoo!" he called. "Can you generate an audio signal that matches a larty's drive profile?"

R2-D2 beeped to say that he could mimic the full range of Republic vessels, and some Sep ones too if he was asked nicely. He obliged with a demonstration that made Anakin's hair bristle, right down to the LAAT/i's close-to-infrasonic note that droned steadily under the rapid puttering sound.

"Master, just tell me . . ." Ahsoka asked.

"We're calling in one of those insects, and we're going to ride it out of here."

Ahsoka just nodded gravely. Maybe she was too tired to argue now. "Okay. I've done a lot of crazier things today. Why the sound effects?"

"The insects think it's an invitation to go on a date. They were all over the larty, remember?"

Ahsoka didn't respond. Suddenly it wasn't something they could joke about, not with a dead LAAT/i crew somewhere beneath them.

"Can you steer?" she asked. The platform took another direct hit from underneath. It was starting to tilt; a pebble rolled a few meters toward the edge. "Provided we can hang on, of course."

"Force-pull here, Force-push there. As long as we take off. That's my priority."

R2-D2 rolled gingerly to the edge of the platform, transmitting gunship love songs to gullible insects. This would be one incident Anakin *could* tell Padmé about. She'd laugh. He wasn't sure he'd ever tell her how bloody the battle had been, though. There were some things he simply couldn't express. He stood as close to the edge as he dared with Rotta on his back, looking for amorous mega-insects on the prowl.

Behind him, Asajj Ventress was close to breaking through the door.

He listened for the machine-like hum of fast-beating, three-meter wings.

LANDING PLATFORM DOOR, MONASTERY SIDE

Ventress had cut a perfect freehand circle into the door, a feat said to be the hallmark of a gifted artist.

As she rotated both lightsabers around a common center, the two separate arcs met, and she gave the thick metal disk a Force push. It crashed onto the landing platform. She lowered her head a little and stepped through the gap, using the excised disk as a step.

There was no sign of Skywalker. The Togruta Padawan and the astromech droid were still there, though. Ventress searched around her in the Force to see if Skywalker was somewhere above, waiting to leap from an upper floor. But there was nothing.

"So, Padawan, he's abandoned you." Ventress took her lightsabers and snapped them together, hilt to hilt, to form a double-ended weapon. Then she sent the astromech tumbling at the feet of her battle droids. She didn't trust it. "It's a Jedi habit."

Ahsoka held her lightsaber two-handed and prowled in a circle around Ventress. Their gazes locked. Ventress felt no pity; nobody raised in the brutal ganglands that were Rattatak could afford that level of emotion. They learned to shut down just to cope. It was excellent training, had she known it at the time.

But Skywalker was too fond of his heroic reputation to let a child like this die in his place. He'd be here.

"Where are you, Skywalker?" Ventress called. "Or would you rather let a novice do your dirty work for you? One of Master Windu's handy career tips, if I recall."

Ahsoka scowled as if she'd been snubbed. "You're fighting *me.*"

"So I am." Ventress let Ahsoka come within striking distance, then twirled her lightsaber from the center like a baton, flicking one end over the other to catch the tip of Ahsoka's blade. "Nothing personal."

Ahsoka charged at her holding her blade high, then dropped to her knees and skidded under Ventress's guard. Or so the child seemed to think, anyway. It was a simple matter for Ventress of leaping backward to avoid the sweep across her legs. Ahsoka was up on her feet again, racing wide to attack again from the rear, making Ventress pirouette to keep her in view. Blades clashed in parry and thrust while Ventress kept one eye out for Skywalker to come crashing to the rescue. But he didn't appear.

Now, forty-five seconds into the duel—and these matters never lasted long, she found—Ventress was impatient, and had seen most of Ahsoka's basic technique; a combination of rapid switches and feints, darting from one side of the battle ground to the other, as if she was trying to exhaust her opponent enough and dart in to deliver the fatal blow. It was very Togrutan.

Ventress countered by making Ahsoka come to her, not by evading or even pursuing her. At one point, Ventress stood still, double blade held to one side with her body exposed, to tempt the child into a fatal error. The Padawan moved in cautiously. As she lunged, Ventress decided Skywalker would not be lured into showing himself, and whipped Ahsoka's lightsaber from her hand with a figure-eight movement before slamming her flat with a Force push and holding her there with an outstretched hand.

"Where's Skywalker?"

Ventress put one boot on her chest. Ahsoka squirmed, trying to push back. "You'll find out the hard way."

"Very well. I can wait." Ventress looked up. "I can start lopping off body parts, Skywalker. Your call."

The landing platform lurched a fraction, opening an ominous crack that ran at right angles from the wall of the monastery. Skywalker's droid beeped plaintively. Well, if the little Jedi prince wouldn't come back for his Padawan, maybe he valued his droid.

"Let's trade," Ventress called. She felt a faint tingle deep behind her eyes; ah, he *was* somewhere in the neighborhood now. She held the tip of her lightsaber a hand's breadth from Ahsoka's throat. "Special two-for-one offer—a Padawan and a droid for one Huttlet. Can't say fairer than that."

Ventress felt a rush of air accompanied by a steady buzz. She'd been here long enough to begin to get used to the oversized insect life, but the creatures still made her wary. She raised her eyes without moving her head, just to note where it was.

It was *then* that it hit her square in the back—something very heavy, very fast, and sharp-edged, a shadow that punched into her like a missile.

She pitched forward, winded, and almost took Ahsoka's head off as she fell. One blade of the lightsaber plunged into the permacrete platform almost up to its hilt. She rolled and was on her feet again in an instant, ready to fight, but in that same moment Ahsoka had also rolled clear.

But that was irrelevant now. Ventress was confronted by a massive hunting fly, a pretty thing with a brilliantly iridescent body and gossamer wings at a safe distance, but, up close, a totally different creature; powerful, fast, predatory, surprisingly noisy, and armed with savage mandibles the size of her hand. The delicate wings with their fine tracery of veins were actually a thick translucent hide stretched on a sturdy bone framework.

And this beast had a rider: Anakin Skywalker.

The Huttlet was strapped to his back.

The hunting fly hovered and darted with the precision of a remote, rising vertically from a dead stop and then hanging in the air, seeming motionless except for a blur of wings that buzzed like a high-speed rotor.

Rifles clicked and whirred in unison as the battle droids took aim.

"Hold fire!" Ventress barked. She flung out her arm in a stop gesture. "Hit him, and you kill the Hutt."

"You catch on quick," Skywalker said, drawing his lightsaber. "I'd like my Padawan back, please."

He clung grimly to the hunting fly one-handed as it made what felt like strafing runs past Ventress, creating its own downdraft. As Skywalker swooped, he tried to reach out to pull Ahsoka on board. It was easier said than done even for a Jedi. The creature's wings made a close approach next to impossible. Ventress spun defensively as the hunting fly zipped up and down the platform like a starfighter out of control, flicking its jointed tail and snapping its mandibles. It was heavy and fast-moving, and if it hit her, it would just run her down as hard as a repulsortruck.

It clearly wasn't enjoying the ride, and neither was Skywalker. He'd hitched a ride on a large, angry predator.

Ventress looked for an opening to unseat him; Ahsoka darted around trying to jump on board. It was going to end in tears for one of them. The hunting fly was getting more aggressive and panicky by the second, shying from the lightsabers and flexing its long body as if it was trying to buck. The platform beneath her boots felt as if it was moving.

It was.

Her horizon tilted violently as the permacrete slab snapped cleanly away from the wall and hung at a forty-five-degree angle for a few final moments, supported only by a few massive brackets, which were pulling free one by one under the sheer weight of the structure. Ventress ducked to avoid an outspread wing that would have snapped her neck on impact. Then she leaped for the door, launching herself into the sudden void.

"Jump!" Skywalker yelled.

He didn't mean her, of course. Ventress landed on the narrow tread of the doorway and clung to the frame. An avalanche of permacrete and durasteel thundered to the jungle floor.

When she looked back, the hunting fly was banking right to begin a vertical climb with Ahsoka sprawled facedown in front of Skywalker, scrambling to get a grip with her legs. The astromech droid trailed them with its rockets on full burn.

"Ma'am." A battle droid's voice wafted from inside the doorway, almost drowned out by the rumbling debris below. "Ma'am—"

"Silence!"

Ventress watched in helpless rage as the Jedi escaped with her prize. For a second, she almost gave the order for the vulture droids to pursue and destroy. The only thing that stopped her was that she hadn't given up yet, and she could still retrieve the Huttlet alive.

She rested her forehead against the wall for a moment, adjusting her plan. Beneath her was a sheer drop of eight hundred meters.

"Electrobinoculars," she ordered, holding out her hand to the droid. She got a focus on the hunting fly, a speck vanishing into the treetop haze followed by the twin points of light from the astromech's jets. "I think I know where they'll try to head next, but their ride might have other ideas. Track them."

"Ma'am, I was trying to tell you that Count Dooku is demanding a report on your mission. Shall I tell him that the Jedi escaped?"

Ventress handed back the electrobinoculars. "No. Because they haven't. They still have to get off this planet. And I'm still going to stop them."

She stalked back down the corridor, checking on her datapad that the vulture droids were monitoring the area. Skywalker had to land somewhere. She opened her comlink.

"Air Control, this is Commander Ventress. I want a vulture tracking Skywalker immediately, and have my fighter ready."

"Ma'am, sensor scans are picking up Republic fighters deploying from a cruiser in low orbit. All vulture squadrons have scrambled to engage them."

"Kenobi," she said.

"Yes ma'am."

"Keep him busy, then. He mustn't be allowed to land troops. Leave Skywalker to me."

"Do you still require the Ginivex to be standing by for you, ma'am?"

"Yes. I may have to intervene personally."

Ventress paused on the stairs. The battle in the courtyard was still raging; and she had to forgo air support in her hunt for Skywalker because the vultures were committed elsewhere. What had happened to the much-vaunted Separatist numerical advantage? So far, an *army* had failed to suppress a company of the 501st Legion—not even battalion strength—and nobody seemed able to detain two Jedi and a baby.

Including me. It's going to be hard to explain that to Dooku.

Droids, she decided, were a liability, but right now they were all she had. She needed to make doubly sure that all the exits were sealed. As long as Skywalker couldn't clear his name with the Hutts, at least there was a negative victory to cling to. She switched to another channel.

"Four-A-Seven," she said, "what's your position? You should have been long gone by now."

"I fear we left too late to slip past the Republic flotilla, ma'am, but I think we have a task to finish here anyway." The spy droid had a talent for being in the right place at the right time. Ventress admired that. He wasn't an average droid. "I've been observing for the last couple of hours. Excellent view of the monastery from here . . . and incoming flights."

Ventress began thinking in terms of putting long-range artillery on the mesa. That could give Kenobi a little surprise if brought into play at the right time. "You have a visual on Kenobi's squadron?"

"I have a visual," 4A-7 said quietly, "on a hunting fly coming in to land, somewhat reluctantly by the looks of things."

Ventress allowed herself a slow smile. "Four-A, I have no idea sometimes what I would do without you."

"Shall I play it by ear, ma'am?" He sounded . . . *satisfied.* Proud, even. "The priority is still the recovery of the Hutt infant, I take it."

"It is."

"Then I shall endeavor to retrieve him."

"I'll join you as soon as I can. You're a very resourceful being, but two Jedi are a challenge to handle."

"I noticed. Perhaps a less combative approach will work this time—they knew you as a Separatist by sight, but I'm just a droid, nothing to put them on their guard." The spy paused. "And I have my battle droid colleagues with me should anything go wrong before you reach me."

Ventress doubted they'd be any help to 4A-7, but he probably knew that. The droid was more of a gentleman and a warrior in his way than most of the organics she'd had to deal with in her life, and a *patriot*—he served the CIS without stinting. An organic agent of his standing would have been awarded honors by now.

And he would never betray the cause, because he couldn't be bought, bribed, threatened, or seduced. She knew exactly what to expect of him, and what drove him. Ventress . . . *trusted* him. She hadn't trusted anyone before or after Narec—dead, buried—except her parents—also dead, also buried—and this droid.

A spy's life was a lonely one, whether flesh or metal. It struck her that 4A-7 was the closest thing she had to a friend, and one day she might tell him that.

"Ventress out," she said.

MONASTERY COURTYARD

For a few minutes, the blasterfire from the droid position paused.

It happened sporadically. Maybe it was the time when they received new orders, new programming, and had to reboot their systems. Rex hadn't worked it out yet, but he took the opportunity to recharge and reload every weapon in the cache they'd assembled, check his comm frequencies for any lapse in the Sep jamming, and whip off his helmet for a precious second or two to cram high-calorie dry rations into his mouth. Without his bucket, as everyone called it, he was blind, deaf, and vulnerable on the battlefield. His helmet meant survival; it was that stark. He wiped his head with the palm of his glove and dropped the helmet back into place again, securing the seals.

Nax glanced at the chrono on his forearm plate. "You think Skywalker stopped to pick up a pot of caf for us?"

"I still can't raise him," Rex said, mouth full. Skywalker couldn't have started out any farther from them than the western boundary of the monastery. A Randorn mollusk on crutches could have covered that in the time since the general said he was on his way. "I just hope it's not connected to the big rumbling noise and the smoke we saw a while ago. But he'll be here. He said he would, so he *will* be."

Coric edged up the barricade and poked a strip-cam over the top. The image appeared in Rex's HUD and he surveyed the view of the droid position. It was just a big courtyard, now almost unrecognizable as a place of contemplation, with a lot of deep craters, dead tanks, and the wreckage of assorted vessels of various sizes. Fires still burned. Rex's squad—he'd stopped kidding himself by calling it a company—was barricaded behind a burned-out AT-TE that they'd gradually reinforced with dead droids and anything else they could drag into position.

It was now just him, Coric, Del, Attie, Zeer, and Nax. The droids knew that.

So the fact that they were still alive after an hour or so troubled Rex greatly. The droids had to have some plan up their sleeves, or wherever droids kept plans.

He didn't know exactly how many tinnies were left, but there were an awful lot more than six of them.

Drive noise overhead distracted him, but he couldn't see what it was, not without moving beyond the barricade. It sounded like vulture droids. Those were the tinnies that bothered him most. Anything packing that much firepower that could fly, run, and learn was his worst nightmare.

And his broken rib hurt. He decided to lay off the painkillers until he *really* needed them again.

"I don't get it," said Zeer, one of the company combat engineers. He had both arms deep in the chest cavity of a super battle droid, as if he was doing heart surgery. "If this had been Jabiim, they'd have been all over us by now and our heads would be stuck on poles. What's stopping the tinnies from doing that? They know how few men we've got because they were guarding us."

"They're dumb," Del said. "At least, the regular tinnies are. If they're not lined up in a row and just firing, they're lost. I don't think the SBDs are that much smarter."

"This barve wasn't, for a start." Zeer knelt back on his heels and began bolting the SBD's plates back into place. "But he's got a new outlook on life."

Nax still clutched his bolt cutters. "They're waiting for that mad bald woman to think for them, but she's too busy looking for the general."

"No, we're bait," said Attie. "As long as we're alive, they know Skywalker's going to come for us. It's him they want, and the slug."

Rex checked his HUD again. No comms, no tactical display worth a mott's backside, nothing to indicate anyone was coming to extract them. He didn't even have access to HNE networks, and when he didn't know things for sure, Rex tended to plan for the very worst.

He hadn't given up on Skywalker yet, though.

"Okay, lads," he said. "Caf break over. Now, we could wait until the tinnies start up again, or we could send our special ambassador to explain our position. How's he doing, then, Zeer?"

"I think he's ready to walk, sir."

The squad maneuvered the eviscerated SBD into a position where it would stand upright again once its power pack was activated. Zeer had loaded the chest cavity with a few thermal dets. The tinny would march back to his lines, rejoin his brothers, and then blow them to pieces when remotely detonated, which wouldn't solve all Rex's problems, but it would certainly ruin the Seps' day and buy some more time.

And, of course, it was a few more scores settled. Ged would have loved to see it. So would Hez.

Rex checked his chrono. He could hear the all-too-familiar sounds of droids moving back and forth, and he wondered what they actually *did* when they milled about like that. It wasn't as if they had the same physical reactions and needs as an organic soldier. He'd spent so much time recently being a hostile next-door neighbor to them, often only meters apart, and yet he felt he knew less about droids now than he did when the war began.

Maybe there wasn't that much to know, only how to line up a Deece's reticle on the best and most destructive point.

"Okay, Zeer," he said. "Let's get into position before we send him back to the bosom of his family."

Where was Skywalker? Come to that, where was Kenobi?

In the absence of any command, all Rex could do was fight, and then either escape or put as big a dent in the enemy as he could before someone killed him. Sitting around waiting for Republic Day wasn't an option.

The clones settled back into their positions, Coric and Del on a repeating blaster that they'd taken off the Seps the hard way, and Attie with his mortar. Rex knelt, sighting up through carefully excavated gaps in the barricade of debris.

Zeer tinkered with something in the SBD's armpit, and then it came to life. Its blaster arm lifted forty-five degrees into the safety position. Rex watched, distracted by seeing the brute mobile, and he only breathed freely again when it crunched its way past the line of the AT-TE.

"Say hi to your mother for me," Zeer muttered, and took up his position between Rex and Attie.

"I hope the stupid thing doesn't fall down one of those craters."

"Nah, sir, they've got independent processors. I've programmed in his target coordinates, and he'll walk the best route avoiding obstacles before he becomes a martyr to the Republic's cause."

The SBD clunked back to his lines. A couple of battle droids on observation points looked up; Rex could see them in his optics. But they just looked, and carried on. He wasn't the enemy. His transponder data said he was still one of them. He marched on through the lines into the heart of the enemy position.

"I'll give him a few more moments," Zeer said.

The vulture activity overhead was getting more urgent. Rex found himself—again—playing the droid commander in his head: pinpointing the location of the Republic troublemakers, estimating their strength, and then blowing the poodoo out of them in an air strike. He couldn't imagine why droids—or whoever tasked them—fought wars this way and didn't use every advantage they had. They were right overhead; why didn't they attack? Okay, they didn't have line of sight, but it didn't take a genius to pinpoint six men well enough to reduce them to minced nerf.

Be thankful for morons.

"Is he far enough in yet?" Rex asked.

"I can see him," Zeer said. "I want him to move into the staging area. Pity it hasn't got a roof. That'd magnify the damage nicely."

"We kill what we can. Count us down, trooper."

Zeer flourished the remote detonator in his left hand, his Deece held pistol style in his right with the muzzle resting on the barricade. "Three . . . two . . ."

Stang, those vultures were really *bothering* Rex now.

He turned his head slightly to look at Zeer's hand. The man's thumb curled down onto the pressure plate.

"One!"

The infinitesimal moment of silence between pressing the det and the explosion always fascinated Rex. It was as if it was never going to happen, as if time stood still and would need kick-starting.

Time did, and it got the mightiest kick in the backside imaginable.

The flash of searing white fire plunged Rex's visor into temporary darkness as the sensors shielded his eyes from the intense light, and then the explosion shut down his audio to a muffled *oomph*. But he felt the shock wave punch up through the ground—through his legs and belly, and finally into his throat. At the same time, the blast wave shoved him in the chest. If it felt like that at *this* range . . . Rex decided that if he was going to go, then he wanted to be at that exact point on the targeting laser, and know absolutely nothing about it.

Nax adjusted his optics, a nervous tic that belied his mocking, casual impression of a sportscaster. "Republic—one; Confederacy of Independent Systems—nil."

"Well, that worked rather well . . . ," Zeer said modestly. "I wonder if they'll fall for it again?"

For a few moments, the entire courtyard was a quiet blizzard of gray ash. Then metal fragments started falling back down from the sky, clattering and crashing on the flagstones. Just in front of the AT-TE, the smaller, lighter particles that had been hurled farther fizzed as they rained down and hit the ground cold, but Rex didn't see a single piece big enough to pick up, let alone identify.

"Here we go," Attie muttered to himself. He slipped a mortar round down the tube and waited. "If we're going to make a tactical withdrawal, sir, it's now or never."

In the next few minutes, any droid that hadn't been reduced to components and metal filings was going to come boiling over that dune of rubble. The lull was almost unbearable.

"Anyone for *now*?" Rex asked, and waited for the answers.

"Not really, sir."

"Yeah, *never*'s good for me, too."

"I'm comfy here. Nothing better to do."

Coric brushed ash from his shoulder plates. Under the fine dusting of gray powder, his once-pristine white and blue armor was charred by blasterfire.

"I saw a holovid like this once." His tone was the deadpan one he used to tell jokes. "All very stirring stuff. The vast enemy hordes besieging the fort were so impressed by the brave stand of the handful of troops defending it that they sang songs of tribute to them."

"How did it end?" Del asked.

"They all got shot."

Rex wanted this moment to be over. It was—as usual—on the cusp of hilarity and sobbing despair. For all his training and his loyalty to the state, all the theoretical reasons why he was doing what was right, the only thing that made him sit and wait for the inevitable was that he was doing it for the men next to him, and for Skywalker—wherever he was—and even for Kenobi, but for nothing and nobody else. That was as far as any man could think. And it was far enough.

The rattling noise began, distant at first, and then resolved into the *chunk-chunk-chunk* of perfectly synchronized metal feet. The sound rose like a tide. It came not only from in front of them, where they expected it to start, but also from behind, and to either side.

Rex knelt back on one heel, and wondered if there was any

point doing the tactically correct thing—fighting from cover—or if it was best to stand up now in full view both of his comrades and whatever it was that made up a droid.

Either way, we fight to win.

He got to his feet, laid his rifle on the nearest flat surface, and took a DC-15 short blaster in each hand.

"Torrent Company," Rex said. *"Stand to."*

FIFTEEN

*I can't define a hero. All I know is that it's someone you probably
don't notice, but when you find out what they did and how
modestly they did it, you can never shake off the feeling that
you're cut from a lesser cloth, and you find that braggarts
suddenly offend you a great deal more than usual.*

ADMIRAL YULAREN, Republic Fleet, declining to discuss the
matter of the Republic's war heroes with HoloNet News

SECOND LANDING PLATFORM,
THREE KILOMETERS FROM TETH MONASTERY

ANAKIN WONDERED IF A THREE-METER CARNIVOROUS HUNTING
fly bore grudges.

He still held the creature in a Force grip as it flew in a straight
line—more or less—toward the ship that held out the last hope of
pulling off this mission. The fly didn't want to go there, and it
didn't want passengers. It took all Anakin's concentration to control its direction and stop it from plunging down through the trees
to scrape off what it clearly regarded either as parasites or an up-
pity lunch item.

"When we get close enough to solid ground, Snips, jump and
run."

Ahsoka was now sitting astride the fly just behind its wings and in front of Anakin. "You think it's *that* dangerous?"

"It's an ornithopter with the mind of a womp rat, and we caught it by luring it with a mating call, so work it out for yourself."

"I thought you were supposed to be good with animals."

"Machines. I'm good with *machines*." And that was what he was banking on; as the landing platform got nearer, he could see that the ship standing on it was a freighter that had seen better days. "I can get anything to fly. But I pushed my luck with *this* guy."

Neither would say it aloud, but Anakin thought it: if he couldn't get that ship airborne, they'd be stuck on yet another plateau in hostile territory, with no way out but down into the jungle, or wrestling with the local flying fauna. Anakin glanced to one side to check that R2-D2 was keeping up. From the backpack, Rotta made awful gagging and wheezing sounds.

"Rotta's sounding pretty rough, Master."

"He's up one moment and down the next, and he's still alive. Do you know how hard it is to kill a Hutt? You can't even poison them. They regrow body parts. They can live for a thousand years. Rotta isn't some delicate snowbloom or anything."

"What *is* it with you and Hutts?"

"I spent too much time with them to ever like them. And that's all you need to know."

Anakin regretted it as soon as he said it. He'd made it sound more as if he had some wild, dark past, and nothing was better guaranteed to keep Ahsoka asking questions than that. If he explained he'd been a Hutt's slave, she'd dig away at it until all the bad stuff came out. It was hard enough telling Padmé, and she was his wife.

Wife.

It was such a serious and wonderful word. It shouldn't have

been a guilty secret. Anakin wondered what would happen if he told Yoda straight out that he had a wife, that he didn't agree with all the arbitrary Jedi rules on avoiding love and attachment, and ask him—respectfully—what he was going to do about it.

He'd have to tell Kenobi first, though. And that was going to be *much* harder, because he heard that Kenobi had faced the same choice as Anakin, but had walked away from the love of his life, and done things strictly by the Jedi book.

How can that be right? How can that make us better Jedi?

No. Anakin would say nothing. He weighed the corrosive effect of keeping secrets from his old Master against the storm that would be unleashed if he confessed to his marriage.

I have a war to fight. And Padmé is nobody's business but mine.

"That ship's looking worse by the minute," Ahsoka said. "But it only has to get us to Tatooine, right?"

"That's the spirit. The cup is half full."

"How are you going to land this bug?"

"Seriously?"

"Yes."

"Okay, I'll make it settle with a Force push and hold it there while you get away with Rotta. Then I'll back away, release the Force hold, and hope it flies off relieved to be rid of us."

Anakin had tried to reach out to the hunting fly in the Force, and calm it the way he'd seen Kenobi do with dangerous animals. But its mind was so alien, so unfathomable, that Anakin had backed off in case he made matters worse. The plateau loomed. What had been a slowly resolving blur of vegetation, ferrocrete, and transparisteel now rushed at him at collision speed.

He checked his comlink again. The frequencies were still jammed.

Rex, I'm coming. I swear it. Just dig in.

Ahsoka hadn't mentioned the beleaguered 501st men since

he'd given her the pep talk. She might have been avoiding a sore subject.

"Here we go . . ."

He visualized *down,* a growing pressure on the fly's back and wing surfaces, and it began to drop at a shallow angle. Then he concentrated on what was, if he thought consciously about it, like a headwind in the Force to slow its approach. Weeds and surface cracks in the permacrete platform passed beneath. The combined Force influences brought the fly down a safe distance from the edge, and Anakin held the creature in position with a steady Force push while Ahsoka scrambled to release the backpack. She hauled Rotta clear and ran for the shelter of a tree.

Anakin leaped down. He would have patted the fly's back, but its whipping tail said he should quit while he was ahead. "Thanks, and sorry for tricking you," he said. "You'll find a nice female fly one day, I promise."

Then he ran, releasing his hold on it in the Force. Without the weight of the Huttlet on his back, he almost felt he could fly himself. The sudden turbo-saw buzz of wings behind him faded fast to silence, and when he dared to stop running and look behind, the fly was gone.

For all he knew, the creature could have been female, soaring away to tell her much, *much* bigger and angrier spouse about this human's outrageous hijack, and Anakin would be on the run from giant hunting flies forever.

Ahsoka fussed over Rotta and eased him out of the backpack. *I don't even want to* think *about cleaning that pack out.* Anakin decided that fussing duties were adequately covered and walked over to the freighter.

The meteor-pocked panel on the hatch read TWILIGHT.

"Apt," he said. *Please start. Please fire up. Please get us out of here.* "The old crate's fading fast by the looks of it."

R2-D2 rolled up next to Anakin and let out a mournful whis-tle.

"Defeatist." Anakin patted him on his cranial dome. "We've fixed worse. Hey, Snips—I'll show you how to hotwire a ship. Essential Jedi training they tend to omit at the Temple."

R2-D2 trundled beneath the airframe, opened a cover plate, and began trying various extending probes in the slots. Ahsoka came up carrying Rotta in her arms. There were water splashes on her clothing.

"I gave him a quick rinse from my water bottle," she said. "Hutts in confined spaces, and all that."

"Good thinking."

Ahsoka had the makings of a good Jedi, and she was going to butt more than a few heads with the Jedi Council. He'd bet on it. Maybe those were one and the same thing. He thought of Rex and his handful of troops, and gestured to R2-D2 to open the hatch.

Hang in there, Rex.

The main hatch popped and air hissed from the seals. Anakin stood back to let the ramp lower.

"Can I help you?" said a voice from behind.

Anakin spun around. He was hard to startle. But he'd been preoccupied, and droids didn't leave impressions in the Force the way living objects did.

"Just leaving." Anakin was on his guard. What else had he overlooked? "Hey, you're—"

"You're the caretaker droid," Ahsoka interrupted, doing that little irritated frown. She'd never make a sabacc player. "Four-A-Seven, right? I thought you looked after the monastery. What are you doing here?"

"Taking care of *myself*." The droid bowed his head. "The monastery has been utterly defiled *again*. I thought those Hutt gangsters were bad enough, but the droid army has reached new depths of profanity." He glanced at Rotta. "No offense, little one. Your path in life may yet be innocent."

"So this is *your* ship," said Anakin, ready to do a deal—or take what he needed—as long as it was *now*. "You're leaving?"

"I've retrieved the few holy scrolls and devotional artifacts that have not been pillaged or destroyed, and I shall keep them safe until I find monks who'll accept them." 4A-7 indicated the packing crates stacked nearby. "Yes, I intend to leave this wretched place, and as soon as possible."

"So do we." Anakin was poised to silence Ahsoka, who just frowned at 4A-7 and seemed to be gearing up for something. "Shall we leave together, then? If you don't have a destination in mind, I can think of a few."

"A reasonable suggestion, sir. Please, board my vessel and make the child comfortable. The monks I served believed that giving aid freely to another being was the highest form of worship."

Anakin was about to start softening up 4A-7 to the idea that he'd have to divert or return to rescue his men, but he decided it was best left for when they were airborne. The droid might have included clone troopers in the *heathen despoilers* bracket. Anakin didn't want an argument on the landing pad, or to be obliged to use force. The ship *was* leaving, Ahsoka and Rotta *would* be on it, and, when he'd worked out the details, it *would* be saving Rex and his surviving troopers. Anything that stood in the way of that—too bad.

He stood to the side of the hatch and gestured to Ahsoka to board the ship. R2-D2 was still trundling around checking its undercarriage and making critical beeps. Ahsoka put one foot on the ramp, then froze, and looked down in defocus at her boot as if straining to hear something. When she looked up again, her eyes were wide and the pupils fully dilated; not fear or surprise, but that feral look again, a hunter who'd detected something to chase or fight.

Sometimes she wasn't the overeager kid at all. It was all the more unsettling for that.

"Snips?"

"Artoo," she said quietly. "Artoo, take Stinky for me, will you? Just for a moment."

Anakin didn't ask any stupid questions, and took her cue. "Smell finally got to you, then?" He watched R2-D2 take the pack and roll quietly away from the ship. "No throwing up, okay?"

She held her arms loose at her sides and took another step up the ramp. Anakin tried to sense what might have spooked her, but he couldn't tell, and combat zones were awash with disruptions in the Force.

"We really must make a move now, sir," 4A-7 said. "The fighting here is escalating. We don't want to be trapped here."

"No," said Ahsoka. "We don't."

She'd drawn her lightsaber even before the first metal boot hit the ramp. Two battle droids suddenly appeared at the hatch, barring her way. Anakin drew his weapon and turned to check on R2-D2, but the droid was well clear, and 4A-7 would have to get past Anakin to reach him.

The battle droids opened fire on Ahsoka. She charged them, swatting aside the blaster bolts and slashing into their bodies before disappearing into the ship. Anakin was going to rush in after her, but she was clearly in control, and he had other business to attend to. He rounded on 4A-7.

"You nearly had me." Anakin held his lightsaber to the droid. There was no telling what else this "caretaker" had hidden. "You're Ventress's droid, aren't you? She's sent you to kill the Hutt."

4A-7 still had that smug calm about him, even now his ambush had failed. "I suppose I'm only obliged to give you my name, model number, and parts code . . ."

Anakin noted that the blasterfire had stopped abruptly. "Funny."

"I have no orders to kill the Huttlet. I'm unarmed."

"Spy, then. You'll be even more useful when your data is extracted . . ."

Ahsoka came running toward them with her lightsaber held so tightly that her knuckles were white. She seemed lost for words for second. But she'd find some harsh ones pretty soon, he knew.

She'll have to do something about that temper. Maybe I'm the wrong Master for her.

"You're a traitor," she said. As her lips moved, Anakin could see the little killer teeth, the ones she usually didn't show. "A *traitor.*"

"No, I'm not a traitor," 4A-7 said. "I'm just not on your side. I serve another government, one no less valid than yours. There is always more than one side to any story, youngling."

She had no answer to that. Anakin realized he now had a logistics problem, as Rex would call it. *I'm coming, Rex. Hang on.* He'd have to take this spy with him, because he couldn't leave him here; and spies were no ordinary prisoners. They were dangerous every second of the day, and a droid spy—it was almost too much to think about. He could be a booby trap or a sabotage device or a surveillance system as well.

Anakin felt he was collecting problems, not solving them. Time mattered.

"Come on," he said, and went to usher the spy droid onto the ship with the intention of having R2-D2 render him safe, like some kind of elaborate bomb.

But Ahsoka was still fuming. If she'd had fur, it would have been standing on end. She had this way of being absolutely still and then exploding into movement. Right now, she was a statue.

"You're still a traitor," she said. She never raised her voice. The S was hiss. "Still aiding a monster."

"If you truly believe that the Republic and the Jedi Order are wholly good, and that the Confederacy is wholly evil, then you're even more dangerous than my mistress thinks."

Ahsoka snapped from freeze to explosion and swung her lightsaber.

Anakin was standing too close; he jumped back instinctively as 4A-7's head hit the ground and bounced once before rolling to the foot of the ramp. In the shocked silence, Anakin could hear the droid's voice repeating something.

He ran to it and squatted down to listen, trying to make sense of what had just happened. 4A-7's voice was fading, repeating snatches of his final words. Anakin had taken the heads off many, many droids in the war so far, and it hadn't troubled him one bit, but the disembodied head—lights still active—and the very human voice still talking gripped something deep in his gut.

". . . you're even more dangerous . . . you're even more dangerous . . . you're even more dangerous . . ."

The voice faded to nothing and the lights died.

Ahsoka stood over him. He looked up at her, for once.

"Creepy," she said.

"Volatile memory." Anakin had to move on to the next task, to the Hutt and to Rex. "Spy droids don't store their data when they're terminated, for obvious reasons. I believe they transmit it."

"So he's scrap."

Anakin watched R2-D2 roll up the ramp carrying Rotta. If Hutts could be traumatized in childhood, that kid was going to be a basket case after what he'd seen in the last day or two.

"Yeah," Anakin said. "You could say that."

He sealed the hatch behind them. R2-D2 had to work some of his astromech magic to fire up the drives, but they lifted clear in one piece.

Scrap.

Where did *scrap* end, and *being* begin?

"You did a great job, Artoo," Anakin said. "Thanks, buddy."

R2-D2 whistled. He said it was a pleasure.

COURTYARD, TETH MONASTERY

Rex had stopped thinking some minutes ago, but he was still on his feet and firing.

The tinnies hadn't knocked him down yet. He reached for a reload. He'd perfected the technique of jamming the muzzle of his discharged blaster in a slot in the AT-TE's carcass to hold it steady while he removed the spent power pack and replaced it one-handed, without needing to stop firing the blaster in his other hand.

It was quite a skill to learn in the last minutes of his life.

"Get down, sir," Attie said, squatting to his left and sliding a round into the launcher. "Mortar surprise coming . . ."

Rex conceded. He dropped and turned his back to the launcher.

"Cover—fire!" *Whoomp.* "Cover—fire!" *Whoomp.* "Cover—fire!"

The explosions had become a continuous wall of noise and smoke. The six men were in a square now, facing out on four fronts, and relying on the generous supply of mortars still in the dead AT-TE interspersed with blasterfire and anti-armor rounds. Zeer had crawled into the wreckage of the walker for some respite while he worked on something. When he emerged, he was hauling a flamethrower.

"New and improved," he said. "Removes those *difficult*, ground-in tinnies that other flamethrowers can't touch."

Zeer defaulted to stock phrases under extreme pressure, as if he had a script he could turn to when he was too hyped up or scared to think. It made him sound like a relaxed wisecracker. Rex knew different. They were all running on empty, spinning a credit, and the moment they stopped spinning it the chip would collapse flat, and that was what would happen to them. They kept moving and they stopped thinking beyond the next second. Even though Rex knew that was how it happened, he was still stunned by it. And he was *proud*.

They were an island sinking in an ocean of droids.

"Just end it," Coric said to himself. He was facing the other side of the assault, almost back-to-back with Rex, emptying clip after clip from a repeating blaster through a gap in the barrier. "Got to stop sometime."

Rex gestured to Zeer. "Hang on to that. Droid flambé for

dessert." He wanted the battle droids a lot closer to make that count. "Coric, you okay?"

"Always am, sir."

"Good man."

Rex had set his helmet comm circuit to cycle automatically through the frequencies. He was only monitoring subconsciously; he fired a grenade over the top of the barrier to give himself a second's grace to get into position, and opened up with both blasters again. Droids fell, but there were plenty more where those came from. Ocean. Yes, it was a good word for it. The scene in front of him was in constant motion, with waves, and the droid shrapnel and smoke forming spray.

They will never stop.

But he still had five men, and to hold off a droid army even for this long was exceptional. It was a shame that nobody would ever know.

You can't give up on Skywalker.

Heavy arty pieces would have been nice. And maybe some air support, which was beginning to take on the mythic aura of spiced creams, a delicacy everyone craved but never found on the menu. He almost didn't hear the burst of chatter in his ear. It was breaking up.

"—Five-oh-first—"

But it wasn't *jammed;* he could hear something.

"Twenty-twelfth inbound—air group—time on target fourteen-oh-seven—"

Now he knew where the vulture droids had gone. Kenobi was here, with the 212th Attack Battalion. It was the help they thought they'd never live to receive, and he was elated, disbelieving, and oddly disappointed at the same time.

The enemy fire stopped. Rex ducked down.

In the relative silence—in the background fires still roared, superheated metal still clicked and groaned—they listened.

"Kenobi's coming," he said. "Listen for the larties . . ."

There was a *chunk-chunk-chunk* of a single pair of droid feet picking its way over the carpet of fallen tinnies.

"Republic cannon fodder!" a droid's voice shouted. "Surrender! You can't carry on."

It was the droid commander. Rex peered through a gap and saw the yellow markings on the torso.

"They're not going to sing a rousing chorus as a tribute to our manly clone grit, then . . . ," Coric murmured.

Rex stood up and faced the droid commander across a gulf of about twenty meters.

"Who're *you* calling cannon fodder, clanker?"

"Surrender immediately."

Maybe it was what droids were programmed to do, and maybe they really did want him and his men as bait for Skywalker. It probably wouldn't matter in a few minutes.

Rex adjusted his external audio pickup to maximum. He heard it: the unmistakable drone of a LAAT/i drive. *Lots* of LAAT/i drives. And the whine of fighters. And a lovely, familiar, whistling note . . .

"I wish you'd asked earlier," Rex said mildly. "Because then—"

The droids behind the commander all looked up at once.

Then they exploded as a missile smashed into their position.

"—you wouldn't have been outnumbered."

LAAT/i gunships rose all around the edge of the plateau as if on cue. That was some flying; they must have hugged the tops of the trees for some distance to sneak up like that. Some of the larties laid down suppressing fire while Clone Commander Cody's troops rappelled down from others to land in the courtyard, firing before their boots hit the ground. The ocean was changing color from dull droid tan to orange and white.

" 'Bout kriffing time," said Nax. "No Skywalker?"

A Jedi Interceptor appeared from nowhere over the monastery and screamed down to land on the flattened roof of an outbuilding. Rex expected Skywalker to come bounding out, batting away blasterfire with his lightsaber, but when the canopy popped, the flurry of brown robes and whirling blue blade that leaped from the roof and landed—perfectly, like a gymnast—right next to Rex was General Kenobi.

"Good timing, sir." Rex reloaded, two-handed this time.

"Obviously not good enough, Captain," Kenobi said. A droid popped up above the barricade, and he Force-threw it back across the lines as if he didn't like eavesdroppers. "Just these men left?"

"Sir."

"I'm sorry. So where's Skywalker?"

"Last known position somewhere in the monastery, sir, but that was some hours ago. We've had no further contact."

"I'll go look for him."

"Watch out for a woman with my taste in hairstyles and a double-ended red light saber."

"Ventress . . ."

"Smack her one for me, will you, sir? She gave me a few fractures."

"Count on it."

Kenobi bounded off. Rex would have liked to have that amount of energy left, but he was flagging. He almost felt that the battle now raging around the temporary and fragile sanctuary of the AT-TE was happening somewhere else. His wrist comlink beeped.

"Captain Rex, this is General Skywalker."

Rex's gut tightened. *So he's alive.* The relief made his scalp prickle. "Go ahead, sir."

"Apologies for vanishing. Been a little busy."

Rex assumed he knew Kenobi and Cody had shown up with all lasers firing. "Comm working now, sir?"

"Ah, yes . . . we've got a problem, Rex. The Hutt kid is getting sicker. I've commandeered a ship and I'm going to transfer the kid to Admiral Yularen's vessel. We're not going to be able to get to you yet. I'm sorry."

Rex often felt sorry for Skywalker. Guilt seemed to get the better of him sometimes. "The mission comes first, sir," he said. "You'd have to wait in line anyway—Cody's lads have taken all the best seats. We can't move for orange stripy armor. Hurts the eyes."

There was a crackling pause, very brief but telling. "So you don't need us, then."

"We're fine, sir. Good luck with the Hutt. I'll let General Kenobi know you're okay, because he's just gone looking for you in the monastery."

"I didn't mean to waste his time."

"Oh, I don't think he'll mind, sir." *Ah, he still worries what his Master thinks of him, even when he's got a Padawan of his own.* "He'll probably take the opportunity to catch up on old times with Ventress."

Skywalker laughed, but there wasn't any humor in it. Rex closed the link.

"Well, that's a relief," Coric said.

The six men, all that was left of Torrent Company, 501st Legion, stood in the center of the chaos that only moments before had been their fort, and might well have been their grave, and felt oddly *irrelevant*. The 212th had taken over and was sweeping back the droids. The adrenaline was ebbing, and though it would take a while to settle completely, Rex already had that shaky, drained, *lost* feeling.

Yeah, we know how it feels not to be needed, sir.

"Well, that's a different ending to your holovid, Sarge," Attie said to Coric. "We all lived happily ever after."

"No," said Del. "Most of us didn't."

Rex holstered his short blasters and picked up his rifle.

"In that case," he said, "let's commemorate them the Five-oh-first way. By wiping out every last tinny on this rock."

Tomorrow, they'd start all over again.

SIXTEEN

○

Enemies are not accidental or unfortunate. We make them,
we earn them, and we nurture them, whether we realize it or not.
If we can't find real enemies, we'll invent them and make them
as big as we can. They become our justification for existing, or excuses
for our own failings. Many of us would suffer if we didn't have them—
who would need Jedi if there were no dark Force users?

LORD GAJAKUR BIUL, Kilian Ranger

TETH MONASTERY

VENTRESS HAD THOUGHT THERE WAS NOTHING LEFT THAT THE
Jedi could take away from her, but she was wrong.

The last moments of intelligence droid 4A-7 unfolded as a
holorecording. After she'd acted on that transmission, coldly ra-
tional, to alert vessels to look for Skywalker's ship, she had a moment to reflect.

She watched it two, three, then four times in the semidarkness
of an alcove in the passageway, shutting out the battle raging in the
monastery grounds outside. Artillery fire smashed into the building and the volcanic rock of the plateau. The floor trembled beneath her feet.

They had to take him from me, too, didn't they? Without a sec-
ond thought.

4A-7 was designed to upload stored data and his temporary volatile memory if he was too badly damaged to function, to stop information from falling into enemy hands. His backup power supply was set to detect a catastrophic failure and then transmit everything, both stored and volatile, to a secure location. When the system finally failed—when the droid died—there would be no data left in his components for an enemy to extract.

So he'd continued to dump data—still running on that short-lived backup power, *still conscious*—even after the Jedi brat decapitated him. That realization disturbed Ventress more than anything else.

It means nothing to you, does it, Jedi?

The droid had been the only trustworthy entity in her world. Ventress heard his words, and saw the events from the perspective of the holorecorders embedded in the side of each photoreceptor. No, *eyes;* he had *eyes,* and the recorded data were his *thoughts.* She refused to use that sterile machine language. 4A-7 had died like . . . a *man.* He was more of a real being than most organics she had to endure. He'd done his duty, and, irrelevant as it was now, he'd told the Jedi some home truths about the dictatorship of the Republic. His termination on active service was as heroic to Ventress as any flesh-and-blood soldier's.

She looked at her datapad. It now contained everything that had been 4A-7—programming, data, and working memory up to the point when his backup power supply had finally failed. In the terms of flesh and blood, she had his soul in her hand.

My resolve has never weakened. But you've strengthened it, Jedi. Again, you earn your enemies.

If she'd never learned to convert pain, loss, and anger into action, she would have died a long time ago. She turned to go back to the battle, reinvigorated.

The comlink bleeped again. She responded, and the empty air in front of her was filled with a hologram of Dooku.

"I hear Kenobi's forces have arrived, Asajj."

"We're dealing with it."

"Have you recovered the Hutt yet?"

You know I haven't. I'd have told you the second I did. "Skywalker still has him, but we'll take his ship before he leaves the Teth system."

"You know the stakes." Dooku never sounded angry. He was always quietly understated, but she knew he was furious in his own way. "It's not enough to create enmity between Jabba and the Republic now. He needs a reason to be seen to reward *us* with sole access to the Outer Rim. We have to be the ones who rescue the child."

"I understand, Master. My challenge, though, is stopping Skywalker without harming the Hutt. The Jedi have been carrying the child at all times, so I'm dealing with a living shield. Normally, that would mean nothing and I would regard the innocent as collateral damage, but in this case, I can't."

"Then you need to think more laterally. And *faster*. Dooku out."

Ventress stared at the empty air where the hologram had been and swallowed her resentment.

Remember—this is the man who won't train me as a Sith. This is the man who's happy to use my skills for Sith ends, but won't let me join the club.

They had a common objective, but he wasn't on her side. She was the hired help. She reminded herself of the ramifications of that.

But there was no point obeying blindly. She was the commander on the ground; only she knew the situation. If Skywalker managed to hand that Hutt over to a Republic warship—and that was now his best option—she stood little chance of preventing the Huttlet from being returned to his father. She paused to transmit new orders to the vulture droids.

If unable to prevent Skywalker from docking with enemy warship, override order to preserve the hostage and destroy the Twilight.

She had no other option. That was the last resort.

In that brief quiet moment, she felt someone coming closer in the Force, a brash fanfare of a presence. She took a lightsaber in each hand and hefted the hilts to focus herself before activating the blades.

"Master Kenobi," she said, not looking up for a few moments. "You're late. Never keep a lady waiting."

Kenobi ambled down the passage toward her. "I was looking for Anakin. He stood you up, then?"

"Consider me on the rebound when it comes to killing Jedi." She held one glowing red blade vertically in front of her face. "You'll do."

She turned and sprinted into a side passage that led to an older part of the site, a different style of construction where the ceilings were flat and supported by columns, rather than the spacious vaulted rooms of more recent architecture. The chamber she found herself in was a stone forest, filled with precise ranks of granite columns that glittered in the low light; less room to maneuver, but plenty of cover from saber strikes and opportunity for feints.

For him, too. Remember that.

Ventress slid behind a column and waited, lightsabers shut down. For a while, she thought he might have resisted the lure, or that he really *was* on other business, somehow unaware of Sky-walker's whereabouts and searching for him. But she heard his footsteps coming closer. If he missed the entrance to the chamber, she'd have to guide him.

But he didn't. She could hear the rustle of his robes coming closer.

"Ventress, there's no point hiding from me . . ."

She stayed silent and turned her head slowly to pinpoint the sound. Footsteps, and the occasional *vzzzzm* of his lightsaber. He was either swinging the blade or spinning around to check behind him.

Kenobi was easy to sense in the Force anyway.

"Ventress, we have Jabba's son. It's over."

His voice was closer. He could sense her in the Force, too, of course. *Come and get me, braggart . . .*

"Ventress . . ."

He talked too much. Maybe he liked the drama, or used it to work himself up for a fight.

"Ventress . . ." The tone was soothing, like calling a pet to come for feeding. "Ventress . . ."

She sprang from behind the column, thumbing both lightsabers to life, and swung one into him. The blades clashed, red on blue. For a split second she saw the look of surprise illuminated on his face. He parried. But she brought the other saber swinging in an arc, and then they were locked in combat. Ventress used both sabers simultaneously in a scissor action to drive him back and force him against a wall or a column, but each time, Kenobi managed to ram his weapon between her blades.

He spun away behind a column. She heard him panting. They both needed a few seconds to draw breath.

"You'll have to do better than that," he said.

"And you'll have to learn to keep your mouth shut." She leaped around the column from the other side. Her blade missed his head by a fraction as he ducked, and sent a cloud of dust sparkling from the stone. Kenobi raced away. She pursued.

He's not invincible. He couldn't take Fett. But he's not trying this time.

Ventress wouldn't trust Kenobi as far as she could spit.

She stalked him, and this time it was his turn to leap out at her and strike. He drove her back against a wall, but she used it as a springboard to Force-push him back before hacking at him with all the raw strength she could muster. It wasn't hard to summon up. She simply saw Narec, and wanted to destroy the whole world in vengeance.

Kenobi's lightsaber spun in the air. For a second she thought it was a trick; but she'd knocked it from his hand. Her blade was at his throat in a heartbeat.

Kenobi looked up at her, chest rising and falling as he caught his breath. "Okay, Ventress, are you going to gloat and give me a speech on the futility of my mission?"

"No," she said. "I'm just going to kill you."

Then he threw her backward with a Force push. She hit a column hard enough to hear something crack, and staggered to her feet. Kenobi summoned his lightsaber back to his hand with a grin.

She was going to have to wipe that smirk off his smug Jedi face the hard way.

THE FREIGHTER *TWILIGHT,* TETH SPACE

Anakin knew he should never have expected things to get easier.

The trajectory he'd set took the *Twilight* close to the action. It was inevitable. He needed to locate Yularen's flagship, *Spirit of the Republic.* Once he handed over Rotta, he could get back to the fighting, or start replacing the men of Torrent Company if the ground engagement was over, or—*anything* but this.

He'd opted for the most direct course. The airspace above the jungle combat zone and up through the atmosphere into space was crawling with V-19 fighters, vulture droids, and warships. Even at maximum thrust, the *Twilight* climbed slowly for a pilot used to starfighters.

We might as well have a big target roundel painted on us.

The freighter shuddered as it climbed. Ahsoka sat in silence with Rotta clutched on her lap. In a confined cockpit, the smell was almost too much for Anakin to bear. He tweaked the fuel injectors a little higher.

Come on . . . come on . . .

Bursts of white light flared against the sky in the thinning layers of the planet's atmosphere. Anakin kept a wary eye on both the ship's sensors and what he could see with his own eyes through the viewport. He could see *Spirit*'s transponder on the screen, but the cruiser was in the thick of it, surrounded by smaller pinpoints of light that indicated Republic and Sep fighters.

"They're too busy to worry about us," Ahsoka said at last.

"I'll try to worry less obviously in future."

"Yularen knows you're inbound."

"Yeah, but so does Ventress, I'll bet. She had her droids ready for us, and she knows this crate's gone. She also knows we won't be crazy enough to head for Tatooine in it. So she knows we've got to do a transfer, and that we don't have many ships to choose from."

"She might not."

"She's smart. If I can think of this solution to our problem, so can she." Anakin adjusted course, looking to divert around a knot of V-19s chasing down a flight of vultures. Rotta whimpered. "What would *you* do?"

"Er . . . booby-trap the freighter to explode?"

Anakin's gut flipped over. He hadn't thought of that one. "No. No, she needs Rotta. That's got to be her plan."

"Admit it, we found this tub *really* conveniently."

It would take a matter of minutes to reach Yularen. "She wasn't expecting us. She couldn't have planned the hunting fly. She'll have vulture droids looking out for us."

"It all hinges on who's the best pilot, then, you or a heap of smart scrap."

R2-D2 chirped and flashed. He said he thought that was a little *organicist*, speaking as a heap of smart scrap himself.

Ahsoka was still learning. "I didn't understand all that."

"I'll give you some sensitivity lessons later . . ."

The *Twilight* began her approach to *Spirit*. Any minute now, a Sep sensor officer or a vulture would notice the freighter on their screen, and then it was all down to nerve, speed, and skill. Anakin knew he was weak on one of those. He realigned his instruments on *Spirit* and lined up with the cruiser's hangar bay.

There was an awful lot of traffic in between.

"Hang on to our slippery friend, Snips. Here we go."

"Yes, Master."

Anakin opened the comm. "General Skywalker to Jedi cruiser, we need hangar bay access. I say again, we need hangar bay access urgently."

A blip appeared instantly on the screen. A vulture had dropped out of nowhere and was skimming just above the cockpit, matching their speed. Anakin couldn't fire the *Twilight*'s laser cannon. It was like a nasty itch in a place you couldn't reach without tearing yourself up. Another vulture peeled off from formation and headed straight for them. It was on an intercept course.

Something hit the *Twilight* hard. Rivets flew from the internal bulkheads as they flexed under the impact. The freighter had taken a hit. Anakin held it on course.

"Maybe she doesn't want Stinky alive after all . . . ," Ahsoka said.

Maybe. "Nearly there. Hang on."

He could see the cruiser and the hangar now. The outline of the opening was picked out in hazard lighting. But he also saw a ball of energy heading directly at the freighter, coming straight from the cruiser's aft cannon position.

"Brace!" he yelled. "Ahsoka, *brace!*"

The cannon round hit the cockpit and Anakin felt the shock wave travel up through the steering yoke to his hands and smack into his elbow and shoulder joints. The freighter shook violently.

"Are they targeting the vultures?" Ahsoka asked.

"No, they're firing at *us*!" The cruiser still had its deflector shields up. Anakin opened the comm again. "Jedi cruiser, this is General Skywalker, this is a Republic friendly, repeat, freighter *Twilight* is a Republic friendly, hold fire, hold fire."

The comm popped in response. "Freighter *Twilight,* you're showing a CIS military transponder code . . . your call."

Stang. Of course: the spy droid and his detachment would have made sure their own forces didn't fire on them. 4A-7 had had the last laugh, then.

"Jedi cruiser, this *is* Skywalker. We're crawling with vultures and we need to drop off a very sick Huttlet. Open the hangar. *Please.*"

After a second's pause, Admiral Yularen's voice came over the comm. "Skywalker, we're going to drop the deflectors, but we need to lose those vultures. Divert to the aft hangar, I repeat, aft hangar. And check your transponder next time you commandeer an enemy vessel. We've had a few suicide runs before, and we shoot first."

"Yes, Admiral." *Wow, consider me put in my place.* An admiral was lord of all he surveyed in his own fleet, and Anakin was just another pilot who should have known better. "Stand by for a possible crash landing."

Anakin jerked the *Twilight* violently to port, leaving the pursuing vultures wrong-footed for a vital moment, and looped under the cruiser. Ahsoka gasped, Rotta shrieked, and the freighter came about facing the cruiser's stern. The hangar doors were open; the aperture rushed up on Anakin like a gaping mouth about to consume him.

The vultures were still pursuing, hammering the hull with laser cannon. How the crate was holding together Anakin would never know, but it was, and that was all that mattered.

Ten seconds.

The vultures were still with them. He couldn't do a deck landing with them clinging to him. The cruiser knew that, and opened up with precision lasers. One vulture shattered and cartwheeled away, showering red-hot debris on the cockpit viewport.

The next shot hit a vulture with unerring accuracy, too. But it was suddenly a ball of flame tumbling ahead of the freighter's nose. It streaked into the hangar, and all Anakin could see was a ball of fire and smoke where sanctuary should have been.

"Pull up! Pull up!"

"Abort, abort, abort!"

Anakin did it without thinking. He jerked back on the yoke and sent the freighter climbing vertically. He didn't have time to worry about the cruiser or the hangar crew, but the ship had its hands full with damage and casualties now, so they couldn't worry about him, either. There was no going around for another approach.

And he was still trailing an unwelcome escort of vultures.

Just as Captain Rex had been, he and Ahsoka were now on their own. The irony wasn't lost on him.

TETH MONASTERY

Kenobi ran.

Ventress chased him through the passages and up flights of ancient stone stairs, slowed by whatever she'd injured—vertebrae, ribs?—even if the adrenaline and endorphins flooding her bloodstream had completely numbed any pain for the time being. She didn't have time to stop and check her comm for an update on Skywalker and his escape attempt.

He'd either beaten the fighter picket and docked, or he was charcoal by now—along with his ship and the Hutt. Dooku would rage in his quiet patrician way, but sometimes the only choice was between a bad result and a worse one.

She could still find a way to pin a dead Huttlet on the Jedi.

At the top of the stairs was a window that ran the full height of the wall, and Kenobi was standing there as if he was waiting for her to catch up. The ornately patterned colored transparisteel of the window itself had been blown out by shelling. He was silhouetted against the afternoon sun.

It was a gesture of contempt. It said that he could take her any time he liked. And it made her angrier than ever.

Just a game for you, isn't it? No family, no lover, no country, nothing to weep for. A sport.

"What are you waiting for?" he said, and jumped.

SEVENTEEN

In a battle between those fighting for a political principle,
and those fighting for the survival of their home and family,
the latter usually win in the long run. They've got nothing more
to lose, and it makes them terrible enemies. Like us.

JABIIMI COMMANDER, on the nature
of fighting the Republic on Jabiim

TETH AIRSPACE

ALL ANAKIN NEEDED WAS A SMALL WINDOW OF OPPORTUNITY TO
climb free of the atmosphere and jump to hyperspace.

Any doubts that the battered freighter would survive the massive forces of acceleration to light speed and beyond were now a
luxury to sweat over later. That was the great thing about problems; there was always a bigger, nastier one to put the rest in a convenient shadow. Anakin's was his escort of vultures, which were
now trying to force him to land.

"I can't outrun them," he said.

Ahsoka had been commendably silent, no helpful suggestions
that he didn't need or cheery exhortations to keep his spirits up. A
Padawan needed to learn when to shut up. She had. She clutched

Rotta to her chest as if he were squirming to get away, but the Hutt hung limp in her arms, eyes half closed, breathing noisily.

If they ever got away, they might be delivering a dead Huttlet to Jabba after all. It didn't bear thinking about.

"Let's jettison something," Ahsoka said at last.

Laser cannonfire streaked past the *Twilight*'s nose, and another vulture droid buzzed the ship, so close to the cockpit viewport that Anakin jerked hard to starboard in pure reflex. Vultures were not dumb tinnies. They seemed to be able to learn from their quarry, and right now they were playing a very good game of nervous nuna—harrying the freighter and making runs at it to test who would blink first.

"What? Can't dump fuel." Anakin checked the gauges. "It's not like it weighs enough to make a difference, and we've got to get to Tatooine."

"Water," she said. "Ballast."

"I didn't check the cargo bay."

"I'll do it," she said, and before he could stop her, she'd strapped Rotta in the copilot's seat and was making her way aft. "I jettison whatever I find, right?"

"Yeah. When you open the cargo hatch, I'll get a red warning light up here, and I'll just bring up the nose and let everything slide out. Don't waste time dragging any crates up to the tail ramp."

She vanished through the cockpit hatch. Anakin concentrated on evading the vultures. Would they really bring him down in flames now, and risk killing the Hutt? He didn't know, and he couldn't take any chances playing brinkmanship with them. As he banked, he could see V-19s beneath him locked in a fight with more vultures. He didn't dare loop over the monastery to see what was happening. He couldn't even allow himself to be distracted by listening in to the GAR comm circuit to see how Kenobi and Rex were doing. He headed out over the jungle and away from the fighting to make sure he didn't add to their woes by dropping heavy objects on them. Even a small crate falling from that height would cause some serious damage.

The cockpit intercom buzzed. "Master, I'm in the cargo bay now."

"Good. What do you see?"

"Plenty of crates, and the reserve water tanks are showing full. That's five tons at least."

"That might do it. Open the drains on the tanks and make sure you're standing behind anything heavy that's going to slide out the back when you hit the big red button."

"I know."

"Just checking. Tell me when you're ready."

There was a crackling silence, and then she was back on the intercom. "Done. Ready?"

"Let's do it, Snips." Anakin looked across to Rotta to make sure he hadn't slipped from the restraints in a pool of slime. R2-D2 chirped to get on with it. "Hit it."

The console warning light flashed to life: CARGO HATCH OPEN. Anakin brought up the nose and the *Twilight* climbed steeply.

He thought he heard Ahsoka say something, but it was drowned out by the noise of air buffeting the bay. The freighter soared. Suddenly there were no vultures ahead of him, and he was heading into darker skies as the ship climbed.

"Time to get out, Snips. Can't leave the atmosphere with the door open." No answer. His stomach flipped again. "Shut the hatch. Snips?"

R2-D2 chirped and shot off. He'd check, he said.

Anakin had a split second to decide whether to level off and wait for Ahsoka to get clear, or carry on and close the inner cargo bay bulkhead from the cockpit, not knowing where she was and probably consigning her to certain death.

Now where're my fine words about making tough decisions as a commander, accepting that soldiers die?

He was running out of time. He checked the altitude readout as it flickered rapidly through ever higher numbers. His hand hovered over the emergency bulkhead controls. R2-D2 would be okay because astromechs were built to operate in raw vacuum, but Ahsoka . . .

It was a terrible way to go.

Don't think about it. Weep later. Just the mission, okay?

Just the—

The red cargo bay warning light suddenly changed to green. Whatever had happened, it was done now. The sensors still showed vultures pursuing the freighter but he had enough of a lead on them now to jump clear. The sky outside changed from deep blue to jet black. The ship was in open space now, and could make the jump to Tatooine.

"If you can hear me," Anakin said, "prepare to jump to hyperspace."

He hit the control. The stars became white-hot streaks as the ship jumped to safety.

Anakin leaned back in the pilot's seat and wiped his hands over his face, exhausted and not as relieved as he thought he might have been to leave Teth behind. Rotta wheezed.

"Snips? Artoo?"

R2-D2 came back into the cockpit first, whistling and burbling something peevishly to himself about smart scrap saving the day yet again, and how a brief lesson on using safety lines might be a good idea. Anakin twisted in his seat to see Ahsoka emerge through the cockpit hatch.

She was soaking wet, and her hands were cut and bleeding. She shook herself as if it was a reflex, flicking water all over the cockpit.

"Don't ask," she said.

R2-D2 volunteered the information that she'd ended up hanging on by her fingertips again, and it was just as well that he could plug into the circuit and shut the bay doors.

She gave him a peeved look, but patted him on the dome. "I owe you, Artoo."

"Seeing as I'm not asking," Anakin said, "let's worry about Rotta. Unless you need some first aid."

Ahsoka shook her head and examined the Huttlet. He was still conscious, and he turned his pitiful gaze on Anakin. The pendulum between relief and worry swung back firmly to *worry* again, and now their effort had to be devoted to keeping the kid alive.

Even that might not prove to be enough. Anakin tried to imagine handing a sick Rotta back to Jabba. He wasn't the kind of individual to nod gratefully and say he could see they'd done their best, so no hard feelings. He'd want the kid back in the condition he'd left him in. The Hutt held the cards, and knew it.

"There'll be a med droid in the hold," Ahsoka said. "Let's see if we can get it fired up."

Anakin calculated the time to Tatooine.

"I hope he's a fast operator," he said.

TETH MONASTERY

Ventress followed Kenobi onto the monastery roof, pursuing him along the ramparts. And now he'd run out of roof. He paused on the edge, and turned.

"I know Dooku set this up to alienate Jabba from the Republic," he said. "But it's not going to work. Jabba *will* know the truth."

"There you go again. Truth. What's that, Jedi truth, or *real* truth? The Jedi variety is a flexible commodity."

"Even if you kill me, Dooku will be exposed."

Ventress held both lightsabers vertical, walking slowly toward him, ready to follow if he was going to jump again. There weren't many places he could leap to from here that didn't involve a plummet of hundreds of meters, and he wasn't *that* good.

"You haven't seen your protégé's award-winning performance on holovid yet . . . ," she said.

"I'm sure he was magnificent, but there's one little snag."

"Go on. The only way I'm going to shut you up is by taking your head off, I can see that. So have your last moment on stage."

Kenobi looked up at the sky. "Feel it?"

Ventress readied herself for another diversionary tactic. She'd been preoccupied trying to contain Kenobi, too busy and angry to concentrate on feeling the subtler variations in the Force, and any suggestion that she should turn her attention elsewhere wasn't going to work. But now that she'd stopped for a moment, she felt it.

Skywalker was gone.

Maybe he's been shot down.

She opened her comlink. "Air Control, report. Where's the freighter?"

"Commander, we sent every available fighter we had, but—"

"I'll deal with you later." Ventress snapped the comm closed, but sent a coded request for retrieval. She couldn't hang around indulging Kenobi's love of theater. Now she had to recover the situation.

"He's on his way to Tatooine with Jabba's son," Kenobi said. "You've lost. Dooku won't be very pleased with you."

"If you'd stopped admiring yourself long enough to learn anything about me, Kenobi, you'd know this." She was utterly crushed at that moment, but she'd been crushed before many, many times, and the only way she knew to deal with that was to get up and start fighting again, and harder. "I don't give up easily. And I always have a plan."

"Lay down your weapons."

He came back at her with his lightsaber raised, and they stood toe-to-toe, locking blades and struggling. She had to warn Dooku that Skywalker was coming. She needed to end this charade. She stepped back to swing again with both blades, but Kenobi caught the tip of one and sent it spinning from her hand.

"Surrender," he said.

She could hear a vulture approaching, and held out her hand to Force-pull her fallen lightsaber into her grip. The fighter slowed as it tracked along the ramparts.

"Not yet," she said, leaping onto it as it passed. "In fact, never."

She was gone before he had a chance to reply, if he replied at all. Knowing Kenobi, though, he had. He always had to have the last word.

JABBA'S PALACE, TATOOINE

Some things couldn't be safely left to others.

Dooku berated himself for delegating too much. Next time, he'd do the job personally, but right now he had to act to salvage the situation. Jabba was demanding an update in person.

Dooku slipped into a storage chamber on the way to the throne room, mind-influenced the two servants working in there to go away and forget they'd ever seen him, and opened a comlink to Ventress.

"Now I have to pick up the pieces," he said.

The hologram of Ventress looked as steady and implacable as ever, hands on hips, boots planted firmly in a wide stance. She wasn't one to cower and beg forgiveness, however deferential she seemed. He admired that. What he didn't admire was her failure to deliver on critical missions.

"I regret that as much as you do, Master. But I haven't given up yet. I have a ship in pursuit. We have no choice left but to destroy Skywalker's vessel and the Hutt with it."

"Stand it down," Dooku said. "It's too late. I shall intercept

Skywalker personally when he lands. In the meantime, prepare yourself for a display of contrition. I have to see Jabba in a matter of minutes, and when I do, I'll question you in front of him, and you'll tell me that the child is dead and that Skywalker is heading for Tatooine. Follow my lead."

"Yes, Master."

"We'll discuss your future later."

Dooku didn't even wait for her acknowledgment before snapping the link shut. He swept along the passage, mentally preparing himself to look grimly determined yet suitably mortified.

Jabba watched him walk up to the dais with baleful yellow eyes. He had his full entourage around him, so a power display was in the offing.

"You'd better have some news," he said.

Dooku took out his comlink and made a show of keying in a code. "Lord Jabba, we may hear direct from my commander in the field. The fighting on Teth has been fierce, but I might be able to contact her. I know no more than you do." He feigned a few failed connections, made an irritated sigh or two, and then the hologram of Ventress appeared. She looked convincingly battle-weary now rather than defiant. Defiant didn't go down well with Jabba. "Commander, what's happening? I'm with Lord Jabba at the moment, and he's very anxious. So am I."

"My lords, I have no easy way to tell you this," she said, all defeat and noble sacrifice. "The Republic overwhelmed us. By the time we fought our way through and searched for Rotta, Skywalker had killed him."

A gasp went around the chamber, and Jabba froze for a breath. Then he bellowed; not his typical stream of abuse and threats, just a terrible animal cry of inarticulate grief. He was beside himself. He didn't seem to care about showing emotional weakness in front of his servants now. And, Dooku suspected, their horrified gasps were more for themselves, their fear of what would happen when Jabba had recovered his composure enough to lash out and go on a rampage of vengeance, not all of which would be aimed at those thought to be directly responsible.

Dooku aimed to appear shaken but still in control. "My condolences, Lord Jabba." He wasn't sure if Jabba had heard him, because the Hutt was now moaning pitifully in a hoarse, bubbling voice. "The Jedi is the lowest kind of criminal, a child-killer. There is nothing worse. Commander Ventress, you killed the scum in reprisal, I take it."

"No, Master, but no effort was spared in trying. He's on his way to Tatooine with his Padawan."

"Where is my son's body?" Jabba bawled. "I demand his body! I want to see what this Jedi monster did to him, and then I shall personally do ten times that—"

Dooku cut in. Improvisation was fine, but this was getting a little too risky. "Ventress, where is the body?"

"He took it with him, my lord, so we'd have no proof. Knowing his respect for life, he may have dumped Rotta's remains out the airlock by now."

Excellent thinking. Jabba gulped in air, outraged. Dooku stayed steely.

"We'll discuss your failure later," he said, and ended the transmission. The throne chamber was silent, waiting for the next explosion.

Dooku doubted Jabba was putting on a display. He felt the Hutt's shock and grief in the Force, like standing too close to a detonation. It was nothing to do with an insult to his power or loss of face. It was a father's bereavement. Dooku, long used to the brutal reality of the war he had to fight, inured to deaths he would have chosen to avoid in an ideal world, saw himself standing shocked in the snow at Galidraan again.

What have we done?

He shook it off. "Lord Jabba—"

Jabba found his voice. "Why does this filth dare come *here*?"

"To kill you, Lord Jabba, and wipe out your entire clan."

Dooku took a few steps toward Jabba, head slightly lowered. "You *know* he hates your people—you've seen the recording, and he has scores to settle from his time in slavery here, no doubt. But it's more than that. This is about the Republic's ambitions, because they're happy to use Skywalker and his feuds as their loaded cannon. They don't want to rely on your goodwill to maintain access to Outer Rim routes. They need to control those routes themselves, perhaps even install their own puppet clan leader."

"And this is Republic *democracy*. Republic *civilization*." Jabba was getting a grip of himself now, coming back harder, angrier, and even more dangerous an enemy. "I'll make them regret this."

That was so understated and quiet for a Hutt that Dooku knew it meant all-out vengeance of a kind seldom seen.

"Lord Jabba," he said, "allow me. I would like to go some way toward making up for our failure to save your son. I have MagnaGuards ready for him, and I'll deal with Skywalker personally."

Jabba drew himself up to full height again.

"His skull," he said. "Remember, I want his skull."

EIGHTEEN

Hatred can be pushed aside, but it will always whisper in your ear.

IRMENU PROVERB

CREW QUARTERS OF THE FREIGHTER *TWILIGHT*,
SOMEWHERE IN HYPERSPACE

"WHY DO FREIGHTERS HAVE EXPENSIVE MED DROIDS?" AHSOKA asked, watching TB-2 examine Rotta on the scan table.

"Piracy." A lot of men had died to get the smelly little slug this far. No, Anakin was going to get Rotta home or die trying himself. "They get shot at a lot. Pays to have good first aid on board. Come, on, Tee-Bee. Get on with it."

The med droid peeled monitors and probes from the Huttlet's skin. They came away with a wet sucking noise, trailing slime. "The patient is feverish and suffering from an unknown bacterial infection. He is also dehydrated and requires an electrolyte liquid. I prescribe a generic antipyretic suitable for Hutts to reduce his temperature, a broad-spectrum antibacterial, and one liter of liquid by mouth per hour."

Anakin had one eye on the chrono, counting down the time to arriving on Tatooine. "We're some way from a pharmacy."

"I can dispense these items."

"Better make it snappy, then, Tee-Bee . . ."

Anakin went back to the cockpit and fretted at the lack of action open to him. It was the first time he'd had literally nothing to do, rare and precious time that he would have welcomed in any other situation, but he couldn't comm from hyperspace. R2-D2 whistled helpfully.

"I know, Artoo. Good time to take stock. But we've still got a long way to go. Ventress knew where we were heading, and if she hasn't arranged a welcome home for me, I'll be very surprised."

Anakin composed a message to Padmé, glossing over the events of the last few days and concentrating on how much he missed her, and then recorded a message for Rex. Once this mission was over, there was a large hole to plug in the 501st, good men who would be missed, and Anakin understood the subtleties of leadership well enough to know that it wasn't simply a matter of replacing numbers. There were friendships, all the more keenly missed by men who had no family, and there was morale.

Anakin wondered how many times he would go through this before the war was over.

"Better make sure we have operational cannon before we land, Artoo," he said. "Leave the deflector shields for later."

The astromech rumbled out from behind an open bulkhead panel with tools in his claspers and whistled. He had it in hand, he said, but nobody could expect a freighter to hold its own against a military vessel. It was down to pilot skill in the end.

"No pressure, then," Anakin said.

Ahsoka came back to the cockpit with Rotta in her arms and something clutched in her fist. "I could do with some help if you're not busy."

"Does it involve anything messy?"

"Not really. He's not eaten anything for a while, so no problems there. I just need an extra pair of hands, literally." She laid Rotta on a seat and held out her unclenched fist. There were two stimplugs in her palm. "I have to get him to swallow them."

"Can't you grind them up in his electrolyte fluid?"

"Did that. He spat it clear across the compartment. Had to mix a new batch."

Anakin rolled up his sleeves. "Okay. What do I do?"

"Grab hold of him and stop him from squirming away."

It was easier said than done. Anakin grabbed Rotta in a two-arm arresting hold that would have done a CSF officer proud, and pinned him. For a sick Hutt, and a tiny one at that, he was still a handful. The layer of slime made it harder. He twisted furiously. Anakin held on while Ahsoka grabbed Rotta's head like a zone-ball and forced the tablets into his mouth. Then she clamped one hand over his mouth while she held on to his head.

They waited.

Rotta held his breath.

"I can wait all night, Stinky," Ahsoka said. "Just give in. You're outgunned and outnumbered."

Anakin was holding his breath, too, and he wasn't sure if he could hang on longer than the Huttlet. He wondered how he'd ever get the smell out of his robes. Eventually there was a *glumph* sound and Rotta shuddered. Ahsoka removed her hand and put her thumb in his mouth to make him open wide.

"There," she said, peering into the open maw. "All gone. Was that so bad? You'll be all better now."

"Impressive," Anakin said, retreating to wipe his clothing. R2-D2 burbled and held out an oily rag to him. "Most impressive."

"You care what happens to him, really. Don't you?"

"No, I don't. But I care what happens to our army. He's a means to that end."

"I don't think you're as callous as you act."

"Don't worry, I'll be on my best Hutt-loving behavior when we land."

"How does it feel to be going home? How long has it been?"

Anakin wondered how she'd rate him on the callous scale if she knew what he'd done in the Tusken Raiders' village. *I kill people. I kill men, women, and children.* But he always had a reason. So far he wasn't ashamed of anything he'd done, only the things he *hadn't* done. He wondered what Rex would make of it, a man who did his fair share of killing but had rules of engagement. He couldn't imagine Rex losing it and going on a killing spree no matter what the provocation.

Rotta the Hutt slept peacefully on a bunk off the main compartment. Ahsoka checked on him every few minutes. Eventually she came back with a triumphant grin and held up a dribble-soaked piece of blanket.

"He's awake, and he's hungry. He's on the mend."

"That is so cute . . . ," Anakin said flatly.

"Try to see the positive side."

"Try to find him something more nourishing." Anakin fumbled in his pocket and tossed a small sealed package to her. "Here, he can have my dry rations. Hutts can digest anything. Just mash it all up with some water."

"Okay, I get it. You want to get Tatooine over with and get out."

Explaining was asking for trouble. He let her go on thinking he was just a Tatooine boy who hated Hutts, like a lot of other humans who came into contact with them.

The *Twilight* dropped out of hyperspace facing the twin suns, its viewport filters reducing the glare to an amber haze. Tatooine was just a black disk against the light.

"Ready, Artoo? Snips? Stinky?"

Ahsoka tightened her restraints. Rotta lay oblivious of his destiny on a ledge in the cockpit. "He's fed and sleeping."

"Okay, this is it. Snips, watch the scanner for anything that isn't supposed to be there."

Anakin set the *Twilight* on course and had the laser cannon on standby. He wondered if this would be one of those rare, lucky times when the predictable worst didn't happen, but life wasn't like that, and Dooku was only thinking the way Anakin would have in his position.

Tatooine loomed in the forward viewport, a mottled black and red dusty ball with high, wispy clouds that gave the false impression of seas on first glance. They'd hit the atmosphere soon. If anything was going to go wrong—

Sensor alarms sounded.

"Master, there's two traces on the scanner, moving on an intercept course," said Ahsoka.

Bang. Something smashed into the *Twilight*'s hull. Anakin knew laserfire impact when he felt it.

"Ahsoka, stand by. I need to do a little maneuvering."

Anakin swung the freighter in as tight a loop as he could and came about to face the attacking ships. He was expecting vultures, the ubiquitous air asset of the Separatist forces, but when he checked the scanner's magnified image what he could see picked out in the raw light from the twin suns was much, much worse.

Two MagnaGuard fighters—the elite personal guard of General Grievous—were pursuing the ship.

Anakin was nose-to-nose with them in terms of the scale of space. The cannon was charged and primed; his only option was to open fire, because he'd never outrun those, not even if he jettisoned every last bolt in the ship. The MagnaGuard fighters peeled away in opposite directions, looping to start an attack run on his blind spots.

Because that's what I would do if I were them.

He could fire on only one. He picked the first one that flashed in the reticle of the targeting array, and squeezed the button set in the steering yoke. White bolts of energy streaked toward the fighter, and it was swallowed in a ball of white fire.

"Wow, good shooting!" Ahsoka gripped the armrests of her seat as if she were digging in claws. "One down, one to go!"

But, as Anakin had already worked out, life wasn't like that. He hated denting Ahsoka's faith in him to save them. Taking out a MagnaGuard with a crate like this was lucky, *very* lucky, and Anakin had used up most of his lucky quota for the day. The other MagnaGuard was nowhere to be seen. Then the trace showed up on the scanner again, and Grievous's finest looked as if it was making a run on the *Twilight*'s stern.

It was. Laserfire smacked into the cargo bay section, setting off alarms across the console and throughout the ship. There was a hull breach; atmosphere was venting. The hull creaked and screamed as if something was going to shear off.

"Hang on," Anakin said, as if there were anything else they could do. "I think we lost a maneuvering thruster as well."

The freighter rolled. Ahsoka snapped off her restraints and dived like a bolo-ball goalkeeper to grab Rotta before he rolled off the ledge. R2-D2 thrust out a clasper arm to steady himself. Anakin was now ahead of the MagnaGuard fighter with no functioning aft cannon and a lot of space between him and a landing— if he could land at all. The ship shuddered again as more laser rounds hit it. Without an aft canon, Anakin needed to find a way of firing astern.

"Artoo, can you move the forward cannon past its safe range?" The arc of fire was limited so that freighter crews wouldn't blow their own vessel apart by firing too close to the hull. It was all too easily done when frantically emptying a magazine into a hostile vessel. "I need to move it one-eighty degrees."

The droid plunged a probe into the console and bleeped, explaining that he was overriding the safety control, but that it was a very bad idea.

"I think that's going to be academic, buddy," Anakin said.

More direct hits shook the freighter. "We won't have much hull left at this rate anyway."

R2-D2 burbled to himself, and Anakin waited long seconds for the okay to fire.

"Artoo, sometime before we plummet in flames would be good . . ."

Then the *Twilight* shuddered dramatically as if in its death throes. Anakin waited for a ball of flame to come rolling through the ship, but the scanner showed an expanding ball of hot debris in the freighter's wake.

The MagnaGuard fighter was gone. R2-D2 spun his dome antenna in celebration, whistling happily. It was a *very* tight shot, he explained, and best done by a precise robotic hand, not a human, however good a gunner that human might be.

"Nice shot, Artoo," Anakin said. "I'll be out of a job soon if I don't buck up. If we useless meat-bags don't make it through a landing—you know where to take Rotta."

Hutts didn't have bones, and they were basically an immensely strong bag of muscle. Stinky might survive a crash that killed humanoids.

"Sorry, Snips. I got you into this." Tatooine rushed up to greet him, and with an out-of-control ship, Anakin was even less pleased to see it than he'd imagined. Comm silence wasn't an issue now. He needed to get a message to Kenobi, just in case it was his—and Ahsoka's—last. "Master, this is Anakin. Are you receiving me? I'm making a crash landing on Tatooine. Rotta's alive, hostiles in pursuit, and—"

He lost the comm frequency on reentry. But at least Kenobi now knew they'd come this far. He looked around to see Ahsoka shielding Rotta with her body. He didn't have the heart to tell her that she could have used a Hutt as a crash bag.

"Brace for impact," Anakin said. "Because this is going to hurt a bit."

PALPATINE'S OFFICE, SENATE BUILDING, CORUSCANT

Palpatine enjoyed Yoda's company, because the longer he sat smiling benignly at Yoda, and the longer the greatest Jedi Master failed to recognize Palpatine for what he was, the more satisfying the situation became.

So this is where centuries of wisdom—and power—gets you. Oblivious, smug, and self-serving.

General Kenobi was present at the meeting, too, but as a hologram. He was still mopping up the Separatist forces on Teth. "Anakin's reached Tatooine," he said. "I've received a message that Jabba's son is alive and well, but the ship was under attack. I'm now convinced this kidnap was all part of a plot by Dooku to frame the Republic and alienate the Hutts."

Palpatine shook his head very slowly. "And will Jabba believe Dooku? He's not the most trusting of beings, even for a Hutt."

"If Jabba this believes, then ended is our hope of a treaty with them." Yoda frowned. "In Skywalker, the Republic's only hope lies. Return the Huttlet personally, he must."

"As ever, Master Yoda, you summarize the dilemma perfectly," said Palpatine. *Yes, restate the obvious. Very effective leadership, Yoda.* "General Kenobi, is Skywalker up to this task? I know he's an excellent soldier, but this is verging on a diplomatic assignment."

Kenobi nodded emphatically. "Don't worry. Anakin has more experience in dealing with Hutts than most of us. If anyone can placate Jabba and get him on our side, he can. Kenobi out."

The hologram vanished and Palpatine was left looking at Yoda. The Master had both hands clasped on the top of his cane, nodding, an image of senescence that didn't fool him one bit. Yoda might have let the Jedi fall into slow decline and comfortable expedience, but he still wasn't safe to write off.

Palpatine leaned forward on his desk, fingers meshed. "Master

Yoda, should we send young Skywalker some support? Do *you* think he can do this?"

"Impatient, the boy is. Given to emotions, too. But in dangerous situations, the most likely to succeed."

Palpatine noted that. "I'll place my faith in him too, then. You must excuse me, Master Yoda, I have political business to attend to. Senator Amidala is due here for a meeting."

Yoda rose to leave just as Padmé Amidala entered the office. They bowed politely to one another in passing, and Padmé sat down opposite Palpatine's desk.

"We were going to discuss the new security measures on Naboo. My security advisers tell me more fighting has broken out in the Outer Rim."

Palpatine liked to see how much information he could shake out with a statement rather than a question. "Yes, I've just been talking to General Kenobi about the engagement he and Anakin Skywalker have been involved in."

Padmé's brow creased slightly. "Anakin? Is he all right?"

"I'm afraid a negotiation between the Jedi and the Hutts has gone badly wrong." Padmé's reaction—all Anakin, no Kenobi—confirmed his suspicion that this wasn't just professional political concern. "Lord Jabba believes Anakin kidnapped his baby son."

"Anakin would never harm a child," Padmé said, indignant. She recovered herself a fraction of a second too late to fool Palpatine. "No Jedi would. Let me intercede on behalf of the Senate. I can talk to Jabba and explain to him that this is some mistake, and conclude the negotiations."

"That's very courageous of you, Senator, but Jabba has refused all further contact with the Republic. It's far too dangerous for you to visit Tatooine. We're dealing with organized crime, not a democratic state."

"Jabba's uncle Ziro has a palace here," she said. "I'll try to get him to act as an intermediary."

The more Padmé was dissuaded, the more determined she became. Palpatine found that he almost pressed that button now simply to see if it worked every time. It did, although it served no extra purpose to involve her in this. He was simply gathering intelligence.

"Do you think that's wise? They're *gangsters*."

"Diplomacy is about dealing with those you'd rather avoid," she said, getting up to leave. "And we must need Hutt assistance very badly in this war for Jedi to be willing to negotiate with Jabba."

Palpatine nodded sagely. "Yes, sometimes we have to put aside our principles for the greater good. I'm glad the Jedi feel able to do this, and don't cite their consciences as a reason for not fighting this war." Padmé glanced back at him from the door, and he smiled his best paternal smile. "Do be careful with those Hutts, Senator."

DUNE SEA, TATOOINE

The *Twilight* was full of fire-suppressant foam, sand, and smoke, but it had landed, and everyone was alive.

Anakin scrambled clear and checked for enemy activity, but the desert looked as empty and lifeless as ever. His next thought was to open a comm frequency to Kenobi. It was just static.

"Snips, have you got a comm channel to me, or offplanet?"

She checked, frowning at the comlink. "No, just noise."

"They've jammed everything, then. I'd hoped I lost Kenobi's signal because of reentry, but obviously the Seps are getting smarter." He pulled the hood of his tunic over his head to protect himself from the blistering sun and beckoned to Ahsoka. "All clear."

She crawled out of the wreckage with Rotta tucked in the backpack. The Huttlet was now alert and curious, with no sign that he'd ever appeared to be at death's door. "Wow, feel that heat. How far do we have to go?"

Anakin gestured to the horizon at a cluster of turrets and extravagant domes shimmering in the heat haze. The sand slowed even the fittest, and they had no survival kit, which didn't bode well; they also had a slug with them, a species not exactly fitted to dry, dusty environments. "That's Jabba's palace, and we've got a few hours' walk ahead. Not a great idea in this heat."

"Should we wait until it gets dark?"

"I don't think we can afford to delay, Snips." Anakin was used to the desert, but he still didn't underestimate its capacity to kill him as surely as Dooku would. "So I'll take the Hutt. You grab as many water bottles as you can carry."

R2-D2 rumbled out of the wreckage, beeping plaintively. Ahsoka coaxed him out. He didn't like sand.

"Come on, Artoo," she said. "I know. Nasty abrasive stuff. Don't worry, we'll give you a full service when all this is over."

Anakin knew there would be eyes on them. There was nowhere to hide in open desert. But the attention wasn't directed at them—not yet, anyway—but at what was left of the *Twilight*. A couple of hundred meters into their hike, he looked back over his shoulder to see scavenging Jawas swarming over the wreckage like insects, dismantling sections and forming a chain to carry away everything they could detach or lift.

R2-D2 swiveled his dome to watch, too, and beeped. He didn't fancy meeting Jawas in a dark alley, he said. It was the hydrospanners that disturbed him.

"Don't worry, it's never going to happen to you, buddy," Anakin said. "Come on. Keep up."

All they could do was keep putting one foot in front of the other, and not concentrate on how far they had to go. Ahsoka had made a bonnet of sorts out of a sheet of bulkhead insulation, and draped it over Rotta's head. Anakin could hear it rustling against the edge of the backpack.

"It's a shame you can't see him, Skyguy," she said. "He really does look cute."

"If we see a vendor selling Neuvian sundaes, I'll buy him one . . ."

"So this is home."

"No."

"Tell me about it."

"No."

"Okay . . ."

"The more you talk, the more you dehydrate." Anakin wasn't sure if that was true, but he thought it was good advice for both of them. "The desert's a killer. It takes everything from you in the end."

"I understand," she said quietly.

Yeah, he had a horrible feeling that, even without knowing the details, she probably did.

They kept up steady pace all afternoon, stopping for regular water breaks and to check on Rotta. He gurgled happily. For a slug, he seemed to be coping with the dry heat well. Maybe it was the slime acting as a protective barrier. By the time the twin suns were edging close to the horizon, the temperature had fallen from near-unbearable to a balmy stiflingly hot. In a few hours, though, it might plummet close to freezing. The desert was out to get the unprepared every moment of the day.

Anakin felt a chill now, but it wasn't the climate. He stopped.

"Feel it?" he asked.

Ahsoka half closed her eyes. "Yes. We're not alone."

"It's the dark side. It's Dooku. He's coming for Rotta."

"He's not going to get him. Over my dead body."

"Oh, he'll oblige, Snips . . . time to split up."

"Master, I can do this. I don't need protecting. We should stick together."

"No, I need you to get Rotta back to his father." Anakin scrambled up a slope and squatted on the top of the ridge, pointing out features in the desert that were almost invisible in the unending sand. "See that gully between those rocks? It's part of a network of ancient riverbeds. Take Artoo and follow it. Watch out for Dooku's droids, too. If he's borrowed any more hardware from Grievous, they'll be out searching, and there's not much cover out here, even at night—they've probably got infrared sensors."

Ahsoka looked at him blankly for a moment as if digesting the enormity of the mission. "But Dooku—"

"I'll deal with Dooku. He'll come after me."

"You're crazy."

"You're best suited to a stealthy approach, and I'm the more experienced at fighting the likes of Dooku. You can't argue with that logic."

"No," she said. "I can't."

"But you will."

"No, Master, I won't."

It was getting easier. They'd cracked it now, this Master and Padawan business. Maybe it took a war to shake things down, because he didn't remember falling into line that fast, and he wasn't sure he ever had.

"Give me the backpack," he said. "We need to make a decoy so that I look like I'm still a devoted guardian of Stinky."

NINETEEN

Why not just let them cede from the Republic?
Why do we need to have a war about this?
What's a republic if it's not about allowing beings
to decide who governs them? I don't get it.
CALLER TO HOLONET NEWS OPINION SHOW

DOOKU'S SHIP, TATOOINE

"YOUR PLAN'S FALLEN APART," ZIRO SAID. "I'VE GOT A SENATOR here begging me to tell Jabba the kidnap is a plot by you to discredit the Jedi."

Dooku had no time for panickers, especially not when he had to hunt down Skywalker. He stood in front of the hologram in his best you're-not-backing-out-on-me-now pose.

"*My* plan, is it? Let's not forget this was an agreement for mutual advantage."

"Okay, *our* plan. It's still in tatters."

"Think this through, Lord Ziro. Of *course* there'll be those who think the Separatists are behind this. And there'll be those who think the Republic is. I'm certain that Jabba thinks *both* sides are equally capable of it and trusts neither, so all he wants is proof of who's guilty *this* time. I've got it under control. I've told Jabba that the Jedi murdered his son, and that they're on their way to kill him, too."

Ziro wobbled with exasperation. "Jabba will kill the Jedi on sight!"

Dooku pulled on his gloves. The desert was chilly at night. "Will you lose any sleep over that?"

"No, but . . ."

"If Jabba kills the Jedi, then the Jedi Order, exercising their great moral authority, will be obliged to bring Jabba to justice. Which means you're left to take control of all the Hutt clans. That's what you want, isn't it?"

Ziro's ghostly blue image considered Dooku in silence for a moment, as if the Hutt lord had suddenly realized something. "Ah. So *that's* how you intended to do it."

"Does that not meet your needs?"

"It does, Count Dooku."

"It meets mine, too. I get a dead Jedi or two out of it, and my armies get sole access to the Outer Rim. Why does the strategy come as a surprise?"

"Jabba would lose authority if he was seen to be held to ransom by the Republic. That would have been enough to unseat him. But your way is *much* more emphatic."

Dooku smiled. It was reassuring to think that it looked so seamless from the outside. Yes, it *was* planned, but the plan had needed constant adjustment every time one component had failed—and it still did.

"I'm glad we're both happy, Lord Ziro."

"But what do I do with this Senator?"

"Ignore her. What else would a Republic Senator claim? Of *course* she'll accuse the filthy enemy of doing something outrageous. Counterpropaganda, conspiracy theory, call it what you will—governments in wars accuse one another. It would only be worthy of attention if she *didn't*."

"I can't ignore her."

Ziro was very slow on the uptake sometimes, considering his flashes of subtle gamesmanship, and for a moment Dooku wondered if he was trying to get him to say something incriminating on record. That struck Dooku as amusing, given recent events. He checked the chrono and cast around in the Force for Anakin Skywalker. He had to cut this short. He had Jedi to kill.

"Senators are very accident-prone individuals," Dooku said. "See that she has one, and my contacts will ensure that's how it's recorded. A tragic waste of a young and promising politician. State funeral. You know the drill."

There was a faint scuffle at Ziro's end of the link, and the Hutt turned suddenly as if someone had come into the chamber. One of his sentry droids appeared in the image dragging Senator Amidala.

"No, I meant that I have no option to ignore her," Ziro said. "She shot a sentry droid when he caught her spying on me. So an accident is the only choice now."

Dooku looked at her, and that meant she could see him. This was why he often preferred audio-only comlinks, but the fact that she'd seen him changed nothing.

"Senator," he said, bowing. "How are you? I'm late for another appointment, so you'll have to excuse me."

She looked contemptuous of him. She usually did. "So *you're* behind this, you poisonous traitor."

"Senator, I wish we could get one thing straight—I'm not a *traitor*. I was never on your side. I'm called *the enemy*." He had to leave now. "Lord Ziro, you might want to rethink my accident suggestion. Some of my Separatist allies will pay you a handsome price for her."

Ziro blinked as if he was basking in warm sunlight. "Excellent suggestion, Count Dooku. I can defray the costs of replacing my droid, too."

"Keep the change," said Dooku, and shut the link. He stepped out into the cold desert night, lightsaber ready, and mounted his speeder bike.

THE DESERT, FIVE KILOMETERS FROM JABBA'S PALACE

Anakin was almost grateful that he could feel Dooku coming. It stopped his thoughts wandering too far.

He sat meditating in the cold night air, a backpack strapped to his shoulders, staring at the three moons without blinking so that they became a blur and quieted his mind. His breathing had slowed; his pulse rate had dropped dramatically. In that state—and he reached it rarely these days—things spoke to him, and he didn't always want to hear them.

There were layers in his awareness. At the top, he searched for Ahsoka moving through the dunes toward Jabba's palace with Rotta, and—he hoped—R2-D2. They should have been almost there by now. He couldn't detect his astromech, however hard he tried, only the disturbances to living organisms that the droid sometimes created. Ahsoka had faded, too, drowned out by the Force impressions in the deeper layers, where Anakin felt Dooku—precise, targeted, controlled, a firaxa shark slicing through an ocean. In the depths, though, there was Tatooine.

It wasn't just memories. It was the accumulated misery, greed, and desperation of ages, generations of beings in poverty and servitude, and his small experience of that was barely visible in the mass. It was the voice that got to him. A wordless voice whispered, asking why he did as he was told and never asked the obvious questions, or demanded answers.

Why didn't you make them come back for her? Why didn't you see she was throwing you to safety, sacrificing herself and sinking back into this terrible ocean so that you could have a chance at life? Why didn't you come back sooner, change the course of events, and rescue her before it was too late?

He never needed to define *her*. She was his mother. Tonight, she blotted out everything, even thoughts of his wife. The irony of his task—saving a Hutt—teetered on the brink of being a final message, an ultimatum to his sanity.

You must save who you can from now on. You must save those who deserve it.

Dooku got closer. Anakin rose from the depths of the Tatooine that never left him, surfacing through eddies of Dooku and Ahsoka and breaking a surface that was simply ripples made by distant strife on other worlds. He adjusted the straps of the rock-laden backpack.

Dooku must have known that the sound of the speeder bike carried a long way in the desert at night. Anakin wondered why he didn't attempt an ambush. But neither of them needed physical evidence to find one another, and they couldn't hide.

Anakin heard the drive cut out a few meters away. Each footstep crunched in the sand. Finally, Dooku stood before him, robe flapping in the breeze. Something else caused a disturbance in the Force, but Anakin could concentrate only on Dooku now, and ignored it. He stood up, adjusting the pack of rocks on his back, and activated his lightsaber.

"Give me the Huttlet, Skywalker," Dooku said quietly. "Or I'll have to kill you."

He'd swallowed the ruse, then. "I think you were going to do that anyway."

"Very well."

The tone of the confrontation was strangely courteous, like an Irmenu noblemen's duel. Dooku threw out his hand and sent Force lightning crackling across the sand toward Anakin, lighting up the night. Anakin evaded the bolts and channeled the lightning to his lightsaber.

"You're making progress," Dooku said. He lunged forward with his lightsaber, forcing Anakin back, then somersaulted over him. "Being here is painful, isn't it? Your home. Too many ghosts to contemplate. Stayed away too long, perhaps—"

Anakin whipped his hand up almost without thinking and sent a Force whirlwind of sand sweeping from the dunes. It spun toward Dooku, enveloping him and almost knocking him to the ground. The Count crouched for a moment as it passed over him, cloak pulled tight around him, and then stood again, lightsaber outstretched.

"Was I being insensitive?" He walked forward. "We all have to face our ghosts, Anakin. I face mine. They never go away, you know. They can be a burden, like that Hutt you're carrying, or a teacher, if you learn to live with them."

Did Dooku know about Shmi Skywalker? He seemed to know everything else, or maybe it was the trick of a fortune-teller, casting generalities to get a client to react and reveal specifics. Whatever it was, Anakin couldn't walk away from it or shut it out. He felt every shred of pain, his and his mother's, and lunged for Dooku with his lightsaber. His attack was blind and ferocious, oblivious of the dead weight on his back, slashing and whirling at the Count until he drove him back to the softer sand where he'd lose his footing.

But Dooku had been a master duelist, even among Jedi, and Anakin forgot that for a pain-blinded moment. Dooku ducked under his frantic sweeps and spun around behind him, slashing through the rigid backpack almost to Anakin's spine. The sudden movement of the rocks packed tightly inside made Anakin pause to get his balance.

"Oh dear," Dooku said mildly. "I seem to have cut Rotta in half."

"You wish." Anakin held out his lightsaber to fend off Dooku while he released the straps and let the backpack fall to the sand. Rocks spilled out.

Dooku raised his eyebrows. "Good grief, not a Hutt at all . . ."

It dawned on Anakin too slowly that Dooku wouldn't have been so easily fooled. *This is a game. He's playing for time.* Just when Anakin thought he'd passed that elusive finishing line that said *adult, experienced, seen it all,* he realized he was still twenty, Jedi or not, and the wounded boy in him still rose to the surface—

provoked into angry violence, scared of abandonment, and still in need of approval.

Dooku was playing decoy.

"You're too late, anyway," Anakin said. He had to choose: fight Dooku to the end, or make a run for it and try to get to Ahsoka. He had his eye on the speeder bike. "She'll be at Jabba's palace by now."

"You'll note I didn't ask where she was," Dooku said, taking a holoprojector from his cloak. "And I know you can't comm her. But I can show you some friends she's run into."

Anakin thought it was another trick, but the blue holoimage that sprang into life looked real enough. The angle suggested it was being recorded by something much taller than Ahsoka. She backed away from two MagnaGuard droids, stumbling in the sand, Rotta on her back in the makeshift harness she'd made.

Was this real? Anakin didn't trust anything he saw now.

"Jabba's son is still a casualty of war, alas, but your Padawan is being delivered to Jabba alive." Dooku carved a slow figure-eight in the air with the tip of his lightsaber. "He needs to vent his grief on something, and he won't have you to play with, will he?"

Anakin sprinted for the speeder.

He had it airborne the moment he settled into the saddle. Dooku seemed to give chase, but Anakin lost him in a cloud of sand.

As he raced for Jabba's palace, he had no idea whether this was still part of Dooku's maneuvering. *Am I really stronger than him, or did he choose to let me escape? Why did he show me the hologram, to fool me or to demoralize me into dropping my guard in a fight? Why did he—*

Anakin stopped thinking. It would only distract him. He'd made his decision; he had to follow through. The only thing he knew was that Dooku had tried to delay him for a reason, and he had to take the risk that the decoy wasn't simply to provoke him into rushing to the palace.

Maybe Ahsoka had run into MagnaGuards after all. Maybe she was already at the palace, reuniting Jabba with his son.

The only way to find out was to get there.

TETH MONASTERY

"What a mess," said Cody. He kicked a scrap of droid casing out of the way as he crunched through the carpet of destruction in the courtyard. "And get your hair cut."

Rex, helmet under one arm, scratched the stubble that had sprouted on his scalp since he'd last had a chance to shave. "Yeah, I'll be tripping over it next."

"We're going to have to start fighting a lot smarter than this. Or we'll run out of men."

"Tell me about it."

"Not the first company we've lost. And it won't be the last."

Rex chose not to take it as Cody's offhand reassurance that it wasn't his fault. He knew it wasn't. "It's the first company *I've* lost, *sir.*"

"Pays not to think about it too much, Captain."

"I'll try that. Trouble is, if we don't think, we might as well be droids."

Cody didn't press him further. They ambled around the battle-field, at a loss for something practical to occupy them beyond see-ing what technology and intelligence had been gleaned from captured droids—or what was left of them—and learning from the mistakes. Kenobi wasn't around. The two clone officers held their own private washup to decide how to do things better next time, knee-deep in enemy dead. It was just as well they were fighting in-organics. Rex imagined the scene with flesh-and-blood casualties on this scale and hoped he never saw it. It was bad enough hauling out his own men and recording the armor tallies of KIAs, although that was a task that had fallen to the 212th, who now picked their way through metal recovering what they could. He'd hoped some of Torrent Company would turn up alive, but that hope hadn't lasted long. He'd kept the last five standing, though. Or they'd kept him standing. He suspected it was the latter.

"Well, next time we don't attempt this without air cover," Rex said. "Crazy. Larties aren't enough. Vee-nineteens, that's what we need."

"It wasn't supposed to be an infantry battle."

"Hostage extraction in a heavily defended and pretty inaccessible position? We should have sent in special forces to prepare the battlefield, then established air superiority and landed airborne troops. Not crawled through the jungle and lost a quarter of our men before we even started. And this needed battalion strength, not a company. It was supposed to be a critical mission, and they should have resourced it accordingly."

"Okay, everyone learns." Cody stood with hands on hips, looking down at the ground. "But don't expect things to improve any time soon."

Rex wasn't sure who to sink his teeth into. Skywalker didn't have any more say in the assets he was given than Rex did. Kenobi probably didn't, either. The problem was higher up the chain; and one thing he'd worked out fast after he left the confines of Kamino, where they learned only the military solutions and how to be the best soldiers, was that politicians didn't think like soldiers, and did stupid things for reasons best known to themselves.

Rex had heard Skywalker mutter occasionally about the Jedi Council and his . . . disagreements. Now he understood. It was down to the Jedi Council to tell the Chancellor to pick his battles carefully.

Rex swallowed his frustration for the time being. He could tell Cody was getting restless by his habit of rocking back slightly on his heels.

"Okay, tinnies really are useless in nonstandard situations and confined spaces," Rex said. "Proven. All they seem to know how to do is stand up and march forward firing. If we do the same, we just run out of men. We need to avoid engaging them on that kind of terrain. Maybe commit fewer ground troops and hit harder from the air. Maybe Kenobi can feed that back up the chain."

"Where's Skywalker?" Cody asked.

"Crash-landed on Tatooine, but the Hutt's still alive, according to General Kenobi's report."

"Mission accomplished, then. It wasn't in vain, Rex."

Rex was going to say that if the access to the Outer Rim routes was matched with a more realistic approach to the number of battles they could fight, then it had achieved something. But he had a feeling that it wouldn't change a thing, but just spread the Grand Army more thinly.

He had faith in Skywalker, because the man was in there with them, in the thick of it, and he understood the stakes. Rex found his faith was like the atmosphere, getting thinner the higher it went.

"I'll go round up my men, then," Rex said, turning to the aid station set up in one of the gunships that had landed on the perimeter. "It won't take long."

TWENTY

We've secured the Hutt location, sir. Senator Amidala's unharmed
and she's returning to the Senate with her protocol droid.
We have Lord Ziro in custody. He's claiming he was forced
into the kidnapping of Jabba's son by Count Dooku. Zero casualties—
unless you count droids, of course.

CLONE COMMANDER FOX, reporting a successful
hostage extraction to GAR HQ

JABBA'S PALACE, TATOOINE

"LORD JABBA, WE'VE LOCATED SKYWALKER." THE CAPTAIN OF THE
Nikto guard came in at a brisk walk. "He's approaching the palace
on a speeder bike. I've positioned snipers on the roof. Permission
to use lethal force, my lord?"

Jabba concentrated on not letting grief overwhelm him. Anger
was a good temporary antidote, a brief respite of cold focus.

"No, bring him to me alive," he said. "I want him to tell me
what he's done with my son's body. After that, I don't want to be
too hasty about killing him. I'll spend a few weeks about it, perhaps. And then the Sarlacc will take a few thousand years to digest
him. No, I won't spare Skywalker with a quick death."

Jabba had his full entourage assembled. He wanted to crawl

into a dark corner and bellow until the agonizing emptiness in his chest stopped, but he had to be seen to be strong and still in control. If he wasn't, the kajidic families, and so Hutt society, would fall into chaos and leave Hutts weak. He needed an audience to witness that even in his darkest moment, he remained in command.

A Nerrian piper played a lament in the background. Rotta's crib lay empty to one side of the dais. Eventually, Jabba heard droid footsteps, and TC-70 walked in carrying a lightsaber.

"Skywalker surrendered his weapon without a fight, my lord," said the droid. "He asked for his Padawan."

Nikto and human footsteps came down the passage. Skywalker entered almost casually, certainly not a human preparing to die, and looked around as if he expected to see something.

His focus seemed to fall on the empty crib. Then he looked at the piper.

"Lord Jabba, where's my Padawan?" He spoke Huttese with a strong Mos Espan accent. "Where's your son?"

The piper stopped in midrefrain. Jabba didn't dare look away from the Jedi in case his rage now boiled over and left him helpless.

"My son . . . is where you *left his body*, you murdering Jedi filth."

"Your son is alive, unless Dooku's MagnaGuards killed him along with my Padawan. She was bringing him—she should have been here by now."

Jabba edged forward a little. "If you were any other human idiot, I would take your feeble attempt to deceive me as simple stupidity. But you *know* us, Skywalker, because you were raised here here, a *shag*, a common slave, and so you know you *insult* me in my grief."

Skywalker paused for a moment, blinking, and then reached out his hand. The lightsaber TC-70 was holding flew across the chamber and into the Jedi's grip, and within seconds the Nikto guards had crashed against the wall as if thrown by an invisible hand. Skywalker ignited the weapon and batted away blaster fire before leaping onto the dais and holding the glowing blade to Jabba's throat.

Jabba should have been outraged, but for a moment he felt that it would have been an end to the pain he was in. Then he found habit taking over. He did what he had always done; he sat defiant and unmoved. Hutts couldn't run. They'd made stalwart defense into a tactic instead.

"So Dooku was right," Jabba said. "You killed my son, and now you come to kill me."

Jabba knew the Nikto guards couldn't open fire. They risked hitting him, and Skywalker might kill him simply by deflecting the bolts. Everyone froze.

"No, I didn't come here to assassinate you." Skywalker actually looked into his eyes. Jabba could see that it was a struggle for him. "I came here to negotiate."

"Then you'll still die, *shag*."

"Somewhere out in the desert, my Padawan is making her way here with Rotta. She's been attacked by MagnaGuards, I know that. I've fought Dooku to get here. Instead of having your heavies make themselves useless here, why don't they get out and *look* for her?"

"Another feeble attempt at a trick, Jedi?"

Skywalker couldn't stand here forever. He must have known he would be overwhelmed sooner or later, so he was buying time. Jabba felt no fear. He had no room for it right then.

"Guards," he said. "See if the Jedi's reinforcements are coming. Then kill them." He swiveled his head to stare at Skywalker, trying to see something in the human's face that would explain how he could kill an infant. Humans—most sentient species, in fact—were disarmed by something small and helpless, even if it wasn't their own kind. It was a very primal instinct. Jabba even found baby humans quite appealing—until they grew up, of course.

But Skywalker killed children. It made him something danger-ous and *different*. Jabba consoled himself thinking how easily hu-mans broke, and the many ways he could break them.

The minutes ticked away.

Skywalker's time was running out. Jabba could see sweat on his top lip.

"My lord Jabba!" The guard's voice rang down the corridor, the nearest Jabba had heard to a Nikto sounding *excited*. "The Jedi's here with her droid! She's got him! It's not an explosive de-vice!"

Him?

It took Jabba a few moments to take that in. He turned his head slowly, steeling himself against the inevitable plunge into deeper grief at a dashed hope. It couldn't mean *that*. It couldn't.

A tiny Togruta female—disheveled, streaked with blaster burns, caked with sand—stumbled into the chamber carrying a bundle on her back that was too big for her. She twisted from the hip, almost collapsing, as she set it down on the dais.

It's not an explosive device.

"Well done, Snips," Skywalker said. He let out a long sigh and shut down the lightsaber. "You look awful."

The Togruta unwrapped the bundle, and Jabba didn't quite manage to maintain an icy dignity. His composure slipped, but he caught it quickly.

"My . . . son," he said. Rotta gurgled and squealed happily at the sound of his voice. "Hand . . . him to me."

TC-70 stepped in. "Lord Jabba says to put his son in his arms."

And she did. She looked as if it was one more effort she could hardly make, but she lifted Rotta into his arms. His son felt lighter and thinner, but he was alive. He was *alive and well*.

"There you go, Stinky," she said. She gave him one of those smiles, all teeth. "Safe with Dad again. I'll miss you."

Jabba would have replied in her language, in Basic, but he had an image to maintain. This was *his* world. Foreigners spoke *his* language.

The court seemed to breathe again. The piper struggled for a happier tune, and the servants chattered excitedly.

Jabba had his son back. He was barely able to believe it. Dooku had conned him, but so had the Jedi. They were all the same, these humans, only after his favor for what they could wring out of it in their interminable little squabbles. He wouldn't let relief get in the way of business yet.

"Now, Jedi," Jabba said. "You still die."

ANAKIN DECIDED he should have known better. It would take more than a tearful reunion—if Hutts had that depth of feeling in them—to make Jabba see reason.

"Okay, I'm the one you've got the problem with," Anakin said. "Let Ahsoka leave with my astromech. She saved your son a dozen times since we found him on Teth. She doesn't deserve this."

Ahsoka's eyes darted from face to face; she didn't speak Huttese. She had no idea what was going on, other than that the trouble wasn't over. She looked like she'd fought off an army. MagnaGuards weren't battle droids. Anakin was amazed she'd survived.

She saved Rotta. In the end, she saved him, I didn't. I can't save anyone even when I try.

"Tell Lord Jabba," she said to TC-70, "that he needs to speak to Senator Amidala. I got a comm message when jamming stopped. General Kenobi said she needed to speak to him urgently about his uncle Ziro. He's been arrested."

Jabba moved to the comlink on his dais even before TC-70 finished two words. So Jabba understood Basic just fine; Anakin noted that. He'd always suspected the Hutt did. But the terror of the moment was so intense that even the words *Senator Amidala* didn't set his pulse pounding.

Padmé. My wife. Hey, that's my wife.

The hologram of Padmé appeared instantly, as if she'd been waiting for a long time to take the message.

"Lord Jabba." She bowed her head, ever the diplomat. "Your uncle Ziro has been arrested after conspiring with Count Dooku to kidnap your son and depose you, and incriminating the Jedi to sabotage negotiations with the Republic."

"Prove it," said Jabba.

TC-70 translated. "Lord Jabba says prove it."

"You can speak to Ziro now, Lord Jabba, from the custody cell." Padmé leaned out of the margin of the image, and her place was taken by a hologram of a Hutt.

"You better have a good story, Ziro . . . ," Jabba said.

Ziro started begging right away. "Nephew, I would never harm Rotta! Dooku made me do it! He threatened me, he threatened to kill me—"

"You should have let him," Jabba said. "Because when I get hold of you, I'll make you understand that Hutt does not betray Hutt. I've seen enough. Put me back to the Senator."

Padmé reappeared. Anakin edged into the transmitter's field of view so she could see him. She smiled, a little distant, but he could see she was playing the politician today. Their marriage was a secret as much for her sake as his.

"General Skywalker," she said, bowing her head again. "Thank you for your assistance in resolving this."

"And thank you, Senator." Anakin hoped he was doing his gritty warrior expression, but judging by the look on Ahsoka's face, he wasn't succeeding. It was hard to stand at the brink of death and have your secret love intervene, and not let that show on your face. "Padawan Tano, Captain Rex, and Torrent Company of the Five-oh-first were all instrumental in achieving this."

And there goes Padmé, saving me.

She smiled her professional smile again, but she almost winked.

"Lord Jabba, perhaps we can now agree on Republic use of your routes for military traffic, and bring this war to an end."

TC-70 translated. Jabba, bouncing Rotta on his belly the way a human would use their knee, laughed raucously, like his old self.

"Tell the Senator it's a deal. And I want Dooku brought to justice, too."

That was the moment at which Anakin felt he could safely let his legs give way to the adrenaline, and fall off the dais. Instead, he simply stepped down, beckoned to Ahsoka to follow him, and walked out of the chamber to find R2-D2.

If he ever came back to Tatooine again, it would be too soon.

DOOKU'S SHIP, LEAVING HUTT SPACE

Dooku waited for a dressing-down from Sidious, but it never came. The hologram of the Sith Lord sat in composed calm as if hearing a minor inconvenience.

"Master, I regret to tell you that the Jedi succeeded, and now have their agreement with the Hutts," Dooku said. "This will make the Outer Rim far harder to hold."

"You're aware of the saying about battles and wars, are you not, Count Dooku? You can lose one and yet win the other?"

"I am, Master."

"Then allow them this victory. It makes little difference to the overall course of the war. It stretches their forces more thinly. It makes them overconfident. In fact, losing this small skirmish may well be their downfall when history views the war in years to come."

Dooku had considered that, but as a consolation. Sidious made it sound as if it was *intended*. "You're very gracious, Master."

"No, Count Dooku. I'm very pragmatic."

The hologram was gone, and Dooku was sitting at his apocia desk again in the darkened compartment that, if he ignored the flashing console on the bulkhead, could have been a study in a grand castle.

Galidraan loomed in his memory once more, snow-shrouded and accusing. Dooku pondered on yet another ferocious battle that had ended in a way he hadn't bargained on, and repeated the question: *What have we done?*

He had done his duty.

And he'd do it again. He'd do it until the day he died, until the Jedi were destroyed, until Mustafar itself froze as white and cold as Galidraan.

EPILOGUE

REX WAITED IN THE HATCH OF THE LAAT/i GUNSHIP WHILE Kenobi and Yoda sat inside, talking. He didn't listen to the Jedi Masters' conversation, which was barely a few words anyway.

He was waiting for his general.

Skywalker and Ahsoka appeared severed in half at first, caught in a mirage of hot air that shimmered over the sand. As they drew closer, they resolved into solid shapes, with the astromech droid rumbling ahead of them. Rex jumped down to meet them halfway.

Skywalker held out his hand and Rex shook it. "I'm glad to see you, Captain."

"Me too, sir."

"I'm sorry I didn't return."

"No problem, sir. It gave General Kenobi something to do, anyway. You know how bored he gets."

Skywalker laughed. He looked a mess and he reeked of Hutt. "Bad news for me, though?"

"Five men."

Ahsoka looked up. "Five dead?"

"Five *alive*. Plus me."

"Oh," she said, in a surprisingly small voice. "Oh my. The men I was talking to in the hangar . . ."

"Yes, littl'un. Them too."

"Give me a report," Skywalker said quietly. "Not the usual official record. I want to hear it all. Names. I want to hear how six of you held a droid army at bay, Rex."

"Oh, boring stuff." Rex turned to the gunship, almost unable to bear the thought because they'd have to get up tomorrow and do it all again. "It's not that important, is it?"

"It is to me," Skywalker said.

"And me," said Ahsoka.

Rex nodded.

It made all the difference.

ABOUT THE AUTHOR

Karen Traviss is the #1 *New York Times* bestselling author of four *Star Wars: Republic Commando* novels: *Order 66, Hard Contact, Triple Zero,* and *True Colors;* three *Star Wars: Legacy of the Force* novels: *Bloodlines, Revelation,* and *Sacrifice;* as well as *City of Pearl, Crossing the Line, The World Before, Matriarch, Ally,* and *Judge.* A former defense correspondent and TV and newspaper journalist, Traviss has also worked as a police press officer, an advertising copywriter, and a journalism lecturer. Her short stories have appeared in *Asimov's, Realms of Fantasy, On Spec,* and *Star Wars Insider.* She lives in Devizes, England.